T0146474

GUIDEBOOK TO
MURDER

A Tourist Trap Mystery

GUIDEBOOK TO
MURDER

A Tourist Trap Mystery

LYNN CAHOON

KENSINGTON BOOKS
KENSINGTON PUBLISHING CORP.
www.kensingtonbooks.com

KENSINGTON BOOKS are published by

Kensington Publishing Corp.
119 West 40th Street
New York, NY 10018

All Kensington titles, imprints, and distributed lines are available at special quantity discounts for bulk purchases for sales promotion, premi-
ums, fund-raising, and educational or institutional use.

Special book excerpts or customized printings can also be created to fit
specific needs. For details, write or phone the office of the Kensington
Special Sales Manager: Kensington Publishing Corp., 119 West 40th
Street, New York, NY 10018. Attn. Special Sales Department. Phone:
1-800-221-2647.

Kensington and the K logo Reg. U.S. Pat. & TM Off.

First Electronic Edition: April 2014
eISBN-13: 978-1-60183-238-2
eISBN-10: 1-60183-238-9

First Print Edition: April 2014
ISBN-13: 978-1-60183-304-4
ISBN-10: 1-60183-304-0

Printed in the United States of America

The proverb "it takes a village to raise a child" could also be said for writing a novel. If I listed off all the people who had molded me during this journey, we'd be here forever. That being said, there are a few who need a special shout-out:

Thank you to my husband, Jim, who believed in me from day one. To Laura Bradford, who taught me the magic comes from the work. And to my MoRWA chapter, who challenged me, critiqued my pages, and cheered my success.

Thanks to Esi Sogah, my editor, for laughing in all the right places, and believing in South Cove and its quirky residents.

Finally, I want to thank my sister, Roberta Gowin. Who would have guessed my visit during a long-ago spring break would have sparked the Tourist Trap mystery series?

Chapter 1

Empty shops are the death knell for small businesses. The thought nagged at me as I read, curled up in my favorite overstuffed armchair. Wednesdays were notoriously slow for all the South Cove businesses. Not many tourists included the day in an impulsive California coastal weekend getaway, but I liked to be open, just in case a random busload of quilting seniors decided to stop for a shot of espresso and a few novels to read while they traveled to their next stop on the tour. It had happened.

Once.

The mortgage papers on the building listed me as Jill Gardner, owner of Coffee, Books, and More, the only combination bookstore and coffee shop within sixty miles. But as anyone who's gone through a divorce or lawsuit knows, paper only tells half the story. I might own the shop, but I'm also one of the world's biggest suckers.

When I moved to South Cove five years ago, I realized to survive in the small tourist town I'd need to patch together a few different jobs. So I'd jumped at the chance to serve as the business liaison between the local businesses and the city council.

Now I regretted my impulsive nature. And as if to highlight my error, the fax machine on the back counter beeped and started printing out a message.

It could be a catering order coming in. Hope springs eternal and all that. I jumped up from my chair to glance at the half-printed page.

The South Cove city letterhead sparkled on the top. Then Mayor Baylor's scrawl appeared over the sheet. Short and sweet, he wanted the agenda for the next Business to Business meeting in his office by five on Friday.

As the new kid in town, I'd been honored when the city had offered me the position. I should have known there was a catch, because none of the other more-established business owners wanted the job. Working with His Honor The Mayor was a nightmare. But I was stuck with the job—at least until I could sucker the next victim into taking it on. Planning this month's get-together had been on my to-do list for three weeks. I wrote it there myself, right after I'd left the last meeting. I left the fax on the machine and went back to my book.

With a steaming hot mocha within reach on the table, I snuggled in to devour the latest installment from my favorite mystery author. Customers could come tomorrow. The mayor and my to-do list could wait another day. The sunshine warmed my skin, and the smell of deep, dark coffee hung in the air. I tried to ignore the nagging going on inside my brain.

I'd read two pages when the phone rang. My plans for a quiet morning of reading weren't working out. Running the few steps to reach the phone, I felt breathless when I answered. "Coffee, Books, and More, how can I help you?"

"Jill, is that you?" Miss Emily's high-pitched voice blared over the phone line. Man, for being in her eighties, the woman could really project.

"Yes, it's me. What's going on?" My heart slowed a few beats. I needed to get into better shape. I grabbed a dust cloth, happy for the cordless phone. Conversations with Miss Emily were never short.

"Those rats at the council are at it again." Miss Emily's ongoing argument with the city was a popular topic of discussion not only with me, but with anyone who stopped by her house to visit.

"What did they do now?" I walked over to the closest bookshelf and started to wipe away the dust that had already settled since I cleaned yesterday. I loved my little store but sometimes I felt like it owned me, my time, and what was left of my rapidly shrinking savings account.

"They want me to sell out to some charlatan who's building an apartment complex for wealthy seniors. And they're offering me a condo at a reduced price in the complex. Can you believe it?" Miss Emily sounded near tears.

"They can't make you sell." I tried to calm her.

"The letter says they can. It says the council can condemn the property and just take my house. Can they do that?" Miss Emily rattled the pages hard enough that I could hear the crinkling over the phone.

"Just put that letter away and I'll look it over on Sunday. When do you have to answer?" I was starting to worry. The council had never threatened to condemn her property before. I'd have to check with Amy, she'd know the details. Having the city planner as a friend came in handy.

"The end of the month."

"We have plenty of time. We'll call some lawyers on Monday if we need to." One more thing on my to-do list.

"I'm buying a rifle to keep those carpetbaggers off my land," Miss Emily declared.

"Don't buy a gun!" Miss Emily sounded determined. Determined enough to shoot anyone who knocked on her door and ask questions later. Maybe I should close up shop now and go over to keep her out of trouble.

The bell over the door announced a customer, taking the option out of my hands.

"Someone just came in, I'll see you Sunday?" I nodded a friendly greeting to the woman in a white sundress. The woman's eyes passed over me as she headed toward the bookshelf filled with local history books. Tourists loved the "local charm" books, as I called them. I stocked as many as possible as they flew off the shelf faster than any other category. I focused back on the phone call. I had a couple of minutes before I'd be needed.

"Don't worry, I'll behave myself, as long as they don't come on my property."

"Miss Emily!" I walked back toward the coffee counter to greet the woman who was now wandering around the shop, a couple of books tucked under her arm.

"Go take care of your customer, I'm joking." Miss Emily chuckled and then hung up on me. I would have been worried except she ended all of her phone conversations that way. No good-bye, just dead air. Even when you weren't done talking.

The woman pushed her Jackie O–inspired sunglasses to the top of her flowing blond hair. She portrayed a more Hampton feel than central California coast girl.

"What a quaint little bookstore." The fashion Barbie leaned down to her purse and talked into the bag.

What the heck was she doing?

Today was turning out to be anything but slow. Working with people made me like my books so much more. I put on my retail smile. "Can I help you?"

The woman jumped as she turned to the sound of my voice. "Oh, there you are. Precious and I didn't think anyone was here." She walked toward the counter, books in hand.

"Precious?" She'd named her purse?

"Precious, meet—I'm sorry, I didn't get your name." The crazy Barbie clone focused on me.

"Jill, Jill Gardner. I'm the owner. We're the only bookstore and coffee shop in South Cove," I said with not just a little pride. I loved the little shop I had built over the last five years. The shop and South Cove felt like home more than any place had felt in my entire lifetime.

"Precious, meet Jill." The woman pulled out a red, toy-sized Pomeranian from her tote bag.

I never knew Coach made dog carriers. "Nice to meet you, Precious." I reached out to pet the cute little dog.

Precious took one look at my approaching hand and curled his neck back like a cobra and struck.

"Ouch." I pulled back my bleeding hand. Walking back around the counter, I went to the sink to rinse off the blood.

"Bad boy." The woman and her evil dog came closer to the coffee counter. "Are you all right?"

"Yeah, I'm fine, thanks for asking . . ." I stopped talking, realizing her comments had been to the devil dog, not me. People. I wanted this woman to leave so I could get back to my book, or write the agenda for the mayor, or even clean the stockroom. One lost customer wouldn't hurt. Instead, I took a deep breath, then asked, "Can I make you something?"

"Iced coffee, skim, no whip. Put in an energy boost. I'm dragging today." The woman slipped "Precious" back into his bag, but I could hear him growling through the leather. "I'm missing my coffee shop at home, they have the best supplements, I swear."

"Sorry, I don't sell supplements." I started making the coffee, hoping to get this nightmare out of my shop. "Are you visiting South Cove? There's a great place down the street where you can watch them blow glass."

"My boyfriend is working out a deal on some sort of development here. We won't be in town long. You'll be amazed at how he can take a run-down town like this, bulldoze it over, and have nice, new, clean buildings back up in no time." Precious's owner ran a finger over my counter, holding it up to look for dust.

"I'm sure bulldozing buildings isn't part of any plan the city would approve. Most of these buildings are on the historic register. South Cove's development plan is based on renovating existing structures to modern uses." No way would the council approve a slash-and-burn development.

Fear gripped my stomach, twisting the mocha I'd sipped on all morning. Could this be the complex Miss Emily had mentioned? I'd call Amy to get the real story, right after this woman left. I handed her the iced coffee. Then I glanced at the books she'd set on the counter. "This book on South Cove history was written by a local. His son still runs the Main Street Bed and Breakfast."

"Why, that's where we're staying." She thumbed through the book. "Maybe he'll have some stories to add."

"I'm sure he'd love to talk to you about his father's research." I pointed at the other book. "This one tells the history of all the Spanish missions on the coast. The author did a road trip when this book was first published, stopping at all the mission sites. The launch was quite the production."

"I'm sure it was." She glanced at her watch. "So what do I owe you?"

I guessed girl bonding time was over. "Three-fifty for the coffee and thirty for the books."

"I can't believe how cheap everything is here. You'd be shocked at what I pay for a coffee in Santa Barbara. You just got a regular customer. Besides, you're much nicer than that other place." The woman counted out thirty-five dollars in bills. "Keep the change."

Big tipper.

"Thanks for stopping by." I tried to sound a little friendly.

"I'll see you tomorrow." She headed to the door, then turning back, she struck a pose and smiled. "By the way, I'm Bambi."

Bambi, of course.

"See you." Maybe it was time to hire staff so I could avoid selling Bambi her daily iced coffee.

Bambi didn't hear my response; she was too busy talking to Precious. "Aren't you the little pit bull, protecting Mommy? What a good boy."

The bell on the door rang again, announcing their exit from the shop. I grabbed the phone and dialed Amy's number at the city office.

"City of South Cove, Amy Newman." Amy served as city planner, historian, secretary, and part-time receptionist for South Cove. By combining a lot of the little jobs, she had carved out a full-time position allowing her to use her architectural design degree without living in the big city. Besides, working for Mayor Baylor gave her plenty of time for her true love, surfing.

"Can you meet me?" One customer for the morning was enough.

"I can be at the diner in about ten minutes?"

"See you then." Amy would blow a gasket if she found out the mayor or the council had talked to Bambi's boyfriend/developer without getting her input as city planner. Having her out in public might lessen the steam that would flow out of her ears when I told her.

I hung up and went to the window to post the CLOSED sign. I grabbed my purse and locked the door behind me.

Main Street was empty. A few cars sat parked on the redbrick street, but no one walked down the sidewalk on this side of town. I caught a glimpse of the woman who owned The Glass Slipper, washing the inside of her display window. Another thing I needed to do soon.

The brightly painted flower planters were overflowing with summer annuals, including my favorite, petunias, making the small business district look more like a Swiss Alp resort than a California coastal town. But I loved the old-fashioned lamp posts the council had put in last year. The lamp posts added to the European flair of the downtown core, and a lot of customers had told me how much they loved walking through the town.

Diamond Lille's was the only restaurant in South Cove (unless you counted my coffee shop). Lille and I have an understanding; she doesn't make caramel mochas and I don't serve dinner. That way I can close early and she can open late. Lille has the upper hand in the compromise. She's been a part of South Cove culture for over twenty years. Everyone ate at Diamond Lille's at least once a week. I'm still working on developing regulars after five years.

"Hey!" Amy waved at me as I walked in. Like I couldn't see her among the tables filled with farmers eating their lunch. The smell of apple pies baking floated out of the kitchen.

I slipped into one of the red tufted booths lining the back wall. Diamond Lille's had been decorated as an old-fashioned western saloon meets rocking fifties diner. An iced tea with lemon waited for me, the humidity from the restaurant condensing on the outside of the glass. I took a long sip. "Thanks, I needed this."

At thirty, Amy got carded more than most twenty-one-year-olds we knew. Her short blond hair was cut into a pixie. Perpetually tan from spending her weekends surfing the California coast, her obsession also kept her stick-thin. I, on the other hand, carried an extra twenty pounds because I spent my weekends reading and tanning on the roof of my building. That is, after I closed down the shop on Saturday.

"So what brings us to lunch on a Wednesday? Usually you are too deep into your latest book to even remember to eat." Amy closed the menu, when our hostess appeared at the side of the booth. "Hey, Lille, what's up?"

"Oh, the stories I could tell. People are just weird, that's all. Some girl tried to come in with her dog. I had to throw her and the mutt out." Lille peered over her glasses. "So, ladies, what can I get you?"

I was dying to hear more about Bambi's appearance, but I knew if I pushed, Lille would just clam up. So I settled for ordering lunch. "I'll have the Asian chicken salad with the dressing on the side."

"Give me the house burger with everything. And fries." Amy handed the menu back and shrugged her shoulders at me. "What, don't look at me like that, I had a small breakfast."

Sure, probably a three-egg omelet, sausage, and bacon with a side of hash browns.

I shook my head. Watching Amy eat made me feel like I was

doing something wrong with my perpetual dieting. And I probably was—not exercising. Who had time? "I met the girl Lille threw out."

Amy sputtered through a sip of her strawberry milk shake. "What? When?"

"Just before I called you. She and her dog, 'Precious'—who is anything but—came in for an iced coffee." I stared at the milk shake, imagining the creamy drink cooling my mouth. *I don't like strawberry*, I reminded myself. "Then, after the dog bit me, she told me her developer boyfriend was going to bulldoze the town and rebuild better stores."

"She said what?" Now Amy wasn't interested in her milk shake. Maybe she wouldn't notice if I just took one sip.

"Yeah, that's what Bambi, her name and description, said after she ran her hand down my counter to check for dust." I took a long sip from my iced tea. *I love iced tea*, I tried to convince myself. "Seriously, I would have thrown her out if she wasn't my only customer of the morning. So, what have you heard about a new developer being in town?"

"Nothing." Amy appeared shocked at my announcement. "Really, there isn't anything going on, except . . ." She took another sip of her shake. When Amy played poker or lied, she had a tell. Amy stalled.

"Except what?" This couldn't be good news.

Amy sighed and leaned back while Lille slipped the platter filled with burger and fries in front of her. I could the smell the grease from the fries. My salad looked wilted.

"The council wants to issue Miss Emily another letter about her yard. I've held them off for a while and told them I'd talk to you. But I can't hold them off forever. She's got a week before they meet again."

"Crap. I've been meaning to find someone to mow. It's not easy. She's gone through all of the teenagers who live in the area; none of them will even walk by her house now."

"It's not just mowing. They want her to replace that fence in the front." Amy dug into her burger, ketchup running out of the side of her mouth.

"Wait—what? You said they *want* to issue a letter? According to the call I got from Miss Emily this morning, they already *have* issued her a letter. And they threatened to condemn her house."

"Not possible. They just met last night, and I was stuck sitting through their discussion until nine. The only good thing about last night was they ordered Lille's fettuccine Alfredo for dinner." Amy took another big bite out of her burger, juices dripping down the sides of her mouth.

I handed her a napkin as I searched for more mandarin oranges in my salad. "You sure they just talked about her yard and fence?"

"Positive. I typed up the minutes from the most boring meeting in the world when I got in this morning. I planned on calling you to give you a heads-up tonight." Amy wiped her mouth, then waved a French fry at me. "I tried to call last night but all I got was your voice mail. You let your cell die again?"

Busted. I was horrible at remembering to plug the thing in. Amy and my aunt were the only two people who called me, and they both knew to try the shop first. The odds were better I'd pick up the land line. Trying to change the subject, I ducked my head and asked, "They want her to replace a perfectly good fence?"

"You have to admit, it looks pretty bad, especially compared to the rest of the houses on Main Street." Now Amy attacked her steak-cut fries, dipping two at a time into Lille's famous ketchup/horseradish sauce.

I'd run out of mandarin oranges so I started eating lettuce. Yay. The way this conversation was going I should have ordered the fish and chips. "The council does realize she's the only real home left on Main Street. The rest of those houses are converted businesses."

"That's their point. They want her to sell out to someone who will turn the house into retail." She scrutinized the regulars in the café before she whispered, "I think they're tired of waiting for her to die."

"I wonder what letter she's talking about, then. She was hot when she called. You don't think she's reading an old letter, do you? She's not that old to become confused." I'd first met Miss Emily on a visit six years ago when I was playing tourist here. The first vacation I'd taken after the divorce and six months of seventy billable hours a week at my law firm.

Visiting South Cove had been a weekend diversion after a week from hell. I walked down the street with my ice cream cone from Lille's and realized I'd arrived at the end of town, my bed-and-breakfast nowhere in sight. Miss Emily sat on her porch, watching me.

"Lost?" she called out.

"Kind of," I called back. "Do you know where Beal Street is?"

"I do." Then she just sat there in her rocker knitting, her gray hair twisted up in a bun and a small smile on her face.

"So, can you tell me?" I felt hot and tired. Playing games with this little old lady was not restful. And I wanted restful. I came here for restful.

"Don't get your knickers in a bunch. Come on up on the porch and have a sit. You look all red from the heat." The old lady didn't even look up from her knitting. "I've got a glass of iced tea waiting for you."

Waiting for me? How could it be waiting for me?

I pulled open the wood gate, latched closed with a circle of barbed wire over the post, and headed up to the porch, walking gingerly through the tall grass on a stepping-stone path.

"Sit down, child. Tell me what brings you to South Cove." Two hours later I'd laid down the misery composing my life and had made a decision to move to the small town that already felt like home.

I'd be damned if the city council would railroad my friend out of her own house just because she was taking too long to die. They'd have to go through me first.

Chapter 2

The weeds Miss Emily called a lawn were ankle-high Sunday morning when I pushed through that same gate, off-kilter and rusted with age. The gray weather-stained boards didn't match up with the fence that went past the lawn and down the side of the house. The fence at that point changed to barbed wire circling around a pasture that had many years ago held in a few black and white cows and a horse or two. Now the city council called the old pasture a fire hazard. At the end of town, Miss Emily's house was the first thing people saw driving into the small community.

The town of South Cove made its living off the tourists who found their way off Highway 1. The road meanders north up the coastline from Los Angeles toward San Simeon and The Castle. On weekends, tourists flock into town for lunch and to shop in the craftsmen's art studios that fill the block.

After an hour of calls yesterday, I still hadn't found a kid to mow her yard. I would have to do it myself. The last kid I hired had mowed down her fairy circle, a natural ring of mushrooms in the middle of the yard. Miss Emily had run out of the house brandishing her cane wildly above her head, her long gray hair down to her shoulders, and started swinging at the fifteen-year-old. He stopped the lawn mower where it stood and ran out of the backyard.

His dad called that evening and told me he had to go and get the mower because his son refused to ever go back to that "crazy old woman's house." I had to pull my mower out of the garage and go over to finish the job. Maybe I could put a wire fence up around the fairy circle.

I walked up the steps, grabbing her newspaper from the porch. It was already past ten. Miss Emily always got an early start, reading her paper while she drank her coffee on the front porch. Today she wasn't there. Her rocker sat empty.

"Miss Emily," I called as I opened the door. Setting the paper on her foyer table, I called out again, "Are you in the kitchen?"

Walking through the living room, I headed to her kitchen and the heart of the house. She wasn't there. The back door stood ajar and I stepped out on the porch, scanning the yard, hoping she hadn't fallen and broken a hip. You always heard about old people breaking hips.

She wasn't in the backyard. I sighed, looking at long grass waving in the slight wind. I couldn't wait to find a new kid to mow. I'd be mowing the lawn this afternoon, instead of finishing that mystery. I slipped back into the house.

Where could Miss Emily be? She knew I planned on coming over. She would have called me if she'd gone to town.

I walked through the back of the house toward her bedroom. Fear gripped my stomach, and I took a deep breath, trying to calm down. Pushing away the bad feeling that had settled in my gut, I lightly knocked at her door and called out again. No answer.

I pushed the door open and saw her, lying on her bed. She appeared to be asleep. I walked over and touched her wrist, using the techniques I'd been taught when I worked my way through college at the local nursing home. Nothing.

"Oh, Miss Emily." I brushed the hair out of her eyes. On the pale skin of her neck, slight dark smudges showed. Her body looked peaceful, younger somehow, like all the pain had left her face.

Sitting down on the bed, I felt energy drain from my body. I'd been complaining that I wanted to spend my Sunday relaxing, not mowing a lawn that didn't even belong to me. All the time I groused—my friend had been dead.

I held her hand for a few minutes, trying to understand what I was seeing. Looking around her room, nothing appeared out of place. A teacup sat on the nightstand. I picked up the book lying next to the cup. She'd been reading her favorite author, a woman who wrote historical romance set in Regency England. A happily-ever-after Miss Emily wouldn't ever know.

I walked out of the bedroom and dialed 911 on my cell phone. The bastards didn't have to wait for her to die now.

Toby Killian, South Cove's part-time officer and local heart-throb, arrived first. The man could be a model for the romance novels I sold. He plastered yellow police tape all over the front yard like there were tons of people waiting to storm the scene. After he'd completed that, he stood in the kitchen watching me and waiting for his boss, Detective King.

I sat at the kitchen table, drinking a cup of coffee I'd made while I waited. Coffee I couldn't taste even though it was the best blend my shop sold. At least the warmth of the brew warmed my chilled hands wrapped around the cup.

I willed myself not to cry. Not here where Toby could watch as I fell apart. Miss Emily had been more than just the crazy old lady who lived down the street. She'd replaced the mother I'd never had. All the memories of my mother centered around her glasses of Fresca and vodka on ice that started daily at noon.

Miss Emily listened when I talked about my days at the coffee shop and the regulars who came in for their light sugar-free hazelnut mochas over ice. I'd tell her about the tourists who always asked how a smart girl wound up owning a coffee shop in this tiny town, asking whether I missed all the bustle of the big city.

Miss the traffic, the hour-long commute to my job, the working through a pile of family court paperwork, and representing women who were either angry at life or totally bewildered that their lives had changed in the middle of a conversation at dinner? Divorce court wasn't fun, even on the easy cases.

No, I didn't miss my old life.

I watched as the stretcher carrying Miss Emily was wheeled out of the bedroom, on the way to Flannigan's Funeral Home in nearby Bakerstown. South Cove didn't have its own funeral home. Tourists didn't like to be reminded of death on vacations. I stopped the EMT guys. Pulling back the sheet, I bent down and kissed her gently on her cheek. "I'll miss you."

Detective Greg King had finally arrived and followed me back into the kitchen where he poured himself a cup of coffee. His sandy blond hair hung in his eyes, and in shorts and a sleeveless shirt, he was dressed for a run on the beach rather than a crime scene. He sat down beside me, his large frame squeezed onto the small wooden chair. "It's hard to see them go."

"She was so sweet. Who would do this?" I didn't know Detective King well. He'd moved to South Cove last year. I celebrated the loss of my new resident status until I found out the new guy with a six-foot frame filled with muscles had grown up here. He'd been married at the Methodist church down the street. He was one of them.

I'd be celebrating my fiftieth anniversary of opening Coffee, Books, and More and townspeople would still call me the new kid.

"People die, especially people Miss Emily's age." He put his hand over mine in a practiced motion of comfort for the overwrought. Although the touch both warmed and tingled on my skin, his words left me feeling frustrated.

"Are you sure she just died? Did you know the council wanted her property?" I stood, sweeping my hand out from under his. "You'll run tests, do an autopsy, right? She wasn't sick, I just saw her last weekend. Hell, I talked to her Wednesday, and she was fine."

"Now relax. This is a small town, not San Francisco or Los Angeles. Sometimes people just die. I'll have Doc Ames do an autopsy. Going quietly in the night isn't the worst thing that could happen." Detective King took a last swig of his coffee and dumped the leftovers into the sink. He pulled out a wallet and handed me his card. "Call me. I should have the results by the end of the week."

I took his card. I felt like he wasn't too happy about having to look at this as more than just an old lady passing. I bet the coroner would agree with him. I followed Detective King out of the house, locked the front door, and pocketed the key. I'd come back later and try to find a number for her son. Miss Emily hadn't talked about him often, but I knew his name was Bob.

"Miss Gardner, please try to leave the investigation to us," Detective King called to me as he got into his car. "I promise, if there's something there, we'll find it."

Fat chance.

The town might be smaller than San Francisco, but this cop's attitude reminded me of some police officers in the city. They didn't want to see anything that would cause them work. Years of reading through police reports that barely listed the abusive husband's name or the wife's injury had taught me to be cynical. Just because Detective King's eyes were so blue you could swim in them didn't mean he wasn't trying to keep the paperwork down.

I didn't have to open the coffee shop until Tuesday, so I had an entire day to figure out who killed my friend. Or at least find some evidence so Detective King would believe she was murdered. As soon as I woke on Monday, I went into my galley kitchen and started making a list. If there was no next-of-kin, I guessed I would handle the arrangements. Doc Ames had called last night and asked me to come for some kind of meeting today. He served as both funeral home director and the county coroner. He assured me a full autopsy had been scheduled for today on Detective King's orders. On the other hand, the funeral still had to be planned, murder or not.

I wrote *meet with Doc Ames* as my first task on the sunny "I'd Rather Be Surfing" pad Amy had given me on my birthday. The last funeral I had attended had been my dad's. I'd been five. I wondered if the yellow police tape was down or if I was even allowed back in Miss Emily's house. I needed to go through her files and find her son's address and phone number. That conversation should go well. "Hi, I'm Jill from South Cove. Your mom's dead. Can you come and plan the funeral?" Maybe Detective King had already found the son.

Another reason I should call the town's detective that had nothing to do with the way I felt when I thought about him.

I wrote my second task: *Call Detective King.* I poured myself a cup of coffee. Then, I wrote down the names of everyone from the mayor to Bambi's developer boyfriend as my list of suspects. I went back over the list. Did King know all these people had motive? I didn't know how seriously he'd take a list that had his boss and the entire city council listed as possible murderers, but it was time to find out. I went to find my cell phone.

I punched in the number for the police station, with a separate entrance but in the same building as City Hall. There were three members of the police staff. Esmeralda was a part-time clerk who handled all the paperwork and the phones during the day. Detective King ran the office. And Toby was responsible for handling night and weekend calls. Toby got to do all the DUI arrests. Five last year.

Having a winery right outside of town brought in the tourist crowd who either bunked in one of the town's three bed-and-breakfasts, or took a chance driving home and being spotted by Toby.

"South Cove Police Department, this is Esmeralda." The voice sounded low and menacing.

"Is Detective King in yet? This is Jill Gardner." I knew Esmeralda from her visits to the shop for coffee and coffee cake for the police department's Monday meetings. Lille might cater all the City Council meetings, but at least I got the breakfast business from City Hall.

"Sorry to hear about Miss Emily. When I saw her name on the weekend report, I was shocked." Esmeralda's voice flowed over the phone, now warm and concerned. "Are you okay? I know the two of you were close."

"I still can't believe she's gone." My voice choked up. I still hadn't cried. Crying made it real, and I didn't want this to be real. Not yet. Maybe not ever.

"Maybe we should do a session. See if she's hanging around, looking for vengeance or something. The earlier we reach out, the clearer the signal." Esmeralda sighed. "I'm stuck here answering phones until three, but I could stop by your apartment if you want."

After Esmeralda got off her part-time shift at the sheriff's office, she ran what appeared to be a successful fortune-telling business. Her house, just down the street from Miss Emily's, felt dark and foreboding, paint peeling off the shingles and a herd of cats that came and went at will. Apparently she'd never been approached by the council about upholding community standards. Having the mayor as one of her clients had served her well.

"I'm sorry, I've already committed to running up to Bakerstown to take Doc Ames some clothes." Now, I felt glad I had an actual excuse. Having to tell Esmeralda no sometimes didn't work in your favor.

"Well, we'll just have to wait then. Call me if you need anything. I know Miss Emily wasn't a regular churchgoer, but I've already called Pastor Bill from the Oak Street United Methodist. He's getting the women's group to put together a little something for after the funeral." Esmeralda paused. "Unless you already had something set up?"

When Esmeralda had joined the Methodist choir a few years

ago, several of the deacons had complained, uncomfortable with her profession. I hadn't been at the church meeting when Pastor Bill flat-out challenged anyone to prove Esmeralda a witch or that she'd committed an evil act. And since no one could find fault with one of the nicest women in South Cove, the pastor had held up his arms and said, "He who is without sin, cast the first stone."

After that, the matter had been settled, and Esmeralda's smooth soprano wafted through the halls of the church every Sunday. I tend to think that if she'd been tone-deaf, the pastor might not have fought so hard to keep her in the fold.

I had to get over to the house and find this long-lost son before I screwed up something big. Everyone was counting on me, and I didn't know the first thing about how to honor my friend. "No, that's fine, I mean, I haven't planned anything."

"You poor thing, you must be overwhelmed. Pastor Bill said he'd meet you at the funeral home." Esmeralda was talking to someone in the background. "Greg just got in. I'm going to put you on hold, and he'll be right with you. You call me if you need anything, even just to talk."

"I will." I realized she hadn't waited for my response. I'd been talking to the prerecorded Lawrence Welk–era hold music.

"Jill. I'm glad you called." Detective King's voice came over the line, warm and husky. "I just finished a meeting with the mayor, and I'm supposed to tell you that you're allowed to return to Miss Emily's house anytime. And you've been cleared as a suspect."

"I was a suspect?" I stopped fiddling with my pen.

"You were on the scene when I got there."

"I called the police." I couldn't believe this.

"I know, but it's standard procedure." Detective King sounded like he was kicking his toe in the dirt while he talked to me. "Doc Ames says he'll have the preliminary report back to me this afternoon. The tox screens will have to be sent to the county lab, so we probably won't see any results for two weeks."

"I suppose we can't do anything before that, like a funeral or anything?" I didn't want to sound totally stupid, but I was treading deep water here and I needed some sort of a lifeboat.

"There's nothing holding you back from doing all the arrangements. I haven't found any record of next-of-kin, so I guess you're the one responsible." The sound of pages being flipped came over the phone, and I realized he had me on speaker. Not a good time to read out my list of suspects.

"I'd planned on stopping by the house this morning to find information about her son. Do you want me to call if I find something?" If I did find something, then the detective could call him and not me.

"That would be great. Well, if there's nothing else, I've got a pile of weekend reports to go through."

I thought again about telling him about my suspicions, but he'd already written Miss Emily's death off as just one of those things. I'd wait until I had something solid to give him. "No, that's about it."

I remembered something when I started to hang up. "Wait."

"Yes, Jill?"

"Have you heard anything about a new development here in South Cove?" He'd just had breakfast with the mayor; maybe they had talked about Bambi's boyfriend's development.

"Nothing new. A request came in for a rezoning from residential to commercial at the last council meeting, but I think that's a glass blower starting up her own shop. Why?"

"I'd heard a rumor down at the coffee shop."

"I'll let you know if I hear anything. Take care." The phone went dead.

After talking with Detective King, I wasn't able to think of anyone else for my list of suspects even after finishing my pot of coffee. Instead of donning my usual summer outfit, I pulled on a sundress. I'd never planned a funeral before, so I wasn't sure about proper attire, but I was sure cutoff jeans, a worn tank top, and Hello Kitty flip-flops would be frowned upon. Pulling my dark curly hair into a ponytail, I swiped on mascara as my homage to the makeup gods. I hoped the tears I hadn't shed for Miss Emily wouldn't come and give me raccoon eyes for the day.

Grabbing the keys to my Jeep, I drove over to the house, even though I could have walked or biked the three blocks faster. I didn't want to have to come back for the Jeep in order to make my appointment with Doc Ames. From my parking spot in front, the house looked empty and unloved. Strands of yellow police tape flapped around the fence, reminders of the tragedy that had played out yesterday. The grass on the lawn was long enough to wave in the wind. I would have to pull out my mower tomorrow night. As I glanced around the yard, the size of the chore overwhelmed me.

At least now the council should put off any rush to condemn the house since Miss Emily was gone. They had gotten their wish. Not the most Christian thought, I'll admit, but they caused this mess.

Unlocking the door, I walked in the living room. The house felt cool, the windows open to let in the ocean breeze that floated over the town at night. I went around shutting the windows against the afternoon summer heat. I half-expected Miss Emily to walk up and ask if I'd had breakfast.

I went to her bedroom first. Doc Ames had asked me to bring clothes. When I opened the closet, I found a line of the cotton dresses Miss Emily wore every day. Clean and ironed. Who irons nowadays? A black garment bag was shoved in the back of the closet. The word *funeral* had been written in Miss Emily's shaky hand on a strip of masking tape stuck on the outside. I pulled out the bag and laid it on the bed. I opened the bag and found a dress, shoes, underwear, and a note. I sat down to read the note.

> *Jill,*
>
> *I'm sure you will be the one handling these arrangements, so I want to make it as easy for you as possible. You always think of yourself as a strong woman, but on the inside, honey, you are soft as butter. That's why everyone takes advantage of you. And I'm sorry I have to ask you to do this final request for me. There just isn't anyone else. I've made all the plans with Doc Ames and talked to Pastor Bill about what I want, so you'll just have to follow my wishes and this will all be over soon.*
>
> *Please remember me and know when you came into my life, it was a blessing from God. Jill, I think of you as the daughter I never had, so take these words as they are offered, in love.*
>
> *Stop letting everyone use you. Be strong. Find yourself. You are an amazing woman and deserve to be happy. Don't wind up old and alone, rocking on the porch, like me.*
>
> *Love,*
> *Emily*

P.S. I've left a surprise for you. Call Jimmy Marcum over in Bakerstown.

P.S.S. Don't let Doc Ames put panty hose on me. I don't want to spend eternity itching. And no jewelry. I don't want grave robbers digging me up in a few years just for a few ounces of gold.

Oh Miss Emily. I examined the blue paisley silk dress she had never worn, kept for this special occasion. Tears filled my eyes as I felt the softness of the fabric.

My cell rang.

Sniff. I dug the phone out of my purse and grabbed a handful of tissues from Miss Emily's nightstand.

"Hello?" Blowing my nose, I dabbed the tears from my face. I knew mascara had been a mistake. I'd be sporting raccoon eyes all day.

"Jill? Are you all right?" Amy's voice was sharp. "I'm at your apartment right now. Answer the door."

"I'm fine but I'm not there. I'm over at Miss Emily's getting clothes." I closed my eyes. "God, Amy, she had them all picked out with a note to me pinned to the front. She's planned the whole thing. All I have to do is put it in motion." The tears welled up again.

"You aren't doing this alone. I've taken the day off. You should have called me Sunday."

I zipped up the garment bag and took it into the living room. "I didn't want to ruin your weekend."

"I know, sweetie. I'll be right there."

I hung up the phone and contemplated the living room. I still hadn't given up hope she had a son somewhere to take over this nightmare. Even if Miss Emily said I was all she had, that just couldn't be right. How does someone die without anyone caring?

I went over to her desk and started shuffling things around. Checkbook, bills, advertisements where Miss Emily had circled the deals for groceries and household items, a lot of paper. She had been planning a trip to Bakerstown this week to shop, not someone who thought her days were numbered. She hadn't even said anything about feeling off the last time we talked.

A door slammed and I jumped. "Amy? That was quick."

No one answered. The house sat quiet. Too quiet. The hair on the back of my neck flared as I remembered Esmeralda's words: "Sometimes they hang around." I stood and walked into the kitchen. "Amy?"

The back door stood open, the screen door to the porch unlatched. I walked over to latch the door, and the screen door flew open before I could touch the hook-and-eye lock. The door banged three times. Then sat still.

I had to be seeing things. Esmeralda just had me on edge, that was all. I reached again, and the screen flew open again.

"Okay, I get it. You don't want me to lock the door. What do you want?" I held my breath, wondering how I'd get my answer. I should have let Esmeralda come by; she knew how to talk to these things.

"Who says I want anything?"

I screamed and turned to face Amy, who'd come in the front door. Amy's eyes widened.

"Are you okay?"

I collapsed into the wooden kitchen chair and pointed to the door. "It's open."

Amy frowned and walked over to the screen. She pulled it closed and put the hook into the eye to keep the door shut before closing the outside door and turning the lock. "The wind's really kicking up out there. We should go around and make sure all the windows are closed before we leave, too."

The wind. All it had been was the wind. "I guess I got spooked."

Amy sat next to me and rubbed my arm. "You've had a bad week. You're entitled to a case of the jitters."

I took a few deep breaths and smiled. "I guess."

"We don't have to do this today. We could just go find an all-you-can-eat buffet that serves alcohol." Amy's tone was light, but I knew she worried.

"Come help me look for an address book or something." I stood and nodded to the living room. "She has to have some relatives, somewhere."

The desk had a drawer for folders on the side. Pulling open the drawer, I flipped through the files. Each month had its own folder for receipts, bills paid, etc. Then there was a thick file labeled Council.

I smiled at Amy and pulled the file out. Years of letters from the council and copies of her responses stapled to the front of each letter spilled out. Miss Emily's handwriting got shakier throughout the years and her responses, shorter. The last one just said "Mowed!" with her signature. And as her letters shortened, the council letters lengthened. I read the last letter from the council, sitting on top. The letter gave her thirty days to clean up the property with an attached list of infractions or else further action would occur.

A letter sat on top of the desk. The letter Miss Emily had told me about. But this one was on different stationery. I pulled out my notebook and wrote down the lawyer's name and phone number from the top of the letter. I'd have a talk with him right after I called the mayor. "Amy? Who's this lawyer? Why is the council using out-of-town lawyers?"

"They don't. We have a Bakerstown lawyer on retainer. It's a lot cheaper. Why?"

I handed her the letter. "This guy's out of San Francisco. If they have a lawyer on retainer, why wouldn't they use him to send a property infraction letter?"

Amy studied the letter. "This isn't right. The council has the item up on the agenda to discuss her property, but they aren't at this level, not yet. You know they take forever to make any decisions." She fingered through the other letters from the file.

"This is the only one from this attorney. All the other ones are from the council. I know, because I typed them."

"So why would an out-of-town lawyer be sending Miss Emily a letter threatening to condemn her property?" I sat back in my chair. "This just doesn't make any sense."

"I'll check the council's list of approved attorneys handling their legal matters tomorrow. Maybe they didn't send this through me because of my relationship with you. But I swear, the last meeting they were just grumbling about the weeds and the fence. Nothing like this." Amy pulled out a receipt from a gas station and wrote down the lawyer's name and address.

"I have paper."

"This is fine. That way I recycle the receipt. I hate to have it only be used once."

Amy collected cans and paper for the county recycling program. She picked up trash on her morning runs. She only used her 1970 Datsun pickup for trips to the beach and walked to work and around town. I think the truck only had fifty thousand miles on it. If one person could save the world through recycling, she'd be the one to do it.

Amy tucked the receipt and her pen back into her purse. "How are you doing?"

"I told you, I'm fine."

"Yeah, I can tell." She reached up and rubbed a spot under my eye. "I have mascara if you want to try again."

I'd forgotten about the raccoon eyes. "I think I'll just wash this off and leave it." I headed to the bathroom.

I heard Amy fiddling through the rest of the files. "Find anything?" I asked when I walked back into the room.

"Did you know Miss Emily had the property surveyed last year? There's a receipt here for the cost but no report. That's strange."

"Maybe she put the report somewhere else. Did you find an address book or anything listing relatives?" I still hoped for a long-lost cousin or anything, even though Miss Emily's note made it pretty clear it was down to me.

My cell rang.

"Hello?" I couldn't think of who it could be since Amy was the only person who called me and she sat next to me digging through Miss Emily's desk.

"This is Detective King. I need you to come to the funeral home."

"I'm supposed to meet Doc Ames at two o'clock."

"I need you here now. We found something during the autopsy." He paused. "You might be right. Miss Emily could have been murdered."

Chapter 3

People crowded Doc Ames's office when Amy and I arrived twenty minutes later. The ride over had been quiet. I had known Miss Emily hadn't gone peacefully in her sleep, but I couldn't wrap my head around who would have actually wanted to kill her. Even with the list of suspects I had drawn up that morning, I felt clueless.

"I'm glad you made it early. I have a few questions for you before Jimmy reads the will." Detective King looked like he hadn't slept much in the last twenty-four hours. I almost felt sorry for him.

"From your call, it seemed like kind of a command performance." I scanned the room for a familiar face but came up empty except for Pastor Bill, Doc Ames, and Detective King. "Jimmy Marcum's here?"

"How do you know Jimmy?"

"I don't."

"Then how did you know his last name was Marcum?" Detective King challenged.

"I found this with Miss Emily's funeral clothes." I thrust the note into his hands and walked toward the front of the chapel. "I need to give these to Doc Ames."

Doc Ames met me and gently took the bag. "Thanks for bringing these. I know going back into the house must have been hard."

"She had them all ready. I'm supposed to tell you no panty hose and no jewelry." I bit my lip. I was not going to cry. Not in front of all these people.

Doc Ames laughed. "Sounds like Miss Emily. She told me the same thing when she came in last year to make her arrangements. I guess she didn't think I listened close enough." He reached in his jacket pocket for a small plastic bag, handing it to me. "Here's her wedding ring and the cross she'd been wearing when she came in."

Coming up behind me, Detective King took the bag out of my hand. "Doc, you know there's an open investigation, that's evidence." He scowled at Doc Ames.

"Whatever." Holding her jewelry just made it too real for me. King could have it. I didn't care. "So, what did you want to talk to me about?"

"Not here. Let's go into the chapel for some privacy." He nodded at Doc Ames. "We'll be right back."

He held my elbow as he guided me to the chapel. Amy tried to follow, but he held his hand up like a stop sign and she relented, sitting in the office to wait.

We sat down in the pew closest to the door, closed for privacy. Too bad this chat was all business. Detective King looked hot in a big-muscle, sandy-brown-hair, baby-blue-eyes kind of way. I've always been a sucker for a man in uniform. He'd never paid this much attention to me before.

Focus, Jill, focus.

"What did you want to talk about?" He wasn't here to ask me out. My emotions must be all twisted with losing Miss Emily.

Detective King pulled a little notebook out of his front pocket. "I just need to clarify a few things about your relationship with the deceased."

"You mean Miss Emily. You don't have to act like you didn't know her." Now he'd made me mad. If I were a cartoon character, steam would be rolling out of my ears.

"Sorry, Miss Emily." Detective King examined his notes. "Now, would you please tell me again what happened the morning you found Miss Emily?"

"I told you, I went over Sunday about ten to talk to her about getting her lawn mowed. Amy had told me the council had mentioned taking Miss Emily to court regarding the condition of the house." I didn't mention the letter from the attorney Amy and I had found in Miss Emily's desk. I could drop it off at the police station later; if Amy couldn't find out anything, then I'd let the professionals handle it.

"Was the door unlocked when you got there?" Detective King stared at me. What was he looking for?

I thought back to yesterday morning. I had been dreading the conversation with Miss Emily since Wednesday. I'd walked into the yard mentally measuring the length of the grass and how whomever I got to mow would have to rake up the clippings, as well.

"The door was unlocked. I didn't think about it at the time. I was surprised she wasn't up yet. Honestly, I was worried she'd fallen in the bathroom or backyard."

"You went into the house?"

"I knocked and then went in. I headed to the kitchen for a cup of coffee and called out to her. When no one answered, I started getting nervous."

"Did anything seem out of place in the house?"

I stopped and thought back for a moment. "Not really. I mean, I've never been in her bedroom before that day. The rest of the house looked normal. Miss Emily collected everything, so there were always piles of newspapers, magazines, and more."

"The mayor insists you're not to be considered a suspect." Detective King narrowed his eyes and stared. "Are you related to the Honorable Mayor?"

"Mayor Bird, I mean Baylor?" Everyone called him Mayor Bird around town. He chirped instead of talked, his tone high-pitched and his words clipped. "I'm not related to him or anyone else in this town."

"So, what brought you to South Cove? I heard you had a pretty nice gig in San Francisco."

"If you call dealing with battered women and the men who love to hit them a nice gig, then yes."

Who was this guy? I was getting pretty tired of the questions. Like I'd moved here five years ago as part of my evil plan to kill Miss Emily on Sunday.

"I heard you were an attorney and married to some stockbroker or something." Detective King glanced up at me.

"Well, the rumor mill got part of it right. I was married to a stockbroker and I was an attorney. I practiced family law, which means I worked more hours than the other associates and made half as much."

"You didn't know anyone here when you moved?"

"Only Miss Emily. All it took was talking to her one weekend, and she'd convinced me to pull up stakes and move here. I spent an afternoon with her drinking iced tea when I stayed for a short vacation at Madison's Bed-and-Breakfast. She got me." I started to tear up.

He checked his list. "Well, that's about it. Let's go back into the office."

"What did Doc Ames find? How did she die?" My mind wandered back over the scene from Doc Ames's office. Who were those people? "And what's happening in the office?"

"I can't go over the specifics of the investigation with you. As a former attorney, you should know that. We need to go back to the office for the reading of the will." Detective King peered back at me. "I've been told you are going to be very happy."

Happy? What the heck was he talking about? Miss Emily lived off her small pension check, using coupons to afford her groceries. "Whatever she left me, I'm sure it will be more sentimental than financial."

"I guess you could call the inheritance sentimental."

I followed Detective King back into Doc Ames's office. Looking around, I spied Amy, who patted the chair next to her when she saw me.

"What did he want?" Amy whispered.

I kept an eye on Detective King to see if he was listening. He headed toward the front, but it seemed like he was going to talk to the tall, skinny guy with Doc Ames. The three of them spoke in low tones and kept glancing over at me. The guy was a royal jerk. "He just wanted to get my story about when I found Miss Emily."

"Are you a suspect?" Amy grabbed my hand. "That's just dumb, you loved that old lady."

"No, for some reason, Mayor Baylor has taken me out of the suspect pool." I watched Amy for any reaction. "What's up with that, do you think?"

"How should I know? He's crazy." Amy started to dig in her purse for something, avoiding eye contact.

"Amy? Did you ask Mayor Baylor to tell Detective King to keep me out of this?" I pressed my friend, who continued to focus on the bottom of her purse.

"Why would I do that? And more to the point, why would he listen to me? The man hates me." Amy's voice sounded muffled from the purse.

I suspected Amy knew more than what she was saying, but if my friend had kept my name out of the investigation, more power to her. I didn't kill Miss Emily, and it would be pretty hard to find out who did from the inside of South Cove's makeshift jail. I'd have to think about taking Mayor Baylor's name off my list, quid pro quo, but not until I talked to him. "Hey, what time does he come into the office tomorrow?"

"Mayor Baylor? Not until nine-thirty, ten. Why?" Amy regarded me from her excursion into her purse. She offered me a peppermint Life Saver from a half-gone roll. My stomach growled. I took the Life Saver.

"I wanted to talk to him about Bambi's developer boyfriend. Have you found out anything?" I hoped this reading would start soon. I realized I hadn't eaten since lunch yesterday. Maybe Amy would be up to a stop at Tuscany Garden before we left town to head home.

"Not a word. Of course I didn't see His Honor before I left today, so I'll see what I can find out tomorrow. You have to open the shop tomorrow, don't you?"

I thought about my crowded Tuesday. I had to order supplies and new books to get the shop ready for the weekend. How would I run the shop, plan a funeral, and figure out who killed my friend? Maybe I could find an extra eight hours a day by not sleeping.

"Good afternoon. I'm happy you could all join us." Doc Ames addressed the small crowd of seven in his office. "Jimmy Marcum"—he nodded toward the tall man at the front—"has asked for the will to be read before the funeral as a final request from Miss Emily. Although this is an unusual request, it's not totally without precedent. Detective King has asked to sit in on the reading. Jimmy?"

The tall man stood by Doc Ames's desk. "Thanks for allowing us to use your chapel, Fred." He nodded to Doc Ames. I'd never heard anyone call Doc Ames Fred before. "I guess you know why we are all here."

Jimmy Marcum pulled out a file from a briefcase sitting on Doc Ames's desk. He scanned the people gathered. I felt his glance fall on me. "Let's introduce ourselves. Miss Gardner? Will you start?"

"I'm Jill Gardner. I run Coffee, Books, and More over in South Cove. Miss Emily and I were friends." I turned toward Amy and sat back in my chair, passing her the invisible introduction torch.

Amy didn't stand. "I'm Amy Newman, South Cove's city developer and Jill's friend." She turned toward the redheaded woman in the pew across the aisle.

"I'm Sabrina Jones and this is my husband, George." She pointed to the slender man perched next to her. "He's Miss Emily's nephew and only living relative."

Sabrina glared at me. "I don't know why we are even having this hearing. We should get all her stuff."

"As I've told you, this isn't a hearing. It's the reading of the will, not a court case. These are Miss Emily's final wishes and the disposition of her estate." The attorney took back control of the room. "Of course, everyone knows Detective King and Doc Ames. Now, if we are ready?" He glared across the room that had suddenly gone quiet.

I peeked over at the unknown George, Miss Emily's nephew. I tried to remember if Miss Emily had ever talked about a nephew. Nothing came to mind. Then I realized Jimmy Marcum had already started talking and I was traipsing down memory lane.

". . . my last will and testament. To my nephew, George Jones, my only living relative and heir, I leave the family Bible and a photo album with our family history, which is in Mr. Marcum's care so George and Sabrina don't have to be burdened with the long twenty-mile drive to South Cove after the reading of the will. Since you were unable to visit me during my lifetime, I'm sure you won't mind staying the hell out of my house now that I'm gone."

Jimmy Marcum stopped reading and pulled a large Bible from his briefcase and a blue picture album. He walked over to George and handed him the books. "I'm sorry for your loss."

I wasn't sure if Jimmy referenced George losing Miss Emily or her earthly treasures.

Sabrina glared at Jimmy Marcum. "Two old books? That's it? She didn't have anything else? No money, no stocks? What about the house?" Sabrina's voice got louder as she listed off the items George wasn't getting.

Jimmy returned to the front. "Please, let me continue. To my friend, Jill Gardner, first, I leave you my thanks. You befriended a lonely old woman who didn't have anything better to do than annoy the council with my lawn."

Amy started laughing. Jimmy stopped talking. Amy pulled out a tissue from her purse. "If I could continue."

He started again. "You put up with my ramblings, my stories, and my complaints with grace and love. I may not have had a daughter of my blood, but thanks to you, I had a daughter in my old age. I'm sorry I put you through so much bother."

Amy handed me the tissue as tears started to fall on my cheeks. Miss Emily had been the one who always believed in me.

"For your love, I leave to you my house, the entire contents of the house, my car, and the funds from my bank accounts, life insurance, and stock. My accountant assures me at least in liquid assets I'm rather quite wealthy, and now dear, so are you. My only request is that you move into the house and live there. Oh, and you need to get a dog. That's it. Have a good life, my dear. I'll miss you."

Jimmy set the will down on the table. "That's all, folks. Miss Gardner? I'll make time for you to meet with me and go over the specifics of the bequest next week after the funeral. I understand your store is closed on Mondays? Can you be at my office about one o'clock?"

I nodded, not trusting my voice. I took the card he offered and put it in my purse. Get a dog. The woman left me her house. And she wanted me to get a dog.

"You okay?" Amy leaned into me and put her arm around my shoulders. "You ready for some pasta?" Amy always knew how to cheer me up. Anyplace that slapped bread down on the table as soon as you walked in classified as my favorite place to eat.

"I'm fine. I'm just wondering what kind of dog I'm supposed to get."

"Jill, I don't think it matters. I think she just didn't want you to be lonely."

"I've always been partial to golden retrievers myself." Detective

King stood by me. "I think my friend has a litter of pups if you'd like to go look at them this weekend?"

I studied the handsome man standing by my side. "I'd like that."

"I'll call you on Saturday, then?"

"It's a date. I mean, that would be nice."

Sabrina Jones pushed her way past Greg. "This isn't over, girlie, not by a long shot." She grabbed George's arm and pulled him out the door.

"She's not happy." I frowned as I watched the couple leave the chapel.

"That's an understatement. Make sure you keep your doors locked for the next few days, maybe she'll cool off." Greg joined me in staring as the couple left the mortuary.

And maybe she wouldn't.

I knew I had two more names to add to my list of suspects.

The sun was setting as we drove back to South Cove from Bakerstown's Italian mecca, Tuscany Garden. I'd ordered their seafood special with a bottle of white wine, of which, looking back, I think Amy had one glass. I polished off the rest. Wine, pasta, bread sticks, soup, the whole experience.

"I'd planned to take off for a couple of days to scout out a new place for the competition next month. But I can put it off until after the funeral if you'd like." Amy turned down the stereo, watching for my reaction.

"Life goes on. I'm going to be swamped around here. I'll probably not even notice you're gone." I laid my head back on the headrest.

Thank God Amy drove because I couldn't keep my eyes open. Blame it on the pasta, the stress, or even the warm summer sun coming in through the windshield, but I fell asleep soon after we headed for home. I woke when I realized we weren't moving anymore.

"Hey, how long have we been here?" I glanced out the passenger window. We were parked on the street outside my shop.

"Just a few minutes. You looked so cute with the drool coming out of your lips I thought I'd look for my camera before I woke you up."

Amy was evil that way. "You didn't!" I sat up and wiped my mouth. I'd probably been snoring, too.

She laughed. "I couldn't find it. And I'm never sure how to use this stupid cell phone camera, so your secret's safe with me, I guess." Amy surveyed the storefront. "Have you thought about closing for a week until you get all this stuff for Miss Emily handled?"

"I'm considering calling in the cavalry. My aunt Jackie ran a coffee shop in San Francisco for years. If I can catch her between jetting off to France or Mexico, maybe she'll come down and run the shop for a couple weeks." I hadn't seen Aunt Jackie for over a year, not since my last visit back to San Fran.

"Well, I think you should at least close for tomorrow. People will understand. Most of them will be at Miss Emily's funeral on Friday."

"That's a good idea. I'll pop in and make a sign right now." Then, I added silently, it's upstairs and straight to bed. Making the sign tonight gave me freedom to not set my alarm. Maybe I'd sleep past five-thirty. I'd call Aunt Jackie as soon as I woke.

I pulled myself out of Amy's truck and waved to my friend, who watched me as I unlocked the store door. You'd think we lived in LA, not a small tourist town more likely to be void of foot traffic than not. Especially at nine on a Monday night, a time known by the local business owners as the dead zone.

Not exactly a comforting thought at the moment.

I flipped on the lights and walked back to my office. Scratching out a CLOSED sign, I dug around in my desk to find some tape. I'd gone back and forth about what to put on the sign. Finally, I decided on a sign that said CLOSED FOR THE DAY, SEE YOU WEDNESDAY. I didn't want to seem drab and dreary, but I also couldn't be bright and cheery. What would people think?

I taped the sign in the window, double-checked the locks on the door, and turned off the front lights, heading to my upstairs apartment and bed. All I wanted to do was slip off my clothes and slide in between the sheets. Sleep, I could do, no matter what was happening in my life.

The next morning, the sunlight shining through my bedroom window woke me up. I rolled over to check the alarm: seven o'clock.

Amazing. I jumped out of bed and started the coffeepot. Heading to the shower, I made a mental list of what I needed to get done today. First and most important on the list was a call to Aunt Jackie to see if I could con her into coming down to handle the store for a few weeks. As the water ran over my body, I played out the conversation in my mind. I knew it was a big favor to ask. Aunt Jackie had worked hard for years to deserve her happy-go-lucky traveling retirement. But maybe she'd at least hear me out.

After getting dressed and fortifying myself with a cup of coffee, black, I pulled out my address book and made the call.

"Hey, Aunt Jackie, it's me, Jill."

"Jill, I haven't heard from you in forever! Did you lose my number?"

Great, guilt with my coffee, and now I was asking for a favor?

"I'm sorry about that. The shop keeps me pretty busy." I hoped that would satisfy her. "In fact, I'm calling about the shop. I've had a problem come up, and I wondered if you could help?"

"Sure, let me grab my coffee and sit down, and then you can tell me what's going on. I'm positive I've probably dealt with something like it over my years."

I could hear Aunt Jackie's slippers slapping the kitchen floor as she went over to pour more coffee. I knew from experience, she wouldn't hear anything I said until she got herself settled and ready to talk. So I waited. Examining my to-do list for the day, I crossed off *Call Aunt Jackie*. I just hoped the call would be all I needed to convince her to come.

"Okay, I'm back, Jilly. What's going on? Problems with a supplier? I told you not to put all your eggs in one basket. You need to have options."

"No, it's not a problem with a supplier. In fact, the shop's doing great."

"Then what do you need from me?"

I took a deep breath. "Aunt Jackie, I've had a friend die. She didn't have anyone, so I'm responsible for getting her affairs in order. I just can't do all that and keep the shop going. Is there any way—" I didn't get to finish the sentence.

"You want me to come down and run the shop?"

"Basically, yes. I mean, I'll be in town to help out if you need me, but there are just so many things I need to do." Who knew planning a funeral would be so time-consuming? Especially when you added in the looking-for-a-murderer part.

The line went dead. Oh God, she'd hung up on me. "Aunt Jackie?"

"Hold on, dear, I'm looking at my calendar. I had a cruise scheduled next month to the Galapagos Islands to see that Lonely George turtle. I hear he's not as lonely anymore." She giggled. "But I'm free for a few weeks. I guess it wouldn't hurt me to spend some time with my favorite niece."

I was her only niece. "So you'll come?"

"I'll drive down this afternoon. We can eat dinner together. I should be there no later than five, depending on traffic."

"Great. I appreciate this." I wrote down *Dinner at Lille's* on my list.

"Do I need to book a room at that lovely B-and-B down the road?"

I hadn't thought about where she'd stay, but then I had an idea. If Miss Emily's house was now mine, it would be more convenient for me to stay there while I pulled everything together. "Nope, don't book anything. You'll stay in my apartment."

"But dear, you only have one bedroom and I'm not a couch sort of girl."

Boy, was that ever true. "You'll have the place to yourself. I have other plans."

"You aren't taking off with some loser and leaving me stuck with the shop, are you?" The words sounded light, almost casual. But the meaning was clear. My aunt considered me a flake.

Ouch, that hurt. "No, I'm not taking off. I'll explain it all when you get here."

"All right, then. I'll see you this evening."

"Drive safe. And thank you."

"No problem, dear. What is family for?"

Breathing a sigh of relief, I made another call. In a few minutes, I had the first appointment on the mayor's schedule for the day. Ten o'clock. I headed to the bedroom to pack a bag for my move into Miss Emily's house.

I sat in a turquoise-blue plastic chair, right in the middle of the row of blue plastic chairs I'm pretty sure came from a rummage sale from the California DMV. Think 1960s-era molded backs with most of the lip at the top broken off. Surely the town could afford something a little more upscale, like the folding chairs they sell at Costco, ten for fifty dollars?

Amy pecked at her keyboard, searching for any trace of the lawyer whose letter we'd found in Miss Emily's desk. My travel bag sat in my Jeep, and I was heading directly to Miss Emily's house after hearing what Mayor Bird had on his mind.

I'd called Jimmy Marcum's office and made an appointment for tomorrow afternoon rather than wait until Monday. I figured I had time to get Aunt Jackie settled in the store before I took off for Bakerstown. My mind was running in a thousand directions when I heard my name.

"Miss Gardner?" Mayor Baylor stood in front of me. I hadn't heard him come out of his office. Amy shrugged and started going through the files on her desk. I noticed her screen had gone blank. She must have shut down the monitor when she heard him coming out. I wondered what she had found.

I stood up. "Thank you for seeing me."

"Not at all. Come into my office. I'm sure the last few days have been trying for you, very trying indeed."

He talked like my grandfather had the few times I had met him. Slow, formal, but rather than Granddad's deep, rich voice, Mayor Baylor's voice pitched higher, more feminine. I appreciated his words of comfort, even though I didn't believe the sincerity behind them.

He put his hand on my back and led the way to his office, a gesture that would have been comforting if his hand wasn't just a little too low. We passed by Amy's desk. "Hold my calls, would you, my dear?"

I shot a look at Amy over my shoulder as we walked into the office. She made a gagging motion, shoving her finger down her throat. Okay, the hand on the back definitely felt creepy. I stepped away from the mayor and sat down in one of the leather high backs in front of his desk. He crossed over the Oriental rug and sat down at his large, antique oak desk. No money had been spared decorating this office. This explained the plastic DMV chairs in the waiting room and Amy's iron circa–World War II desk.

"So, what can I help you with? I assume you're here to talk

about selling Miss Emily's house?" Mayor Baylor leaned back in his chair, his hands intertwined in front of him and a barely disguised grin on his mouth.

"Selling? You think I'm interested in selling the house?" I was shocked the conversation had jumped here so quickly. Maybe Mayor Bird should stay on my list of suspects, even if he had taken my name off Detective King's list.

"Why else would you come to see me? I have several investors willing to pay a premium price for the house, even in its current state. I can't believe she lived there all those years in squalor."

My face felt hot and my hands sweaty. "The house isn't in that bad of shape." Okay, so that was an understatement. The house needed everything, but it wasn't like she lived in a cardboard box.

Mayor Baylor sighed. "I know you considered the woman your friend, and that's honorable, especially since she was so difficult to get along with, but we both know that house should be torn down and someone should just start over."

"Mayor Baylor, I don't know what I'm going to do with the house yet." This interview wasn't going the way I had planned. "Now, if we could talk about something else?"

"I'm sorry, I didn't realize. Are there issues with your shop? I'm sure we can work something out. Maybe we could do a flyer for you in the next *Examiner*? We focus on one struggling store a month and give it some free publicity. Amy can give you the application." He leaned over his computer, clearly moving on to another part of his day, a part done with me.

"No, there's not a problem with my shop." He told me what to do, he insulted Miss Emily, and now he was calling my shop unprofitable? What a jerk.

He stopped going through his e-mail and glared at me. "Then why are you here, Miss Gardner?"

I'm here to see if you have the balls to smother someone in their sleep.

I took a deep breath. "I wanted to know why you told Detective King I wasn't to be considered a suspect in Miss Emily's death."

Mayor Baylor sat back in his chair, his potbelly bursting at the buttons of his white button-down shirt. He looked at me, probably for the first time since I had walked into his office. "I told the officer not everything or everyone needed to be examined and suspected. Until yesterday, this was just a woman dying in her sleep. And you were the poor soul who found her." He fiddled with his pen. "Now that you have been revealed as Miss Emily's heir, it does tend to put a different slant on the picture."

"I didn't kill Miss Emily." I stood to go. This meeting had been a colossal waste of time.

"I'm sure you didn't, Miss Gardner. Just as I'm sure you will be seeing your way to selling that house as soon as possible." He spit out the word *house* as if it were a cuss word. "I understand you are an intelligent woman."

"What does that have to do with me selling the house?"

"I just feel it would be in your best interest. Now, if there's nothing else?"

I turned to leave, clearly dismissed.

"You should expect a visit from Mr. Ammond in the next few days. Don't worry, Jill, he'll give you a good profit on your investment."

Red, all I saw filtered through red. I should have just kept walking. I turned at the door. "My friendship with Miss Emily wasn't an investment. If I find out you had any part in her death, I swear . . ."

"You swear what? Remember, my office has a twenty-four-hour voice tape-recording your threat for future prosecution." Smugly, the rat called our Honorable Mayor went back to reading his e-mail. "Good-bye, Miss Gardner. You may want to expect a visit from Detective King, if you turn down Mr. Ammond's offer, that is."

I slammed the door as I left. Amy jumped at her desk. "Jill, are you all right?"

"He is the worst person I've ever met! And he's a crappy mayor." I said the last part directly to the door, hoping his taping system would pick that up for everyone to hear.

"Amen, sister!" A voice came from the back row of blue chairs. "I've been saying the same thing about Mayor Bird for years."

I traced the voice to Esmeralda. The Gypsy woman sat with a pure black shorthair cat on her lap.

She walked up to me, the cat lounging in her arms. Her green eyes glimmered underneath the long, curly black hair bursting out from the patterned scarf she had tied around her head. Her black boots somehow worked with the layers of skirts and patterns swirling around her legs while she walked. She reached out, touching my shoulder.

"Death surrounds you. You've lost one and will soon lose another."

Chapter 4

Esmeralda's black cat hissed at me, reaching out a paw to warn me away. For the second time this week, someone's pet had taken an instant dislike to me. Miss Emily's wish for me to get a dog appeared more unlikely by the minute. At least a dog that liked me.

"Sorry, I'm not popular with animals lately." I slowed my breathing to calm down after my blowup at the mayor.

Esmeralda smoothed her hand across the cat's back, comforting her. "Your aura is disturbing the animals. Your emotions are mixed up. They can feel your distress."

Her explanation made sense in a weird, Gypsy Oprah kind of way. "It's been a rough week," I admitted.

"You have death floating around you." She grabbed my arm, her long, painted nails digging into my flesh. "You have suffered a great loss. Jill, I see that your pain is not over. Someone else close to you will also be lost. Have faith—everything is not how it seems. Be ready. Stand true."

The air around us felt electric. Esmeralda's eyes were vacant as she talked. A cloud passed over her face, and she let go of my arm.

"Good to see you, Jill. Come by the house anytime and we'll do that reading." She turned and addressed Amy. "The mayor can see me now?"

Amy nodded. Esmeralda opened the door and walked into the mayor's office. Without another word, she shut the door behind her.

"Do you believe that?" My body involuntarily shook, like a cat coming in from a rainstorm.

Amy stared at me like I was the circus sideshow rather than Esmeralda.

"I don't think she realized what she was saying. She comes in to do the mayor's reading every week. I've never heard her talk to anyone like that before. She gives me the creeps." Amy contemplated a file on her desk. "I wonder what she meant about your pain not being over."

"She's a fortune-teller, she has to say something."

"She knew about Miss Emily."

"She works for the police department. We talked about Miss Emily's death. Besides, anyone sitting outside the mayor's office listening to me would know that." I pushed the encounter with Esmeralda aside. I had bigger worries. Would the mayor really have me investigated in Miss Emily's death if I refused to sell the house? And worse, would Greg go along with the plan?

With my favorite dinner sitting in front of me—seafood fettuccini, a basket of garlic bread, and a half-consumed bottle of wine—I should have been in food heaven. But I still heard the Gypsy's words ringing in my ears. *Your pain is not over.* What the heck was that supposed to mean? Coming out of my fog, I realized Aunt Jackie had asked me a question.

"What?" I didn't care if I sounded like a spoiled five-year-old, I felt beat.

My aunt had shown up at five on the dot, and we'd headed directly to Lille's. While I'd been lost in thought and a few glasses of wine, she'd finished her dinner, a medium-rare steak and loaded baked potato. "I didn't think you were listening to me. That's all right, you must be tired. We'll talk about the shop tomorrow."

I pushed around the pasta on my plate. "I don't think I've ever been this tired." Curling up under a big comforter sounded like heaven right now.

She nodded toward my barely touched dinner. "Why don't you get that to go, and I'll drop you off at your new house? You shouldn't drive."

Great, two nights in a row I was too sloshed to drive. South Cove was too small a town to start falling apart. Next thing I knew, Amy would be scheduling an intervention.

All I had to do was get through this week. And figure out what I was going to do with Miss Emily's house and money. *My house and money,* I corrected myself. This felt too weird. I'd thought I'd had problems before. Through my alcohol-induced haze, I knew one thing—I wouldn't sell the house to the mayor's developer friend. No matter what price he offered.

I watched Aunt Jackie pay the check and smiled at the hostess, trying to downplay my obviously drunken state. I followed my aunt out to her Escape and waited for her to unlock the doors. Arguing with Aunt Jackie was just a waste of time. She pulled the car out from the curb and onto the main road.

"You can come back for your Jeep tomorrow." She stared at the road ahead, not turning to look at me. "You did lock your doors, right?"

"Only tourists lock their doors in South Cove." The words had just left my mouth when lights appeared in our lane, headed right for us. "Look out!"

Shutting my eyes, I prepared for the crash. The Gypsy's premonition coming true.

No—I don't want to lose my aunt.

I felt the car jerk to the right and waited for the crash. And waited. And waited some more. I opened my eyes. Aunt Jackie watched me, a slight smile on her face.

"Just some kids, hon. You need some sleep."

I closed my eyes, leaning back into the leather bucket seat. I was jumping at shadows. "The house is at the end of town, just as you come in on Main Street. You passed it on the way in."

"The one that looks like it's falling in on itself?" Jackie could barely hold back the horror from her voice.

"Yep, that's it. My new home, stuffed to the brim with old newspapers and other clutter I need to kick to the curb." As soon as I mowed the lawn so I could find the curb.

"Are you sure you don't want to just stay at the apartment? I wouldn't mind sleeping on the couch."

Now I knew she thought I was crazy. Aunt Jackie never offered to sleep on the couch. "I want to stay at the house. If nothing else, it will keep the local kids from thinking it's their new party place. Besides, that way when I get up I can get a head start on cleaning."

As we drove the few blocks down Main Street, I wondered if Miss Emily had any other living relatives besides the weasel-faced George and his pushy wife. I had been so sure she'd mentioned a son. I felt the car slow and realized we were in front of the house.

"Well, if you're sure." Aunt Jackie leaned around me to stare at the dark house, looking more and more like a horror movie set than the charming Victorian it could be after remodeling.

I handed her the extra key to the shop and the apartment. "Don't worry about me. I'll be fine." I gave her a quick hug and stepped out of the car. "I'll meet you at the shop tomorrow at seven to go over everything. One of Lille's staff will drop off the pastries just before eight. Thanks for coming."

I hoped she was up to it. I didn't get a lot of business during the week, mostly townies who liked their coffee dark and simple. The challenge would be this weekend when the tourists poured into South Cove. Maybe by then I'd be a little more organized and able to help out.

"Not a problem, my dear." She was still looking past me at the house. "Jill, did you leave the front door open?"

I glanced over my shoulder. My breath caught. The door stood wide open. "I guess maybe I did."

I couldn't remember. I'd been cleaning out a bedroom on the second floor after I met with the mayor. I'd lost track of time until Aunt Jackie had called, already waiting in front of the shop. I'd produced piles of garbage bags sorted by things to donate, things to show the antique dealer coming next weekend, and things to trash. But when I left the house that evening, I'd gone out the back door to the driveway where I'd left the Jeep. I hadn't gone through the front all day.

Had it been open since the police visit two days ago? I started walking toward the house.

"Should we call somebody?" Aunt Jackie called out from the safety of her Escape.

"No, it's fine. I'm sure I just left it open." I had my cell phone in my hand, ready if I saw anything out of place. I sobered up quickly. First the close call with the head-on collision and now this.

Aunt Jackie's car stayed running by the side of the curb. I walked to the door, pushing it completely open with my foot. The hand that didn't carry the cell phone reached to the left to search for the light switch. Grasping, I couldn't seem to find it, and my eyes searched the blackness for any sign of movement.

Finally, I felt the switch. Light flooded the living room and pooled out on the porch. I scanned the room quickly. Nothing. Nothing out of place, no masked man in black waiting with a knife. Just the circa 1930s furniture and mail from the last two days, dropped on the floor from the mail slot in the door.

I walked back to the porch. "It's fine," I yelled to Aunt Jackie, who now stood outside her car, watching me. "I'll see you tomorrow." I waved and smiled, hoping that would ease her concern enough to actually drive away.

Aunt Jackie shrugged and got back into the car. She pulled away and made a U-turn on Main Street to head to the apartment. I went into the house and closed the door, listening for the dead bolt to click into place, making sure the door locked this time. Then I headed to the back door to do the same.

When I went to bed, I put a chair under my bedroom door. No one was in the house, I had checked each nook and cranny, but still, it didn't hurt to be a little careful. I lay on the bed, the ceiling fan creaking above me, and listened for other noises that didn't come until finally, I fell asleep.

The sound of my cell phone woke me the next morning. Sun streamed in the window, the lace curtains floating around in the soft summer breeze. I reached over the side of the bed and dug through my purse. "Yes," I croaked. My eyelids didn't want to open.

"Wake up, sleepyhead. Did you forget all about me?" Aunt Jackie's voice sounded all cheer and sunshine.

"What time is it?" I pulled myself up to a sitting position, my eyes crusted over.

"Just about nine. I've had several customers already, all curious about where you are and how you are doing."

"Sorry, I'll get dressed and walk down," I said, remembering my Jeep was still at Lille's.

"No hurry. I just wanted to make sure that the weekly supply order got placed as you are looking pretty low in the stockroom. And your book supplier called. She'll be in about one. Do you have a list of what you want? Or can I make my own?"

"There's a customer wish list on my desk in the back, but we need more stock. I usually let Marcia present her sales pitch and then we go from there. But if you have some ideas?"

"Actually I do. I'll make up a list. Talking with the customers this morning, I got some great suggestions. I don't know why you didn't ask them in the first place. I've sold ten books this morning alone."

Great, now she was making me look bad. I'd be lucky if any of the townies liked me after her visit. "I'll be right down."

"Take your time, dear. I haven't had this much fun in years." The line went dead.

I found a clean pair of jeans in the tote bag I'd tossed in the corner yesterday and pulled them on. I grabbed a T-shirt and headed to the bathroom to brush my teeth and throw on a little makeup.

Five minutes later, I was on the road, power-walking to my shop. Thoughts of sipping on a double espresso and eating one of Lille's cinnamon rolls kept my steps quick. Maybe I'd splurge on a mocha with whipped cream. I wasn't going to fit into any of my jeans by the time this month ended.

I'd made sure to lock both the front and back doors before I left the house. I checked all the windows to make sure that they were closed and locked, as well. If the door was open when I got back, it wouldn't be because I forgot to shut it. Then I could call Detective King without feeling like a fool.

I walked in the shop, surprised to see most of the tables and booths filled. The conversation stopped as soon as I walked through the doors. All glances turned to me. Then the murmurs started back up. As I walked to the counter to greet my aunt, several customers stopped me to express their condolences.

"Good morning, Jill. You look rested," my aunt greeted me when I finally made my way to the coffee counter.

"I can't believe how busy we are." I grabbed an apron from the back and started to tie it behind me.

"Now, what are you doing?" Aunt Jackie stared me down.

"Getting ready to help?"

"You called me to come all the way down from San Francisco to help you out, and now you think I can't do it? What, am I too old?"

"I didn't mean to imply—" My words were cut off by Aunt Jackie's flailing hands.

"Then take that apron off and just show me what you need to get done this week so that you can get back to fixing up that house of yours and handling the funeral arrangements." Her gray-green eyes bored into me.

"Thanks." I took the apron off and started a list of the daily chores, deliveries, and books I wanted her to order. Forty minutes later, the list for the week was done. I'd shown her the stockroom, how to work the equipment, and even the bookkeeping processes and daily deposits.

"Let me know if you need anything." I gazed around the shop that had defined my life for the last five years.

Aunt Jackie gave me a hug. "Don't worry. I'll take good care of the shop."

That was what worried me. Before she retired, Aunt Jackie had run the most successful coffee shop in her neighborhood for thirty years. Even before they called them coffee shops. Asking her in to help felt more like surrendering my life. I hoped I'd be able to walk back in when this was all over.

After handing over my life to my aunt, I went down to Lille's to retrieve my car. I had to head back to Bakerstown today and finish up the details for Miss Emily's service. Maybe I could charm some information from Doc Ames. There must be a reason why the autopsy had convinced Greg that Miss Emily had been murdered.

I practiced my best off-the-cuff questions as I got into my Jeep. I turned the key and stared at a flyer stuck to my windshield. Leaning out the driver's door, I grabbed the offending paper. Probably South Cove Vineyard's weekly announcement of a wine tasting on Sunday. Darla, the winery owner, kept trying to get a steady local clientele built to supplement her tourist crowd.

She'd spoken on local marketing during last month's Business to Business meeting sponsored by the council. I resented getting a flyer on my car every week, but I couldn't fault her tenacity. Planning local advertising for the coffee shop would go on the to-do list as soon as I finished planning the funeral and remodeling the house. Throwing the paper on the passenger seat, I drove to Bakerstown.

The drive took just twenty minutes, but the trip took me smackdab down the coastal highway for a long stretch. A lot of Mondays I made the drive just to clear my head and drink in the ocean's energy. Sitting on a deserted beach with waves crashing calmed my head and my heart. My body recharged, adjusting to the wave rhythm and resetting my internal clock. It might be metaphysical hoo-haw, but the results felt like magic, so who was I to judge? Today I had no time for a stop on the beach, but the drive calmed me just the same.

Last night's open door problem kept nagging at me. Had George and his wife actually made the drive down to see what they missed out on in the will? I figured they were more likely to spend their time with their lawyer, scheming about how to get their hands on whatever money Miss Emily left me. Although I didn't feel totally comfortable with the inheritance, I felt better after meeting the meek George and bull-like Sabrina. Miss Emily must have thought she had a choice of leaving her money to me or the Church of Diseased Cats.

My cell rang in my purse. Keeping one hand on the wheel, I dug through my purse with my right hand, without looking down once. I grabbed the phone and flipped it open. "Yes?"

"Where are you?" Amy's voice came over the speakerphone. "I thought you were taking off on some trip."

"This evening. Listen, where are you?" Amy asked, her voice terse.

"On my way to the funeral home, why?" Amy never called me during the day, unless we were heading to Lille's for lunch.

"Your lawyer's here," Amy mumbled.

"Hold on, I can't hear you." I rolled up the window, cutting out the road noise. I couldn't understand her. I thought she said my lawyer was at the mayor's office. I didn't have a lawyer, unless you counted Jimmy Marcum. My appointment with him had been changed to Monday. "Okay, go ahead."

If anything, Amy's voice got lower. "The lawyer from Miss Emily's letter. He's here in Mayor Baylor's office. He just went in."

I slowed down and considered turning back to South Cove.

"How do you know it's him?" I glanced at the clock on the dashboard.

"I heard the mayor introduce him to Bill from the council. The developer guy's here, too. They're all in the office talking right now." Amy sounded like she'd been locked in a closet. "I left for lunch but forgot my keys. When I came back into the lobby, the four walked into Mayor Baylor's office and closed the door. I don't even think they noticed me."

"Where are you? I can barely hear you."

"I'm under my desk. I didn't want them to see me calling you."

Seriously? What would the mayor and his guests think if they saw a phone cord dangling down under the desk? Sometimes Amy didn't act like she had a master's degree.

"Amy, go to lunch. I've got to meet Doc Ames or Miss Emily won't ever get a proper burial." My loyalty to Miss Emily won out and kept the Jeep heading to Bakerstown.

"I'll call you when I get back if he's still here." Amy's voice got louder.

"Just be careful."

"You don't think they killed Miss Emily, do you?" Amy's voice had a slight quiver. Like when she saw a dead sea lion or an injured bird.

Now I've scared her.

"Just go to lunch. I'll call you as soon as I'm done with Doc Ames."

"I'm going straight to Lille's and ordering a double order of fish and chips and a milk shake."

And she wouldn't gain an ounce. Life wasn't fair. "Later."

I hung up the phone and rolled the window back down to get the wind flowing through the Jeep. I grabbed the granola bar masquerading as my lunch and dreamed of Lille's French fries. By the time I reached the funeral home, I could smell the salt and grease. Tonight's dinner wouldn't be a frozen diet meal. I planned on visiting fast-food heaven before I left the big city. Maybe the salt and fat would ease the pit that had been in my stomach since the reading of the will.

Doc Ames walked me through the funeral process. What would happen, who would speak, even what hymns would be sung. At each step, he'd ask my opinion. By the end of the hour, I'd said "that will be nice" so many times, I wasn't even convincing myself anymore.

And then we were done. Doc Ames walked me out to the parking lot.

"I'm deeply sorry for your loss." He opened the Jeep's door.

Tears filled my eyes. "She meant a lot to me."

"Not everyone would go through all this for someone who wasn't related." Doc Ames shook his head. "Believe me, I've seen too many souls pass through here with no one handling the last requests, no one to grieve. She was lucky to have you as a friend."

I climbed in the Jeep. "That's where you have it wrong. I was the lucky one."

He shut the door and waved. "I'll see you Friday for the service."

I started the car up and headed to fast-food alley. As an emotional eater, I needed to live up to my vice.

When I got back to the house, a black Hummer sat parked in front. Stuffing what remained of the second order of thick steak fries back into the paper bag, I wiped my mouth with my hand. The mushroom and Swiss burger had disappeared soon after leaving the drive-in's parking lot. When I added a vanilla milk shake, the meal had cost the same as one of Lille's rib-eye steak dinners with all the fixings. But it had been worth the price. I'd been starting to feel normal again. Now I had visitors. My stress level ratcheted up as I got out of the Jeep.

A tall Middle Eastern man in a suit that had to have cost more than my Jeep got out of the Hummer and walked toward me. "Miss Gardner?" His voice was deep and smooth, like aged whiskey.

After first wiping my hands on my jeans to remove any last trace of grease and salt, I shook his offered hand. "I'm Jill Gardner, and you are?"

"Admiring your beautiful house caused me to forget my manners. My name is Eric Ammond."

I stiffened, pulling my hand away from his. "Mayor Baylor's friend. Well, you wasted your time. I'm not selling. Besides, under the conditions of the will, I can't sell."

"It's never a waste of time to meet such a beautiful woman." He studied me, scanning my body from head to toe. "It is true. I am interested in buying your lovely home. Can we go inside and talk about what I have to offer?" He put his hand on my shoulder and motioned to the front door.

"I don't think we have anything to talk about, unless you need relationship advice on how to be a better boyfriend to Bambi." What? I was supposed to fall over myself just because he was probably the most handsome man I had ever met, here or anywhere?

Eric laughed. "So you've met my beautiful Bambi. She is the apple of my eye, so light and positive. But you are dark and brooding, intelligent, and amazing. You and I would have a good time, believe me."

I shrugged out from under his hand and headed to the house. "Not interested. In you or selling the house, in case you were confused."

"Not even if I offer three times the market rate for this sad little house?"

"I thought you said the house was beautiful."

He laughed. "The site will be as soon as I tear the eyesore down and put up my condos."

"The answer is still no." I shut the door and engaged the dead bolt, hoping he'd hear the click. I couldn't believe it. He had played the sex card to trick me into selling him the house. Even knowing I knew he had a girlfriend, he'd hit on me. Too bad the beautiful man was evil incarnate.

The mayor's warning about accepting Mr. Ammond's offer echoed in my head, and I couldn't help but wonder what strings he'd pull now.

Chapter 5

Sitting in Miss Emily's kitchen—scratch that, my kitchen—the next morning, I checked my growing to-do list. The funeral had been planned and scheduled for Friday. Check. Detective King had given permission for the body to be buried, which wasn't the way they did it on television, where they kept the murder victim on ice until the vile murderer was caught. But I guess things go differently in real life.

I had two days free to clean the house and decide what I wanted to keep. An antiques dealer from Bakerstown had left his card with Doc Ames, saying he'd be glad to drive out to appraise anything I wanted to sell. I paper-clipped his card to my list and poured another cup of coffee. Looking at my calendar, I could get the majority of these projects completed and be back to my normal life by next Tuesday. And Aunt Jackie wouldn't even miss her next cruise.

The reception would be at the Methodist church right after the service. The church women's group was responsible for providing the food and drinks. Other than sending a thank-you note afterward, half check. Doc Ames had given me a list of what was happening when. When I asked what I needed to do, he said the arrangements had all been made. I didn't understand why he hadn't just called me. I'm not a personal-touch kind of girl.

Calling? My heart sank. I told Amy I'd call her back last night.

I pulled a dead cell phone out of my purse. I'd forgotten to put it on the charger. I was surprised she hadn't shown up on my doorstep, sleeping bag in hand. Then I remembered she was on that scouting trip. Amy chaired the local surfer group, and they sponsored some big-deal competition each year.

I pulled the charger cord out of my bag and found a plug-in on the kitchen wall. I headed out to the garage to get some boxes. I might as well start in the kitchen.

Two hours later, I had dishes stacked on the counter, boxes filled with items for the antique dealer and six bags of trash. I had called the local Bakerstown Home Repair box store, and they were scheduled to come tomorrow with a new dishwasher, range, and washer-dryer set. My credit card hovered near the limit, but my meeting with Jimmy Marcum should solve that problem. Otherwise, I would have to sell a lot of coffee to pay for the changes I wanted to make on this place. Or maybe take on a third part-time job to make the payments.

I made more notes on my to-do list. Paint the kitchen, replace flooring, price out cabinets and counters. The list continued to grow. With all the renovations that my ex and I did on the San Francisco houses, I knew I could lay a wood Pergo floor. Maybe I could con Amy into helping me on that one.

I went to check my phone: no messages or missed calls. I called Amy's office number. After five rings, her message machine came on. "This is Amy Newman, South Cove's city planner. I can't come to the phone right now, please leave a message."

"Hi, Amy. Look, my phone died last night. Call me when you get back tomorrow. I want to ask you something." I hung up the phone but stared at it for a while. When did the council meet again?

I checked the calendar hanging in Miss Emily's kitchen. *Council Meeting* had been written in red on the twenty-fifth, two weeks away. I had plenty of time. Setting the phone down, I grabbed one of the trash bags and carried it out to the side of the garage. My arm pinched, and I rolled my shoulders to ease the stress. I wouldn't think about my friend, even though every plate I picked up reminded me of Miss Emily.

If I could get most of the cabinets cleaned out, I would go shopping tomorrow while they installed my new appliances. My grandmother always said the kitchen was the heart of the home, so it was the first room on my list to remodel. With it done, I could cook dinner for Aunt Jackie next week before she left as a thank-you.

The phone was ringing when I came back through the door. Stumbling over one of the boxes, I grabbed it. "Amy?"

"No, this is Sadie Michaels down at the church."

I poured yet another cup from my second pot of the day. Who needed energy drinks when you could mainline caffeine? "What can I do for you, Miss Michaels?"

"Call me Sadie."

"Sorry, what can I do for you, Sadie?" I sat down at the table. This wasn't going to be a quick call. I could already see that.

"Well, Miss Gardner—"

I interrupted her. "Now, if you're Sadie, then I have to be Jill."

"Well, Jill, the ladies and I just wanted to let you know that everything is set for the service tomorrow. We'll have a ham and several sides, including Aggie's potato salad and Connie's coleslaw. I know you aren't a member of our church family, so I just wanted to assure you that the meal after the service will be tasty. We went all out for Miss Emily."

"I'm sure Miss Emily would be pleased." I was surprised we were having a full meal. I'd expected coffee and cookies. Apparently I had more to learn about this funeral ritual. I wondered what else I was supposed to do afterward. Did I send thank-you notes for the flowers and the food? Did Hallmark sell them? I made a note to call Doc Ames; he would know.

"I wanted to tell you how much you meant to Miss Emily. I'd stop by each week. She was on my visitation route. She would just go on and on about you and that shop of yours."

"She could be a talker." I choked up. I wished people would stop being so nice. One of these times I would start crying. I bit my bottom lip, changing the subject. "So, you visited her? I'm sorry, Sadie. Miss Emily didn't mention you."

Sadie laughed, and the sound chimed over the connection like bells.

"That doesn't surprise me. She could be a little hesitant about anything that had to do with the church. Both Pastor and I visited frequently, especially lately. She seemed to have a lot on her mind. We talked a lot about you, the house, and even her son, Bob."

"Did she ever mention her nephew, George? I was surprised to see him at the will reading."

"He and that wife of his came by last month during one of my visits. I swear they had measuring tapes in their brains, looking at the room. You could tell they were planning a renovation when the house became theirs. I bet they blew a gasket when she left everything to you."

"You could say that." I pushed the conversation further. "Did you ever meet Bob?"

"Bob had already passed by the time I started visiting Miss Emily ten years ago. I think she said he was killed in Vietnam. That entire time seemed such a tragic waste of a war."

"I didn't know when he died." I wrote down *Vietnam-era veteran* next to Bob's name. Maybe he had friends who knew about how he died. Probably a long shot since it had been so many years, but what if he had left behind someone? I drew a box around Bob's name and a question mark. "Is he buried in Bakerstown?"

"Oh, dear, his body was never recovered. Miss Emily told me she had nightmares that he'd been left to die in some rice field during the evacuation. She had to fight the government to get his benefits."

I peered over at the framed military picture of what must have been Bob hanging on Miss Emily's living room wall. His green eyes smiled out at me.

I told Sadie that I'd meet her at the church tomorrow just before the service started.

"Well, don't be late, you won't be able to find a seat. I hear most of the town is planning on coming out. Probably hoping for a catfight between you and the nephew's wife. She's been spouting out all over town what a fraud you are and that they are thinking about taking you to court to overturn the will."

"Me, a fraud?" I couldn't believe the witch.

"Don't worry, the town's on your side. Those two are just sucking on sour apples. Jimmy Marcum wouldn't allow them to contest the will. I hear they tried to focus the murder investigation your way, too, but dear Greg just laughed at them." I heard her muffled talking to someone next to her. "I've got to go, dear, there's a problem in the kitchen. I'm looking forward to meeting you tomorrow."

And with that, the line went dead. So Jack Sprat and his wife were spreading ill will about me in the community. Didn't they realize I owned a business, and if they cost me business, I could sue them?

The phone rang again. "Yes?" I spat out when I answered, still angry about the Joneses.

"Hey, hon, it's Aunt Jackie. I'm at the store and realized that you could open up a huge section of additional seating if you just took out the bookcases."

What? She wanted to redecorate the store?

"Well, the point of the bookcases is to give it a library feel, you know, where people can come and drink coffee, read, and buy books?" I didn't understand why I had to explain my concept to my aunt. Wasn't she supposed to be working for me?

"And you should take advantage of the sidewalk area and set up some tables and umbrellas. You'd get a lot more walk-by traffic that way."

Great idea. I'd already filed my zoning permit with the city last month to allow me to open the outdoor café area.

"Aunt Jackie, I'm already working on that. But thanks." The background sounded quiet. "So, the store sounds quiet. Fewer customers today?"

"Actually, no, there are a ton of customers, but I'm upstairs in the apartment working on the books."

Panic hit me. "Who's in the shop?"

"I hired a nice young man who came in yesterday looking for a part-time job. I think he said his name was Toby."

"You think? You didn't get an application or look at his criminal history? Or anything?"

"Relax. He's one of South Cove's finest, a part-time police officer. He's just looking for a little extra money."

To be honest, so was I. How would I pay for another part-time employee? "I'm not sure I have money in the budget for staffing."

"Oh, don't worry about that. I'm going over the books right now. I think if we stop running the bookstore section, which is losing money, by the way, and just focus on the coffee and pastries, we'll be fine."

"We'll be fine?" The agitation made my voice tight, and I could feel my throat straining when I talked.

"You did call me up here for help, now, didn't you?" I heard the frustration in my aunt's voice.

"Help, yes. Take over, no." Yelling at my aunt wasn't solving anything. I took a deep breath. "Listen, could we talk about this later? Just don't hire anyone else or start tearing up the shop until we do, okay?"

"Sure." The line went dead.

I stared at the phone. My life was falling apart around me. My friend had been murdered. I had to get the house cleaned. I'd scheduled an antiques dealer to come by Saturday to look over Miss Emily's things. And my aunt had already started messing with my shop. Last week I read a mystery. Today I lived one.

Flipping open the to-do list lying on the kitchen table, I knew where to start. Back to basics. Step one, when you are totally overwhelmed, eat the elephant in small chunks. I pulled out the phone book and called a landscaping service. For an outrageous fee, they were willing to come to South Cove and clean up the yard. They would even give me a price on a weekly service and a recommended services list. And they could come on Friday. I gave them my credit card number to pay for the first visit and scratched *mow lawn* off my list. I felt better already.

Chimes that sounded like an old grandfather clock rang through the house. I had never heard the doorbell before. I walked to the front door, still listening to the lovely tune. When I opened the door, a blond Greek god dressed in Dockers and a white polo shirt stood on my porch.

"Jill Gardner?"

"Yes." Hello, papa. The man was divine. My day was starting to look up.

He handed me an envelope. "You've been served."

He turned and stepped through the grass with the grace of a gazelle in a minefield. I hoped he'd trip and fall. Maybe even rip a hole in those pressed Dockers or at least get a grass stain. But no, he maneuvered out of the front yard without incident and back into his shiny red Prius.

"Never trust a man who drives a Prius," I said to the empty porch.

I sat down in one of the white rockers and opened the letter from a law office in San Francisco, the same one that was on the letter Amy and I had found in Miss Emily's files. Scanning the legal document, I found as the proud owner of Miss Emily's house, the city had sent me the correct-or-condemn letter. I had a list of offenses that the house had committed, including the yard maintenance, the fence, the peeling paint, the garage door that barely closed and had several sections missing, and lack of historically appropriate landscaping. I could feel my savings account dwindling just by reading the letter. I had thirty days to make the repairs. Or else.

I took the papers back into the house and called Amy again. She should be back in town by now. No answer on her cell. So I called her office number. "City of South Cove, Bambi speaking. How may I help you?"

"Bambi? What are you doing at Amy's number?"

"I'm filling in for her. Isn't it exciting? She's gone for a few days, and Precious and I get to answer the phones." Bambi stopped talking for a minute. "Hey, how did you know my name?"

"You said your name when you answered the phone. And this is Jill, Jill Gardner from Coffee, Books, and More, the coffee shop?"

"Jill, so nice to hear from you." Her greeting turned into honey like we were long-lost friends. "I adore your aunt, by the way. She's so funny."

Yeah, in a soul-crushing, sarcastic kind of way. I decided to leave that statement alone.

"Do you know where Amy went?"

"No, Mayor Baylor just called my hotel this morning and asked if I could answer the phones for a couple days. I told him I could, but I'd have to bring Precious. And he agreed! He's such a nice man."

"A prince." I didn't like this one bit. "I'll talk to you later, Bambi."

"Okay. And thanks for calling the City of South Cove. Pretty good, huh?"

"You have a knack for this type of work." I hung up the phone. Worried didn't even describe my level of concern. I added *Talk to Amy* to my list, along with *Call painters for an estimate, Call a construction company about replacing the garage door,* and *Find someone to fix the fence.* I needed a new fence anyway, no matter if the council ordered me to get one or not.

Three calls later, I'd lined up appointments that afternoon to get estimates. I needed to hustle to get everything done in thirty days. Besides, the sooner I finished here, the sooner I could get my aunt out of my shop and me back in.

Making myself a tuna sandwich for lunch, I realized I'd used the last can of tuna in the cabinet. In fact, the tuna was the last can of anything in the pantry. *Grocery shopping* went on the list. As I ate, I separated out china to keep from pieces for the antiques dealer. Who needed five sets of china? I saved back a set with a rose pattern, exactly like I'd wanted to have when I got married but the ex-husband had wanted silver border plates. He had won the argument and kept the plates in the divorce.

I heard a rap on the back door. I couldn't believe how busy this place was today. I'd never get anything done.

I pulled open the door. "What?" came out of my mouth just a little too harshly. Especially when I saw Greg, Detective King, standing on my small porch.

He stepped back a half step, probably expecting my head to turn all the way around and vomit to start projecting. "Sorry, is this a bad time?"

"Come on in. Did you come to set up a time to go look at your friend's puppies on Saturday? You could have called, you know." I turned my back and led him into the kitchen and to the table. "Can I get you some coffee? Or I have soda."

I turned around. Detective King still stood on the porch. I walked back, fear in my heart.

"What is it? Am I a suspect again?" I was tired of the legal system. I just wanted to find Miss Emily's murderer and get it all behind me. My back hurt, my feet were on fire, and my day had been filled with unpleasant surprises, including a mouse in the pantry. I might as well hear the bad news now.

"When was the last time you saw Amy Newman?"

Chapter 6

"I talked to her on the phone yesterday at noon. Why?" A chill covered my body, and my legs felt like rubber, so I reached back to find a chair.

Detective King came into the kitchen and shut the back door. He walked over, grabbed a water glass off the counter, and filled it with tap water from the sink. Kneeling before me, he forced the glass into my hand.

I couldn't breathe. Buzzing filled my ears. Nothing made any sense. Amy missing? I thought back on our last conversation and her hiding under her desk. I took a large gulp of the water, letting it cool my throat, trying to slow down my breathing. "The mayor?"

Greg sat down next to me, not understanding my meaning. "The mayor called in the missing person's report this morning when she didn't come in to work. She'd left a note yesterday on her desk saying something had come up and didn't come back from lunch."

Greg put his hand on mine. A warmth flowed up my arm, comforting. "Jill, I'm sure she's just gone off for an early weekend. I didn't come over here to worry you. I just wanted to find out if you knew anything before I called out the troops to find her."

"You can do that?" I glanced up eagerly.

"It was a joke. Maybe not a very funny one, but just a joke." He sat down next to me. "So what did you talk about yesterday? Did she say she was going anywhere?"

"Besides down to Lille's for a plate of fish and chips? She said she was going back to work after lunch. Then out of town for a short trip. But she was supposed to be back today." Should I mention that she was hiding under the desk during our conversation? Maybe not. "Did the mayor mention that he had a meeting yesterday with a council member and an out-of-town attorney? Probably the same attorney who served me with a clean-or-leave summons this morning?"

My voice echoed in the kitchen. I was mad.

"I didn't ask him about his meetings yesterday. Should I have? I'd heard that the city is suing you to clean up this place." His glance fell on my to-do list. Frowning, he picked up the notebook, glancing down at what must have been the possible suspect list.

"I've been trying to make sense of it all," I stammered.

His hand lifted off mine. No more comforting the worried friend, Greg was gone and now Detective King appeared in full force. "Don't tell me that you are trying to investigate Miss Emily's murder all by yourself?"

"No." My almost-whispered lie didn't even convince me. Greg gave me a hard look, then seemed to relax a tad.

"Good. I'd hate to think you were that stupid. Or have to arrest you for obstructing justice." He pushed the notebook across the table and stood. "Are you sure you don't have any idea where your friend would go?"

"No, I don't know where Amy would go. Maybe she got stuck in traffic."

"We don't know anything yet." He walked over to the door. "I'll let you know if we find out anything. You'll call if you hear from her?" It was less a question than an order.

"Yes, I'll call. Thanks for coming by." I wanted him out of my house. Miss Emily's house. Whatever. I needed to have time to think. And his being here kept me from thinking about anything but the way his hair curled over his ears.

"I'll see you tomorrow at the funeral."

Shocked, I asked, "You're going?"

"Part of the job. I liked the old gal. And I want to be close in case something happens."

I could only imagine he thought he'd be needed to referee between me and the Joneses. The funeral. Amy wouldn't have left me alone to face the funeral. Something must have happened. After I said my good-byes to Detective King, I glanced back down to the list of all the things that just didn't add up since Miss Emily died. The list that just kept getting longer rather than shorter.

The first of the contractors to show up was the fence company. The green minivan had a metallic sign proclaiming *The Good Fence Company*. Like anyone would name their company The Shoddy Work and Don't Give a Shit Fence Company. I went out to meet the guy who stood on the sidewalk, his clipboard in hand surveying the combo barbed-wire/wood-slat fence that currently ran around a third of the property. Dollar signs gleamed in his eyes.

"Hi, I'm Jill Gardner. Are you Kevin?"

"Yes, madam. You have quite an eyesore here." He nodded to the fence. "I'm sure we can get you set up with something that is more fitting in no time. I've done a lot of restoration work in the area, so we have lots of options to meet code yet protect your privacy. Good fences make good neighbors, you know."

"Yes, I've heard that." Was this guy for real? "So, where do we start?"

"I'd like to take a walk around the property with you. First we'll have to rip out the old fence. Are you planning on doing any yard work soon?"

"The lawn company will be here Friday."

"Well, I can get my boys out here later this afternoon and we'll get the fence out of their way so the lawn company can clean up easier." Kevin made more notes on his clipboard.

We walked around the property as I told him my want list in a fence. "The front should be lower with a self-latching gate. I'm getting a dog." I hadn't thought about the backyard. I'd rarely been back there except to help Miss Emily out with her garden. "I guess I'd have to fence off the garden from the dog. I'd need another gate near the garage area so I could easily get into the backyard."

As we walked, I realized how far back the property ran. Years ago, Miss Emily and her husband had used this area as a pasture for a few cows and horses.

As we came down the slope at the end, we found a small creek running through a tree-lined area of the property.

"This is amazing." Kevin plowed ahead, crossing the running

water with two steps. "Yep, the old fence ends up just past the trees. This is your property, as well."

"I didn't realize this was even back here." A small barn stood on the right. The horse barn on my parents' farm had been a lot like this, only newer. The barn would have a couple stalls, hay and tack for riding. I headed over to check it out.

"I'm going to measure out the lot. That way I can give you a more accurate idea of pricing for the different types of fence," Kevin called back to me, already walking down the length of the lot, using a rolling counter thing to start measuring.

As I pulled the shed door open, dust sprayed my face. Coughing, I pushed the cobwebs aside and walked in. It had been a while since anyone had been in here. A skylight lit up the small room. Instead of finding saddles and hay, I found the entire shed had been cleaned out and fitted with a newer wood floor. A small loft ran the full length of the back, accessed by a wooden ladder. The rest of the room had blue tarps covering everything. I pulled the first tarp off a pile leaning against the wall and gasped.

Paintings were stacked, five or six deep, against the wall. Pulling off the rest of the tarps, I threw them, unfolded, out the door to the ground. As the minutes passed, the pile of crumpled tarps grew tall. Once I'd thrown out the last tarp, I circled the room. There must have been over a hundred. Miss Emily painted?

The half-done painting on the easel seemed to be a self-portrait of the woman who had complicated my life by leaving me this house along with her fight against the council. Her blue eyes shone out of a face clearly twenty years younger than the Miss Emily I'd known. She smiled at me in that way she had when I would tell her what I was going to do. She'd told me once the only way to make God laugh was to tell him your plans. I guess she had proven that saying true. I never would have thought I'd be here trying to save a house I just inherited and missing my best friends, Miss Emily and now, Amy.

I dug through the other paintings, mostly landscapes, and found a family portrait. The painting showed Miss Emily sitting on a chair, a man in uniform standing behind her, and a little boy, who appeared to be almost five. "So this is Robert and Bob," I said.

Obviously, she'd been painting for years. I gathered several of the landscapes to hang in the house. Looking skyward to the loft, I wondered what treasures it held. Not loving heights, I used Kevin's presence to delay the climb until my next visit.

For a second, I considered calling George and Sabrina about the portraits, but nixed that idea with my next breath. They didn't want family history, just money. I headed back up the hill to the house. Kevin waved from the back of the property. His smile told me all I needed to know. The price of the fencing would hurt.

Coming through the back door, I left the paintings in the kitchen. Knocking echoed through the house and I ran to the front door. The guy standing on the porch tapped at the siding on the house.

"I'm here to do an estimate for a paint job?" The man wasn't as friendly as fence company Kevin. I walked outside to greet him, wiping my forearm over my forehead and probably replacing the sweat I felt with a smear of dirt.

"I need the outside cleaned up and painted, including the garage. I'd like color, but I want to stay historical so I'll have to check with the city to see what's allowable." If Amy ever showed back up to do her job. I'm sure Bambi's paint color advice would match Precious's neon pink collar.

"You have some time here before you decide on a color." The man poked at a shingle on the porch, kneeling to get a better look.

"Actually, I don't. I need the painting done soon."

"I haven't examined the entire house yet, but just looking at the porch area, there's a lot of damage. You're going to need new siding before we paint. I'll leave you the names of a few guys in the area who'll give you a good price." He headed off the porch to check out the rest of the house. He stopped and jumped on a loose board. "You probably want them to check out the porch while they're here. Kind of unsafe."

This day seemed to be getting worse by the moment. I found myself looking forward to tomorrow, when all I had to do was attend a funeral. Seeing Greg again would be a bonus. I had to admit I enjoyed the attention, even if the circumstances were less than ideal.

I went back into the house to check the balance in my savings account online. Maybe Jimmy Marcum would have good news about the money section of the inheritance. I needed a cash infusion to keep the house from being condemned by the city and bulldozed for Bambi's boyfriend's condos.

I booted up my laptop, stealing Wi-Fi service from a neighbor, and put *Call cable company* on my list. As I waited, I peered out the kitchen window and saw another man talking to my painting contractor. He must be here about the garage door. Heading out the kitchen door, I figured I'd get the bad news over quick. *Rip the bandage off fast* had been my motto. Today the bandages were ripping faster than I could recover.

As I walked toward the men leaning against my back porch, I could hear parts of their conversation. Kevin had joined them. I wondered if I should have brought out coffee. Apparently they had gone to the same high school—glory day catch-up time. Looking up at the men, all three over six feet tall, I interrupted and introduced myself. I stuck my hand out to the new guy in the mix. "And you are?"

He straightened and glanced at the other guys, a grin in his eyes. "I'm Todd, from the construction company? Jim here tells me that you have a little more work for us than just replacing the garage door."

"That's what I heard. Can you estimate out the damage for me? I'm on a tight timeline. The council has given me thirty days for all of this."

"A month?" Todd scanned the area around the house and the garage. "And I suppose you need a week for the painting?" He addressed his question over my head to Jim.

"About that." Jim nodded. "Of course, we could add a few guys and cut that by a few days if you need more time."

Of course they could. I felt like I was being grifted by the same group that toured the country after tornados hit. I could feel the price tag rising.

"I think I can estimate you out something to fit into that time frame. But you need to call in someone to check out that roof, too." Todd nodded to the house. "You're going to need that replaced before winter."

Great.

"The good thing is, I'll probably be able to give you a pretty good discount since we aren't busy right now. The economy here has cut down the number of remodels we've scheduled so you caught us in a dead time."

What? This might be a good thing?

"What do you think?" I started feeling cautiously optimistic.

"Let me do up some measurements and check out what's under that siding. We'll have to start tearing down soon if you want this done in thirty days. But it might be doable." He walked to his truck to get a clipboard.

Kevin nodded to me. "I've got all the measurements. My crew will be here this afternoon to tear out the existing fencing. Can I come back tomorrow with a plan and fencing choices for you? Say, noon?"

"How about three?" The funeral started at ten and I wasn't sure how long the thing at the church would last. I didn't want to have to run off right after the service, disrespecting Miss Emily.

"I'll see you then." Kevin walked back to his truck.

"I'll have an estimate to you next week. I need to know what siding you pick before I can determine what type of paint and application you'll need. I'll keep in touch with Todd." Jim handed me a business card.

Looking down at the car, his name jumped out at me. Jim King.

"Are you related to Detective King?"

For once, he stared straight at me and seemed to size me up. "He's my brother. In fact, I was the best man at his wedding."

"He's married?"

Jim King nodded and walked away. Conversation closed.

Chapter 7

The organist played some stylized version of a hymn I remembered from my childhood's sporadic church attendance with my folks. But I couldn't grasp the memory enough to get the words or even the name of the song. Sadie had walked me up to the front pew when I arrived. The Joneses were ensconced in the other front pew to my right. Sabrina sobbed, adding just a little more volume whenever anyone would come by to express his or her sympathy. Aunt Jackie sat next to me in an Ann Taylor suit and black hat with a sweeping feather. Every time she turned to check the crowd, I got a face full of feather.

"Your friend is getting a great turnout." Aunt Jackie lived for the party. "I didn't realize so many people lived here."

"Most of the town is here. Probably to see if I'm going to fall down sobbing on her coffin and confess to killing her." I wasn't in the best of moods. Todd's idea of a discount and great rate for the remodel and mine were in two different ballparks. But I'd signed the work contract yesterday and wrote out another check. Jimmy Marcum had better have some good news on Monday when I went to finalize the will papers. My savings had hit a record low. To make matters worse, even though I had called and left oh, probably twenty messages, I still hadn't heard from Amy.

"Do you have room for one more?" A deep voice dragged me out of my thoughts.

"Detective King?"

"I thought we were past that. Call me Greg."

That was before your brother let the cat slip out of the bag that you were married.

"Sorry, Greg." I felt an elbow dig into my side. "I'd like you to meet my aunt. She's down from San Francisco to help me with the shop for a few weeks."

"Nice to meet you." Greg reached out his hand. Aunt Jackie grabbed his hand like it was a lifeline off a sinking ship.

"Jackie, call me Jackie." She scooted over and patted the seat between us. "Have a seat, Greg. It's so nice of you to comfort Jill in this trying time."

I didn't like the way she said *comfort.*

Greg sat down between us and leaned closer to me, and I could feel the words chilling my neck when he whispered, "Have you heard from your friend?"

"No, and I rang her phone off the wall last night. Have you found anything?" I didn't like the fear in my voice.

"Mayor Baylor said he had a message from a girl on his home message machine saying that Amy had asked him to call because they were going surfing some big wave. She didn't leave a name or number." Greg paused for a moment while a woman stopped by to tell me what a loss Miss Emily would be to the community.

"So, can't you pull phone records or something?" I asked as soon as I was able to break free from the condolence.

"Not without the mayor's permission. He seems to think that she's fine, just needed a few days off." Greg looked back over his shoulder to find his boss in the crowd and make sure he was out of earshot. "Would she just take off like this? I've been told to ignore the missing person's report after that call. But something just doesn't feel right."

"She's always taking off for the big wave, but she'd never leave me like this. She knows how upset I've been. She would have been here for the funeral." I pondered my next words carefully. I had already mentioned the mayor's meeting, but I had left out the part about Amy hiding under her desk talking to me. "Greg, Amy told me that the mayor had a meeting with the lawyer who's processing the city's suit against Miss Emily's house and Eric Ammond."

"And that means what? The mayor has a lot of meetings with a lot of different people." Greg moved even closer to keep Aunt Jackie from hearing my answer.

"She wasn't supposed to be there. She'd left for lunch, and the meeting wasn't on the calendar. She called me from under her desk."

Greg laughed. "Under the desk?"

"It's not funny, she was scared."

"Why didn't you tell me this yesterday? I could have worked this into my discussions with the mayor before he told me to close down the missing person's case." Greg sat back on the wooden pew, folding his arms. "You've got to learn to trust me."

The preamble music suddenly stopped, and the minister stood to greet us. As we bowed our heads for the opening prayer, I snuck a peek at the gorgeous uniformed man next to me.

Stop. Breathe.

I needed to keep him on my side until we found Miss Emily's killer and the missing Amy. Then I could tell him what I really thought of him.

Streams of people stopped by my table after the service to express their sympathy. Or at least it felt like streams of people. Luckily, I had Aunt Jackie. She could make friends anywhere. She kept inviting people to stop by the coffee shop, marketing at a funeral. Aunt Jackie had stopped by the church yesterday and donated several pounds of our daily blend coffee and apparently coffee cups, as well. Coffee, Books, and More's logo was plastered all over the service, including on the drink glasses. Tacky? Probably, but it seemed to be working.

I had a table on one side of the room, and George and Sabrina were camped out on the other side. They hadn't said one word to me all day, but I had gotten plenty of stares from people who stopped by to console the Joneses. I was sure the comments about me weren't good, especially after what Sadie'd told me yesterday. I just didn't have the strength to give them a piece of my mind today.

Sadie Michaels set a piece of apple pie and a fresh cup of coffee in front of me. She plopped her fluffy five-foot-two frame down next to me. "If you aren't coming to my apple pie, my apple pie comes to you." She pushed aside my plate, which had bites out of everything, but nothing had been finished. I'd been too scared to even try the green Jell-O salad. Even my roll had been shredded rather than consumed. Not my best clean plate moment. As a kid, I wouldn't even have been able to see the apple pie, let alone have it delivered directly to me.

"My dogs are barking." She slipped off her worn, black two-inch heels and stretched out her toes. "Eat." She pointed at the pie. "You don't want to insult me, now, do ya?"

"I'm sorry, I just don't have an appetite today." To be polite, I grabbed the fork and took a bite of the pie. The warm cinnamon and caramel sauce surrounding the apples filled my mouth and woke up my taste buds. I took a second bite, this one a little larger. The crust flaked and melted in my mouth. It wasn't chocolate, but the creamy apple cinnamon was the next best thing.

"This is amazing." I handed my fork to Aunt Jackie and pushed the plate toward her. "Taste this pie."

Sadie beamed. "I'm so glad you like it. I've been meaning to come over to the shop. I've been doing mostly wedding cakes, but I've been playing with different pie recipes for about a month now."

Aunt Jackie swallowed her bite, then stood. "I'm going to get a piece."

"You won her over." I watched my aunt float through the thinning crowd, greeting people like they were her oldest friends.

"I didn't have the courage to come and talk to you, at the last chamber meeting," Sadie confided, her eyes on her cup.

"You should have. I'm sure we can work out an order for the shop." My mind raced forward: How many pies could we sell in a week? Adding a new treat to my lineup of breakfast items might extend my customers into the afternoon and early evening. "Sadie, I never thanked you and the other women for pulling this together. I'm sure that Miss Emily would have appreciated it."

"Don't worry about thanking us. We serve God by taking care of those left behind. Most of us don't have a full-time job or a business. We take care of the church and have our visitation routes."

"I'm sure Miss Emily appreciated your visits."

"I was glad to be there, especially when that girl showed up with the baby pictures. I thought Miss Emily would have a heart attack then and there."

"What?" I sat up, my alarms going off. "Who showed up?"

"I didn't want to intrude on family business. The girl was somehow related to Miss Emily. I didn't stay for the whole discussion."

"Did you get a name?"

"Crystal. What was her last name? Dunn. Crystal Dunn. Cute baby, Annie, that's the baby's name."

"How was she related, did you find out?"

"I thought she said the baby was Miss Emily's great-grandbaby."

"I thought Bob was Miss Emily's only child."

"He was." Sadie frowned toward the kitchen. "It looks like there's a crisis in the kitchen. I'll bring a few pies by the shop next week for you to sample."

"I'll let Aunt Jackie know you're coming. Thanks again." I watched Sadie walk back to the kitchen, my mind whirling.

So, how did someone who died in Vietnam come up with a granddaughter thirty years later?

Chapter 8

Saturday morning started like one of those autumn days that make you feel summer would go on forever. The warm breeze gently pushing the limbs of the trees around let the loose leaves cascade to the ground. The white linen curtains on my open bedroom window were floating in the same warm breeze.

Time to move forward. Time to find Amy, figure out what had happened to Miss Emily, and paint the kitchen now that the new appliances had been delivered and installed late yesterday. I didn't realize how tired I would be after the funeral, so when I finally got back to the house, seeing the appliance truck pull up wasn't a welcome sight.

Pulling on sweats and a T-shirt, I headed downstairs to start coffee and start moving the furniture out of the kitchen before laying old sheets down to keep the hardwood floors from being splattered with paint. The kitchen would be sunny yellow by the end of the day, with one accent wall in a spring green. Bright and cheery, and I had just the Miss Emily original landscape to go on the wall to finish off the look. The tile backsplash, although dated, seemed classic in design and thankfully didn't need to be replaced. I started the coffee and called Amy again. This time her answering machine came on immediately telling me that the mailbox was full of my messages and that I couldn't leave another one. Her cell must be dead.

I pulled out my laptop and searched for a phone listing for Crystal Dunn. There were several Dunns listed, most outside the local area, but one, a C. Dunn, lived in Bakerstown. I wrote down the address and phone number. After I finished painting, I'd take a drive over to Bakerstown. Grabbing a cup of coffee, I headed to the study and sat down at the desk. I went through the drawers, looking for the picture that Sadie had seen. I hit pay dirt in the bottom drawer.

She'd been right, the baby was cute. I turned the photograph over, and on the back, someone had written *Annie Dunn, three months*. I put the picture in my purse and called Jimmy Marcum. He agreed to meet me at three in his office.

Why had Miss Emily chosen me to inherit? Maybe Jimmy had answers that would ease my mind. I understood her choice not to leave anything to the Joneses, but the baby should have been an easy choice. There had to be more to the story that I didn't know yet. I had five hours to get my painting done before I had to leave to meet Mr. Marcum. I grabbed some cereal and sat down at the desk to eat before I turned the kitchen into my own art gallery.

"I'm glad you called me. This way I can have you sign today, and by Monday I can have at least the liquid assets transferred to your bank." Jimmy Marcum sat down in his leather chair behind the walnut desk. "I had my secretary get everything together on Friday, and she put it somewhere here." He shuffled through the files that completely covered the top of his desk.

"I wanted to ask you if Miss Emily had any other heirs, besides George and Sabrina, that is." I sat up taller in the chair, trying to see over the manila files.

"Heirs? No, beside George and you, there wasn't anyone else listed in the will." Jimmy contemplated me over the files.

"She never mentioned this little girl?" I handed over the picture of Annie.

Jimmy took the picture and regarded the picture, turning it over. "She said someone had come by claiming to be the mother of her great-grandbaby, but there wasn't any evidence. Since the father was deceased, no one could verify the paternity of the child." He handed the picture back to me. "Here's the file."

"You talked to the girl?"

"I did. She told me that Joshua Williams was the father and

she'd been told he might be Miss Emily's grandson." Jimmy cleared off a space on the desk and started looking over the papers.

"How is that possible? Miss Emily's son died in Vietnam."

"He did. And she had no other children. We figured the girl was trying to run a scam. I wanted to call the police, but Miss Emily refused. I guess she had a soft spot for the baby." He picked up the paperwork and handed it to me. "There are just a few places where you need to sign and date."

I wasn't sure this was the right move. If the baby was related to Miss Emily, she should be getting this estate, not me. "I don't know."

"Jill, I promise you that baby is no more related to Miss Emily than I am. She wanted you to have the house. I'm sure the money will help make the place livable."

Livable and up to code so the mayor and his friends couldn't sweep in to tear it down. My savings account was drier than a load of clothes right out of the cycle. I could certainly use the influx of cash, especially with the construction guys showing up on Monday. I put the picture back into my purse.

"Where do I sign?"

Heading out of Jimmy's office just over a half a million dollars richer, I felt stunned. I never thought I'd be able to feel comfortable even in the perfect job. Bills seemed to always fill in any pay increases I had earned. I had walked away from my former career with a nice nest egg, but nothing like this. I figured getting the house up to the council's code would take close to a hundred grand. The inheritance would refill my security coffers without me worrying about the financial security of the coffee shop. Maybe I could make some of the changes that Aunt Jackie had been talking about at the shop.

Maybe I'd even replace old Betsy in a couple of months rather than a few years. I loved my Jeep, but its repair bills were matching the loan payments. I threw my purse toward the Jeep's passenger seat. I missed the seat and the purse fell upside down, dumping everything on the floor.

Slow down.

I grabbed my wallet, my ChapStick, my notebook and pens, and came upon the picture of Annie. It wouldn't hurt to just go visit and see if C. Dunn was Crystal. And even though Jimmy had totally dismissed the idea of the baby being Miss Emily's great-granddaughter, I needed to feel comfortable before I started spending the inheritance as if it was my own.

But it's your money. Why look a gift horse in the mouth?

My evil side tried to talk me out of opening Pandora's box. That was when I knew that I had to go investigate. I never trusted that voice.

The address for C. Dunn took me just to the edge of the bad side of town. Houses here were small but well-kept, lawns green and flower beds well-established if not overgrown. The mailbox out front just said *Dunn*. No first name. I sat in my Jeep in front of the house mulling over what I would say. "Hi, I'm the woman who got the money you were trying to scam out of Miss Emily?" That seemed a little harsh. As I was still going over opening lines, each one worse than the last, my cell phone rang.

I didn't recognize the number, but I picked up anyway. It was probably the construction crew telling me the house had to be torn down due to ginormous termites living in the basement. "Hello?"

"Hey, where are you?" a male voice asked.

"In Bakerstown." Now I knew there was trouble at the house. It had to be one of the construction guys, since no other guy ever called me. "Tell me, what's wrong with the house now?"

"The house looks fine from what I can see. The outside is a mess and you can't even tell that the lawn was mowed yesterday due to the siding demolition, but I'm sure they'll clean that up before they leave. Why are you in Bakerstown?" the voice asked.

"Who is this?"

"Greg. Greg King. Who did you think it was?" Greg's voice boomed through the phone.

"I thought it was one of the builders telling me the house had fallen in on its foundation." I sighed, relieved that the house hadn't realized that my savings account had been refilled and decided to tap it for more changes.

"So again, now that you know it's not one of the builders, I repeat my question. Why are you in Bakerstown when you are supposed to be here?"

"I stopped by Jimmy Marcum's to sign the final estate transfer paperwork, and now I'm sitting in front of a house wondering if I should go in." I shouldn't have said that last part.

"Sitting in front of whose house?" Greg's investigative tone came over the phone.

I opened the door, I might as well share, and maybe Greg would have insight as to how I should do this. "Crystal Dunn's house, I hope."

"Who's Crystal Dunn, or do I want to ask?"

"I found this picture of a baby, Annie. Sadie from the church said that Crystal had brought Miss Emily a picture of the baby, Miss Emily's granddaughter. Well, great-grandbaby." I continued to watch the house.

"And you thought you'd see if everyone else was wrong? Girl, why can't you leave things alone? You remember that Miss Emily's killer still hasn't been found, and this is an open investigation. Right?"

"I just wanted to meet her." Why did I feel like a teenager being corrected for staying out late?

"Let me do the detective work. It is my job, you know."

"I know, I just thought—" God, I sounded like a whiny teenager.

Greg interrupted. "You didn't think. Now get out of there and get back here. I'm sure there are enough things at the house to keep you busy and out of trouble."

"Fine." I hung up the phone. I didn't need someone telling me what to do. Although I hadn't thought about the possibility that Crystal could have killed Miss Emily. Even though I hadn't met the girl, her being a murderer didn't seem right.

Wait, what was Greg doing at my house? Then I remembered. We were supposed to go and see the puppies today.

I put my phone down and started to pull the Jeep away from the curb, but something caught my eye.

An older sedan pulled into the small driveway. I watched as a young man got out of the driver's side, a blonde woman in her early twenties climbing out the other. They both went to the back and opened the doors. He pulled out two bags of groceries and a twelve-pack of soda. She reached in and pulled out a baby. When they reached the front door, the man pulled keys out of his pocket, and opening the door, gave the baby a kiss on the way in. If this was Crystal Dunn and Annie, there seemed to already be a father attached to that baby. Maybe Jimmy Marcum and Miss Emily were right; the visit had been a con.

I watched the couple struggle with the diaper bags and the groceries. When they finally got everything inside and closed the door, blocking my view, I wrote down the address and phone number from my scribbled note to my notebook. I'd call in a few days if I couldn't get the baby out of my mind. I had run around on some wild goose chase when I should be back in South Cove working on the house and getting a new puppy with Greg.

Married Greg.

Okay, so missing the puppy run probably wasn't the worst idea I'd had for a while. I put the Jeep into gear and headed back to South Cove. First, though, now that my savings coffers were built back up, a stop at the Home Heaven was in order. Both bathrooms needed to be refurbished, and I might as well get some idea of pricing while in town. And maybe a few more cans of paint.

The phone rang again. Probably Greg checking up on me to see if I'd left the Dunn house. I picked up and said, "I'm on my way to the home improvement store. What do you want?"

"Why are you wasting your time fixing up that house? You'll be the next body Doc Ames will cart out of there if you don't sell." The phone line went dead.

Chapter 9

I made it home in record time, all ideas of stopping and leisurely looking at tubs and faucets out of my mind. I called Greg on the way, and when I pulled into the driveway, he sat on the front porch waiting for me.

"Let's go over this one more time. He mentioned Doc Ames specifically?" Sitting in the kitchen on our second pot of coffee, Greg was in full detective mode.

"He only said two sentences, I'm pretty sure I remembered all of it." I felt edgy and annoyed. The coffee was probably to blame for my mood, but I couldn't shake the chill.

"And you're sure it was a man's voice."

Now he was getting on my nerves. "Yes, I'm positive. Why are you still here and not pulling my phone records or something like they do on television?"

"I have Toby pulling your phone records. I'm here investigating. That's what I do. Me, not you. What were you thinking going over to that house? You could have been walking into anything, a drug lab or something, or been accused of stalking. Do you want to wind up missing like your friend?" Greg got louder as the lecture progressed. He stood and walked around the living room.

His words stung.

Was it my fault that Amy had gone missing? Did someone catch her hiding under her desk, talking to me?

"I didn't think it would be this big of a deal. I need to make sure that the baby isn't related to Miss Emily. I couldn't live with taking that money if it was supposed to go somewhere else." I sank down deeper into the kitchen chair I'd shoved into the living room to save it from paint splatters that morning. In my defense, I added, "I asked Jimmy Marcum first before I went."

"And he told you that the girl was a scammer and not related to Miss Emily. I've already talked to him. So you decide to go make sure? What were you thinking?" Now Greg paced from one side of the room to the other, but the kitchen table and chairs were making his progress choppy. He stopped pacing, stood in front of the table, and asked, "Why is this in the living room?"

Desperate to change the subject from my carelessness, I answered. "I painted the kitchen today. Do you want to see?"

"Sure." Greg didn't sound like he wanted to see.

We walked into the kitchen with the new stainless steel appliances and the freshly painted walls. All I needed to do now was have someone come in and reseal the wood floors. I had spent most of last night on my knees scrubbing the floor down and had been pleased with what I had found under the grime. "I'm going to leave the cabinets alone. They need a good scrubbing, but other than that, they're in excellent shape." I opened up a cabinet and showed him the interior. "See, lots of room."

Now that I'd taken out the ten sets of china Miss Emily had stashed.

"This is amazing. It looks totally different." Neither one of us acknowledged our meeting the morning I'd found Miss Emily. "I wouldn't have picked the colors, but they work. Do you want me to help you move the furniture back?"

"I can do it." I didn't need him hanging around helping me with my decorating when he should be with his wife.

"I know you can do it. I asked if you wanted me to help." Greg's gaze poured over my body, making me think of being closer, much closer. "You're not getting rid of me until Toby calls back with the phone records, so you might as well make use of me."

I shivered at the thought of making use of him, my mind clearly in the gutter. "You don't have anywhere you need to be?"

"Nope. Just here."

I didn't believe him. But my shoulders ached from the scrubbing and painting earlier. A little help moving furniture wouldn't be the end of the world.

Just don't look into his eyes. Or touch him.

Two hours later, we sat on the back porch, sipping a cold beer. The kitchen was back in commission, and the first floor bedroom had been stripped of furniture and carpet and was ready to paint. If I could keep Toby from calling for a few days, Greg and I'd have the inside of the house done by the end of the week.

"I'm going to set the room up as my home office. At the apartment, I had work stuff all over the place." I took another drink from the longneck bottle. "This way, I can just close the door on my clutter."

"Does the shop keep you busy?" Greg sat on one of Miss Emily's rockers on the other side of the porch. I could barely see him. The darkness crept from the lawn to the porch except for the light from the kitchen shining through the screen door.

"Between the shop and my consulting job for the city, I'm pretty busy. Or at least until Aunt Jackie showed up. Now I'm stuck in remodeling hell and she gets to sit around and redesign my shop." Ouch, that came out a little harsh. I backpedaled. "It's not that I don't appreciate her help."

"It's just hard to see what you've worked for being changed without your input." Greg finished my sentence. "Toby told me a little about what's happening in the shop. You do know your aunt hired him, right?"

I sighed, bone-tired from the moving. I knew much more lay ahead of me before I could even start to take the shop back from Aunt Jackie. "Yeah, she told me. See, that's the thing. She told me. She didn't ask me. She just read over the books and hired someone. Then she tells me I should get rid of the bookcases and stop selling books because it takes up too much room."

"But isn't that part of the theme? You get to have your coffee and pick out a good book, too?" Greg's voice sounded deep and comforting from across the dark porch.

"See, you get it. I don't think she does. It's not her shop, for God's sake." I hadn't had anyone to vent to since Amy disappeared. Too bad the sexy lawman sitting in the dark on my back porch was already spoken for; otherwise, we wouldn't be on the porch right now. "Shouldn't you be going home?"

"Trying to get rid of me?"

"No, I mean, I'm fine if you need to leave." I stumbled over my words. His leaving was the last thing my body wanted. But my head had to stay in control.

"Someone threatens your life today, and you're fine? You must live a more interesting life than I thought." Greg stopped rocking and stood. "You ready for another one?"

Why not?

"I guess," I said, hesitantly.

"You might as well relax a little. I don't think anything's going to happen tonight. Or it would have already happened." Greg took the bottle I had been playing with for the last ten minutes from my hand. "You need to set up a cooler out here so we don't let the bugs in your house at night getting another beer."

The screen door banged shut behind him.

I needed to set up a cooler? Would we be drinking beer on my porch another time?

My mind raced. Maybe they were separated—divorced, even. Maybe I misunderstood his brother. This was stupid. I needed to ask him, to clear the air. I refused to be the other woman. I'd seen how that game worked out and I didn't need a broken heart.

I watched a firefly dance down by the shed where I found the paintings. Even at that distance, the bug put off a lot of light. It must be huge! I'd loved watching fireflies when we visited Grams at her home down by the Missouri River. They made me laugh just watching them. But tonight I wasn't laughing. Something nagged at me. Greg? Nah, that resembled a raging war inside my head. Something else.

"What has you so deep in thought?" Greg handed me the new bottle, cold from the refrigerator. He offered me an open bag. "I found a bag of pretzels to go with the beer. I hope you don't mind."

"I'm watching the firefly down by the creek."

"You're what?" Greg's voice had gone tight, his cop voice. I turned to look up at him.

"The firefly down by the old shed where I found the paintings."

Greg put his beer down. "Do you have a flashlight?"

"Yeah, right inside the door in that top cabinet. Why?"

"California doesn't have fireflies." Greg went back inside to get the flashlight. When he came out, he turned the light on to check it. "Go inside and lock the doors. I'll be right back."

I stayed frozen on the porch step. "Do you think someone's there?"

"We'll talk after I check it out." Greg started across the lawn. "And get your cell phone, just in case."

I hurried into the house.

Locking the back door, I ran upstairs to my room to grab my purse and the cell phone. On the way back to the kitchen, I checked the front door and double-locked it, too. Then I stood guard at the back door. Glancing out the window, I tried to see Greg or his flashlight. Nothing. I took a swig of the beer he'd just brought me and considered chugging the entire bottle to quiet my nerves.

Changing my mind, I went over and started a pot of coffee. I wanted to be sharp just in case I needed to drive or run or . . . *Or what, Jill? You're building this into something it's probably not. Calm down.*

That's easy for you to say. I pushed back at my calming voice, tired of arguing with myself.

I sat down at the table and viewed the dark backyard, my garage light only covering half of the grassy area. No Greg. I checked the time on my cell. Five minutes had passed. Seriously? It seemed like an hour since he'd left the porch. I grabbed one of my decorating magazines and started flipping the pages.

I didn't want to call the police too soon and embarrass Greg. Besides, Toby would probably be on call and then he'd tell Aunt Jackie and then I'd get the third degree about my non-relationship with the hunk running around my backyard, looking for trouble and nonexistent fireflies.

I heard steps on the wooden porch. Looking out the window, I saw Greg standing there waiting. I unlocked the door and waited for him to come in the house. "What? Was it a prowler? Was someone in the shed?"

He put the flashlight back in the cabinet by the door. Then he sat down at the table. "I'll take a cup of that coffee."

I pulled out a cup and poured. "Black, right?"

"That's fine." Greg wasn't talking.

I gave him his coffee and sat in the chair next to him.

"Thanks."

"What was out there?" I tapped my fingernail on the table. "Tell me."

"Probably kids." Greg hesitated. "You need to get a lock for that shed. I saw beer bottles piled up and a blanket. Miss Emily always turned in early, so they could be used to using the shed for extracurricular activities."

That sounded logical, but it just didn't ring true. "You think teenagers were looking for a secluded place?"

Greg glanced at me over his coffee cup. "Or someone's watching you. I found a set of binoculars in the shed, too. Which story will let you sleep better at night?"

"I'll get a lock for the shed tomorrow." So much for our peaceful night sitting on the porch getting to know each other. Of course we shouldn't be sitting on the porch, together, alone. Married guy, remember? My willpower was weakening.

Greg checked his cell for the time. "It's after ten. I guess they didn't get the phone records yet from your stalker call."

"If you need to go, I understand."

Greg glanced at me, puzzled. "Is my company that disturbing?"

"Huh? No, I love, I mean, I'm having fun, in a creepy Halloween sort of way."

"Then why are you trying to get rid of me?" At that moment, his cell rang. "I've got to take this." He walked into the living room.

Because you're married, I called out to him on the inside. I pulled out a blueberry coffee cake someone had dropped off and cut several slices. I'd just polished off my second slice when Greg walked back in the room. He grabbed a piece and sat down.

"Sarah Jenkins makes the best coffee cake in town." He popped the rest of the piece into his mouth. He seemed to inhale the food. "Toby called. The phone records came back, finally. We traced where the threat call originated."

God, this man loved his drama. "Are you going to tell me?"

The look he gave me when he put his cup down seemed to be mixed with determination and fear. "The call came from one of the extensions at City Hall."

Chapter 10

Greg stayed long past midnight, and after splitting two pots of coffee, I didn't get to sleep for a couple of hours after he left. I checked the locks on the doors and windows three times before, exhausted, I put a chair up against my bedroom door and fell into a fitful sleep. My mind kept going over the recent events. Miss Emily's death, Amy's disappearance, the funeral, my inheritance, the angry nephew, the mayor and his threats, it all kept rolling around, mixing together and not making any sense. Amy sat on a bench crying. I tried to get to her, but piles of roof shingles and siding were blocking my path. I could see her, but I had no way to reach her. I started climbing over the piles when my cell phone went off. I woke up in bed covered with sweat and Amy's cries for help still ringing in my ears.

I had to go to Amy's apartment. I had to find some clue to where she had gone. The thought that the apartment might be considered a crime scene and somehow off-limits crossed my mind for two point five seconds. Shrugging it off, I dismissed the thought. As much as I liked Greg, he wasn't taking her disappearance seriously. He thought she was surfing with some unnamed guy somewhere.

I drew the covers back over my head and prayed for strength. That man was fine. Last night talking and laughing had been comfortable, easy. Not like my relationships with any of the losers I had dated since my divorce. Cute, almost ruggedly handsome, he had weight lifter arms, proof he definitely worked out. I dreamily thought about his chest—did he have six-pack abs? Just the kind of man I wanted in my life.

At least he would be if he wasn't married—my conscience chimed in.

"Arrgghh." I threw the comforter off my bed, swinging my feet to the floor. Pulling on my remodeling uniform of jeans and a T-shirt, I headed downstairs to make a list of things that I had to get done today. The sooner I got settled here and found Amy, the sooner I could get Aunt Jackie out of my coffee shop and back to San Francisco where she belonged.

Grabbing the last pieces of the blueberry coffee cake and a cup of coffee, I pulled out my notebook with my ever-growing to-do list and list of suspects. I added *Visit Amy's apartment* to the list. She'd been gone too long for this to be just an impromptu surfing trip. She would have checked in with the mayor if she was delayed, not ask someone else to call for her. If she wasn't at her desk at nine, I would start my own search for her.

Hammering started outside. I wasn't sure if the source was the men replacing my roof, the siding, or the fence. I must have had half the town working on the house. At least now, with the money Miss Emily left me, I could pay the men standing in my driveway. I added *Buy a lock for the shed* to the list. My office would just have to wait to be painted.

Today I had to figure out if Amy was kidnapped, dead, or just surfing. I hoped it was surfing. Some detective I'd turned out to be. The who-done-its just kept piling up around me. I hadn't added anything to Greg's search except for the bull's-eye on my own back. Shivering, I remembered the call from yesterday.

Why did someone want me out of the house? The development. Maybe Bambi let Eric use the phone while she filled in for Amy. A thought burst into my mind . . . and maybe that was why Amy disappeared . . . to give Bambi access to the city building so Eric could use the phone to threaten me . . .

Okay, that sounded stupid, even to me. I could just hear Greg's voice challenging the theory.

"So, why wouldn't they just buy a prepaid cell and dump it after the call?" imaginary Greg asked.

The doorbell rang before I had the chance to think up an answer.

I spent way too much time alone, having conversations with people who weren't there.

Aunt Jackie stood on my porch with a basket of muffins and a carafe of what smelled like my best chocolate coffee blend.

"Peace offering," she said, walking past me into the house. She stopped at the living room crowded with the furniture Greg and I had pulled out of Miss Emily's bedroom—my future office—yesterday. "I like what you've done with the place, kind of Salvation Army meets Home Heaven."

"It's a work in progress. Let's go back to the kitchen. You'll find it a little more pulled together." I headed to the back of the house, clearing a path through the piles for Jackie to follow. "What are you doing up so early? I thought you'd be taking it easy today."

Aunt Jackie laughed. "I'll sleep when I'm dead." She set the basket down on the table, then, viewing my stricken face, added, "Sorry, wrong choice of words. But, dear, I don't need a lot of sleep."

She glanced around the kitchen, taking in the new paint and appliances. "You've done a great job in here. I can't believe how much you've accomplished in the last week."

"Not having to run the shop has been a lifesaver." I hated to admit it, but it was true. And working on the house kept me from losing my mind over worry about Amy, let alone my new stalker.

She walked up to the landscape that Greg and I had hung on the kitchen wall. "This is good. I mean, really good." She studied the painting. "Did you buy it in San Francisco?"

I chuckled. "No, my gallery's a little closer." I handed Aunt Jackie a cup of the coffee she had brought, the chocolate smell filling the kitchen. "You think it's good?"

"It is. In fact, I'm sure I've seen this artist at one of the city galleries. They billed her as a new local talent. I almost bought one of the pieces, but I was leaving for a cruise and the gallery couldn't hold it for delivery." Aunt Jackie went back to the table and sat down. "I didn't come to talk about art, though."

I stood staring at the painting, wondering if another painter could have copied Miss Emily's style or if more of Miss Emily's paintings were sitting at some gallery. Maybe this was the reason someone had been snooping around the shed last night. Unless Miss Emily had consigned the art to the gallery herself. No need bothering Greg yet—I'd call the gallery myself and check. If I knew the gallery's name. I stopped Aunt Jackie before she could go on to another subject. "Do you remember which gallery it was?"

"I probably have the owner's card in my purse somewhere. I meant to buy a piece once I got back in town, then you called and I wound up here." Aunt Jackie rested the back of her hand on my forehead. "Are you all right? You look a little flushed."

"I've been busy." I sank into the chair next to her and pushed her purse within her reach. "Could you check now? It's important."

Aunt Jackie started digging into her purse. "I don't understand why this is so important. Obviously the artist is selling her stuff to a local dealer here as well as San Francisco. Most artists don't give exclusive rights to galleries." Her voice muddled coming from the large Coach bag. She sighed and pushed the purse away.

"What?"

"It's not in here. I bought this bag on the cruise, so the card would have been in my other bag back at home." Jackie reached for a muffin. "I think I remember the artist's name, though it didn't match the signature at all."

"Who was the artist?"

Aunt Jackie reached for a plate from the cupboard so I couldn't see her face when she answered. "The signature appeared to be an *E*-something." She pointed over to my painting. "See, just like that. Large curvy *E* and then smaller letters."

"How did you know the artist's name was different?" I sat on the edge of my seat.

Jackie came back to the table and handed me a plate with half a blueberry muffin. "It's on the tip of my tongue. Of course, the signature didn't look like the name at all, but the gallery owner assured me that a lot of artists use a different name to sign their work. Didn't make sense to me, though."

Questions filled my mind. Had someone else been selling Miss Emily's paintings? If so, was it with or without her knowledge? Could it be the same someone who wanted me out of the house? I felt hopeful for the first time in days. I pushed the question, again, "So, do you think you could remember which gallery it was?"

"I'm not senile. Of course I can remember the gallery." Aunt Jackie took a bite of her muffin. "One of the new ones over on Market Street. Why are you so interested in another painting? The one you have is perfect for this room."

"Miss Emily did the painting. And maybe whoever's been selling the paintings killed her for them. Maybe she found out." My logic wasn't even convincing me.

"Someone could have been selling the paintings for Miss Emily. You never know, dear. This could all be a misunderstanding."

"Then why wouldn't they tell the gallery owner that she was the artist?"

The room went silent. Then Aunt Jackie spoke up. "Grab your laptop, and let's see if we can find the gallery. I know I'll remember the name as soon as I see it."

I grabbed the laptop off the counter and powered it up. "Thanks."

"No need to thank me yet. I haven't told you the gallery name."

But my aunt had given me another reason why someone might want Miss Emily dead. Maybe she'd caught the thief stealing paintings from the shed? And that was motive—if it panned out, Greg would have to investigate. I could stop fingers being pointed at me if we could find out who had been selling the paintings. It was a long shot, but right now, it was the only lead I had. I signed on to Google and keyed in *Market Street Art Galleries*. A list of ten pages filled the screen. Why so many? I was sure I must have done the search wrong, but then I saw the link to the article "Art's New Mecca—Market Street Galleries Revive Neighborhood."

It was going to be a long morning.

Three hours later Jackie stood and brushed muffin crumbs off her lap onto my just-swept floor. Buying a Swiffer went on my mental to-do list.

"I can't believe there are so many galleries in that little stretch of town."

"Me, either," I groaned. This detecting stuff seemed a lot easier on the television shows I loved to watch. They would have found the body, the murderer, and had their trial all within an hour. I was still trying to find the name of the gallery selling Miss Emily's art. Maybe I should tell Greg. He already knew that someone had been in my shed. "I guess we should just give in for the day."

My aunt stared out the kitchen window, her eyes wide.

Was my prowler becoming more daring? Or was my caller showing up to do the deed? When did my life start including the bad guys I read about in my mystery novels? Jumping up, I grabbed my cell phone just in case and ran to her side. She put her hand up to slow me down. I flipped open the phone, dialed 911, and put my finger on the SEND button. Then I looked out the window.

Three deer grazed in my backyard. The male had a rack of antlers. A doe and a younger fawn walked close by. I closed my phone and let the adrenaline flow out of my body. Time to get a grip. Now I jumped at wildlife. As we were watching, my doorbell rang. The buck lifted his head at the sound and bounded out of the yard, toward the back shed. The others followed.

I headed to the door, Jackie following me like the doe had followed the buck.

I unlocked the dead bolt and swung open the door.

"What, you don't check to see who's out here before you open the door? I could have been your mystery stalker, sheesh." Greg leaned against the doorway, a new padlock in his hand. "I stopped by the hardware store this morning and bought you a present."

"You didn't need to do that. I had it on my list to do today, I just got sidetracked."

I felt hot. Looking in his eyes, all I could think of was how he'd kissed me in my dreams last night. His lips parting mine . . .

Aunt Jackie stepped out from behind me, breaking the lightning that must have been shooting out of my body toward Greg. "Detective King! I was just telling Jill what a pleasure your Toby is to work with. He's such a nice boy."

"Well, I've never heard him called a 'nice boy' before, but I'm glad he's working out for you. Toby needed a hobby." Greg's glance stayed locked with mine. "I didn't realize you had company. I can come back later."

My stomach did a backflip. Oh my God—had he realized what I'd been thinking about? I broke eye contact first. "No, come in. I need you to hear something."

He handed me the padlock. "And can I install the lock? I'd feel better if I knew it wasn't just sitting on your kitchen counter tonight."

Jackie poured Greg a cup of coffee and told him her story of seeing a similar painting in the city. I showed him the list of galleries we had been reviewing to jog Jackie's memory. Greg stayed quiet while we talked, sipping on his coffee. After we had finished, Greg stood up, stretched, and walked over to the landscape he had helped hang yesterday.

"Well, this could explain your prowler." He stared at the painting. "I don't get why the thief would take such chances on a few paintings. They can't be worth much."

"Now there's where you're wrong. A local artist can bring in the low thousands for originals, especially if the gallery is smart at promotion," Aunt Jackie responded to Greg's comment. "The art isn't just something to use in decorating your home, it's marketed as an investment. That's the hook that the gallery used to try to sell me, a new up-and-coming artist whose work hadn't been discovered yet."

"Well, that's true, most of Miss Emily's paintings are still under tarps in the shed." I patted my aunt's hand. "And if you hadn't been tempted to buy a painting, we wouldn't have known that someone had been stealing them in the first place."

"Now don't jump to conclusions here." Greg used his cop voice again. "One, we don't know that it is one of Miss Emily's paintings."

I glared at him. "If Aunt Jackie says it is—"

Greg interrupted me before I could finish. "And two, even if it is, she could have asked someone to try to sell the paintings for her. I'm sure a gallery owner would be more open to working with someone younger and less opinionated than Miss Emily. She would know that she wasn't the best salesman." He took out his cell and snapped a picture of the painting. Turning back to me, he said, "Let's go see what else is in that shed."

Another day with Greg. My heart beat faster. All I needed to keep him visiting was to keep getting death threats and have people stealing from my shed. *And forget that he's married*, my rational side kicked in.

Well, there was that, too. I turned to Aunt Jackie. "Want to go with us? You could pick out a painting for your condo and avoid the gallery markup."

"Maybe later, dear. I think I'm going to head back to the apartment and rest awhile. It's been a busy morning." Aunt Jackie grabbed her purse and gave me a kiss on the cheek. She whispered in my ear, "Don't do anything I wouldn't . . ."

With an evil grin, she headed to the door. "So nice to see you again, Detective King."

Greg grinned at me. "Are all the women in your life that fiery? No wonder you and Miss Emily got along so well."

I considered showing him how fiery women in my family could get when I heard voices in the hallway.

"She's right in here." Jackie stood at the kitchen door. "Jill, you have another visitor."

Eric Ammond walked through the door. Seeing Greg, he stopped short. "I didn't realize you were entertaining, Miss Gardner. I can come back later."

"I'm not entertaining. What do you want, Mr. Ammond?" Something must have come out in my voice because I could feel Greg's body almost touching mine as he moved closer.

Eric's gaze went from Greg to me. A slow smile crossed his face. A smile I didn't appreciate in the least. "I see. I am interrupting. I will come back later."

Crossing my arms in front of me, I asked again, "What do you want—I don't want you to come back later. I've told you before, I'm not interested."

"But you haven't heard my new offer." Eric pulled out a piece of stark white paper that contrasted against his dark silk suit jacket. On anyone else, the suit jacket with jeans would have made them look like an off-strip Vegas performer. Way off-strip. On Eric, it made him look hot, sexy, and dangerous all at once. Just the type of guy I would have fallen head over heels for just five years ago. And the fact I knew he had a girlfriend would have made him more of a challenge, not a detriment. Thank God I was past that now.

Yeah, now you're hot for Mr. Married Cop standing next to you.

Sometimes I hated my inner voice.

He held the paper out in front of me. "Aren't you even going to look at it?" His brown eyes danced with a joke I hadn't heard. He focused on Greg. "You are the town police detective, correct?"

Greg appeared to pull up his shoulders and gain five inches in height. "Detective Greg King." He didn't hold out his hand to shake hands with Eric; instead, he put one hand on the small of my back.

Eric seemed amused by Greg's posturing. He turned his attention back to me. "So, you should feel safe enough to read my offer, correct?"

I ripped the sheet out of his hand. Glancing down at the paper, I gasped at the final offer, one point six million dollars. Half at signing and half in five years. "I don't understand. I don't have to sell for five years?"

"My attorneys inform me you are contractually bound by the terms of the will. I can wait. The deposit money just makes you more inclined to accept my offer. A carrot, if you will." Eric pulled out a chair from the table and sat down. "Of course, if the amount is not to your liking, we can negotiate."

He leaned back in the chair and waited.

"One point six for this place?" Jackie sat down in the chair next to Eric. I'd forgotten she was still here. "You could buy a chain of coffee shops for that kind of money. Maybe even a piece of Starbucks?"

"Mr. Ammond—"

He interrupted. "Eric, please call me Eric."

"Eric," I began again. "I told you I wasn't interested in selling. I'm not sure what type of development you and Mayor Baylor are planning, but you'll just have to build it somewhere else."

I pushed the sheet of paper back toward him.

"Now, Jill, don't be too hasty. I'm sure Mr. Ammond would want you to take some time to think about this generous offer." Aunt Jackie grabbed the sheet of paper before Eric could take it back.

"Your aunt is an intelligent woman. That is exactly what we need to do." Eric stood, brushing a piece of imaginary lint off his suit jacket. "Please take some time to think about my offer. I'll be glad to answer any questions that may come up."

He pulled out a business card from his pocket and laid it on the table. "Call me. I'll find my way out."

I watched as he nodded to Aunt Jackie and glanced at Greg before he walked out of the kitchen and down the hallway to the front door. Only when I heard his Hummer start up at the front of the house did I take a breath and slip into one of the chairs.

"I can't believe you turned down almost two million." Greg sat next to me, his hand now covering my shaking hand.

I laughed—the sound coming out tinny and fake. I'd taken the high road and honored my friendship with Miss Emily instead of taking the money. Principles, they'd bite you every time. "What's a few million dollars?"

Chapter 11

After another trip to the hardware store for a stronger latch for the shed door to install the lock on, Greg laid the keys on my table. "Between that new lock and your new fence, someone would have to be pretty determined to get into your shed now."

I'd been going through boxes of Miss Emily's papers, trying to determine what if anything I needed to keep. "Do you know if dead people have to file taxes?"

"What?"

"I'm going through Miss Emily's files, and I don't want to throw away anything important." *Please tell me he knows something about this pile of paper*, I prayed.

"You probably should ask Jimmy." Greg nodded at the refrigerator. "You got a soda in there?"

"On the bottom." I grabbed my to-do list and put *Call Jimmy* on the top of Monday's list. Twiddling my pen between my fingers, I glanced at Greg's back and quickly added *Go see Crystal*. I needed to put this inheritance thing out of my head so I'd know if I could start making plans for the money that would be sitting in my bank account tomorrow. At least the money that was left after I paid off my credit cards and restocked my savings account from what I'd already spent. If I had to give away the house, I would at least reimburse myself for what I'd already spent.

He plopped down in the chair next to me, popping open the top of the can and tipping his head back to drink. "That chore took longer than I thought. We'll have to visit the puppies next weekend."

"I'd like to have the fence done before that anyway." *And figure out if I should keep the house*, I added silently. It wasn't that I didn't love the house. I did. But if Miss Emily had a legitimate heir, besides her scammy nephew and his wife, the estate should go to that heir, no matter what Jimmy Marcum said.

"Where do you want to take me to dinner?" Greg polished off the can of soda in one more gulp.

"I'm taking you to dinner?" I closed my notebook.

"I guess you could cook me dinner, but I'm not sure if you know how." Greg leaned back in his chair, playing with the keys from the shed lock.

"I can cook." I didn't know where we got from visiting the puppies to me making dinner for him. "But you saw the fridge. I'm pretty low on supplies right now."

"So, let's head to Bakerstown. They have a great seafood restaurant." Greg stood. "And we'll make a stop on the way home and I'll buy you a housewarming gift."

"I thought the shed lock was my housewarming gift." Examining my jeans and T-shirt, I deemed them clean enough for a casual dinner.

"Nope, that's so that I don't get called out here on a prowler call when I'd rather be watching football next Sunday." He smiled. "I'm charging the cost to the city's community safety enforcement account."

"I'll be sure to thank Mayor Baylor the next time I see him," I said dryly.

"Why do you have to be hateful? Didn't you ever hear you shouldn't look a gift horse in the mouth? Besides, you'll like my gift." He grabbed my arm and pulled me up to a standing position. Standing way too close to him. My heart started racing as he put his hands on my arms. "I hope we'll get a lot of use out of it." He stared into my eyes and leaned forward.

I closed my eyes. I might be going to hell for this, but at least I could enjoy this one kiss. I waited. Nothing. Then I felt a quick tap on my nose.

"Let's go then. I'm starving."

I opened my eyes, and Greg was no longer standing in front of me. I turned and saw his nicely formed backside heading out to the front of the house to his pickup.

You read that all wrong, I chided myself.

Feeling silly, I grabbed my purse off the counter, checked my hair in the hallway mirror, and followed my cop. I tested the lock, making sure it had engaged before I left the porch. If this door stood open when we got back, I could be sure someone had been in the house.

Greg waited in the cab of the truck when I closed the gate. "Door locked?"

"I checked twice." I threw my purse on the seat and climbed into the truck using the grab bar on the side to pull me upward. "You ever think about adding running boards? I feel like I'm in a semi, we're so high off the ground."

Greg laughed. "I don't have a lot of passengers."

That's surprising.

"My Jeep is tall, but this is ridiculous."

"Hey, I'm a big man, what did you think I'd drive, a subcompact? At least in the truck I can stretch out my legs without breaking through the engine compartment." He headed the truck down the road that would take us to the highway. "Besides, it's not a Hummer like your boyfriend's."

"Eric Ammond is not my boyfriend." I thought about the offer I had sitting on my kitchen table. "Why would a developer be willing to wait five years to take possession of a property? It doesn't make sense."

"He's putting a lot of money on something that won't pay him back for years." Greg paused. "I don't know a lot about real estate, but I know there has to be a payout somewhere for him, that's just common sense. And I don't see any business in South Cove making that kind of money."

"I paid a steep price for the building with the shop, but nothing even close to what he's offering for Miss Emily's place." I watched the landscape pass by the window. Usually I drove even when Amy and I went to town. I missed my friend. Amy would know the reasons behind Eric's offer and why he could wait for the property.

"Have you heard anything about Amy?" I watched Greg's face for any tells that he knew something he didn't want to say.

"She's off the grid, that's for sure. I had a buddy from the bureau run her credit cards, and there was nothing since she bought a dress a month ago at one of the boutiques in South Cove." Greg shook his head. "The mayor's theory about her being off surfing sounds plausible, except wouldn't you need money on a vacation?"

"Unless you aren't on a vacation."

"Yeah," Greg said. We sat in silence for several miles. I watched the seagulls fly and dive over the ocean and thought about my friend out there somewhere, hopefully riding the waves safely on her surfboard—as safe as you could be surfing. A thought crossed my mind. "Greg, have you been to Amy's apartment yet?"

"That's my second stop tomorrow after I see if she shows up for work." Greg glanced over at me. "Why?"

"If she's surfing, she would have taken her board and gear." Amy had told me that it had taken her years to find the right board for her. She wouldn't head out for mondo waves without it.

Greg kept silent for a few moments, considering my words. "You're sure she wouldn't just use rental stuff when she got there?"

"Greg, she shipped her board to Australia so she didn't have to use rental stuff. She said it was like cheating on a husband: Once you found a board, that's the one you used."

"I'll look into it." His tone of voice changed, and I took his clipped reply to indicate he was done talking about it. But I knew I'd stirred some doubt.

Neither Greg nor I spoke the rest of the drive. I twisted around thoughts about Amy and where she could be if she wasn't surfing. Miss Emily's voice broke through the fog: "No use worrying about tomorrow—there's plenty to keep you busy today." I laughed at the memory of her sitting in a rocker, shaking her knitting needle at me.

Greg slowed down and turned into the parking lot for the restaurant, Sea Delights. I hoped the food was more creative than the name.

"The food's great here, really."

I blushed. "I wasn't laughing at the restaurant. I just remembered something Miss Emily told me once." Great, now he thought I'd second-guessed his choice in eateries. "She always told me not to get tied up in things I couldn't control."

Greg turned off the truck and leaned back into his seat. "Deal with today's fires and let tomorrow be?"

"Yeah, something like that. One day I sat on her porch complaining about not having someone in my life, about the store, about my family." I paused. "I guess she got tired of it and told me to stop."

"My grams used to tell me the same thing. She said there wasn't no point in worrying about something that might never happen." Greg stared out the truck window. "And I have to agree, I never thought my life would lead me here. A big city cop or a fed, maybe. Not stuck in the same small town where I went to high school—dealing with drunken tourists and bored kids."

"Believe me, living in the city's not all it's cracked up to be. I couldn't wait to get out and have a second to breathe." I put my hand on Greg's arm, wanting to comfort him. His arms were steel. I wanted to squeeze and run my hand up and down his shoulder, checking for muscle. Touching Greg felt like holding on to a statue. My body reacted in ways I didn't want to admit.

I pulled my hand away. *Just friends, just friends*—I chanted my new mantra.

"Well, enough of the deep heartfelt confessions, let's eat." Greg bounded out of the truck and walked over to open my door. "You'll love this place, I promise."

We entered the dark building, and the smell of homemade bread made my stomach growl loud enough for Greg to hear.

"I told you." He went up to the hostess stand, where a young woman in a white shirt and blue skirt had just finished taking a phone reservation. When she smiled at us, I gasped. Both Greg and the woman stared at me.

Crystal Dunn stood to greet us.

"Are you all right?" Crystal asked, apparently not recognizing me from my semi-stalking incident from yesterday.

"I'm fine. I mean, I just remembered something." Greg stared at me while I rambled. "Do you have a restroom?" Dodge and weave, dodge and weave.

She pointed to her right, the restroom sign clearly visible. "Do you want me to wait and seat you when you're back?"

"I'll wait." Greg appeared concerned.

Great, now he probably thinks I'm about to throw up or something. "No, go ahead. I'll catch up." I needed a couple of minutes alone with Crystal to feel her out on the Miss Emily stuff. She didn't look like a killer, although a long shift as a hostess could drive anyone to murder under the right circumstances. I headed to the restroom and waited long enough for Crystal to escort Greg to the table. Thank God the room smelled of pine. I'm not a big fan of public bathrooms, but sometimes a girl has no choice.

I cracked the door and peeked out. Crystal stood alone at the hostess stand. As I headed toward her, she stopped reading from the textbook.

"I'll show you to your table."

"Actually, can we talk a minute?" I walked closer to the stand, hoping this wasn't a mistake. I tried to peek over the top of the stand to see if she had a knife tucked behind the stand. Nope, just a copy of a child physiology book. She saw me glance at the book.

"I'm taking night classes." She held the book up. "Are you in Professor Caldwell's class, too?"

Here we go. I took a deep breath. "I'm Jill Gardner, and I own Coffee, Books, and More in South Cove." I waited to see if any glimpse of recognition of the town crossed her face.

"Why do you want to talk to me?" Crystal seemed confused, not angry or scared.

"I wondered if you knew someone who lived in South Cove, Miss Emily?"

Sadness filled Crystal's face, and she nodded toward the seating near the windows. "Let's sit down. I have a few minutes, the dinner rush hasn't started yet."

We sat on tan upholstered settees facing each other. I waited for her to continue.

"Let me guess what you think you know. You and that lawyer guy have me all figured out, right? I'm some gold digger trying to con an old lady." Crystal fought back tears now.

"Jimmy Marcum?"

"He came by my house one day after I had tracked Miss Emily down and left her a picture of Annie." Crystal's eyes were distant as she watched the traffic pass on the street. "He said he'd investigated me. He called me a fraud."

"Why do you think Annie is Miss Emily's great-granddaughter?" I put my hand on the young woman's arm, hoping to calm her.

"Because Henry told me she was."

Totally confused, I asked, "Who's Henry?"

"Henry is . . . was . . . married to Mary, Joshua's mother. Annie's grandmother."

"So Joshua is Annie's father." I started to think I needed a program to keep all the names in my head.

"He was killed in a car accident. When she found out, Mary just kept repeating, she'd lost them both. Henry couldn't calm her down at the hospital."

"Both? Joshua and who?" I needed my notebook to write this stuff down.

"Bob, Joshua's dad. He died in Vietnam before Josh was born, just like what happened to Annie." Crystal eyed the dining room but I ignored her visual cue.

"And Bob was Miss Emily's son." I finally tied the pieces together. I glanced at Crystal for confirmation, but she stared past me.

"Sounds like motive to me," Greg's voice came over my shoulder. He glared at me. The ride home would either be very quiet or I would get my head bit off.

"Greg, this is Crystal Dunn. The woman I told you about?" I'm sure my polite introduction wasn't going to calm the waters now, but I could try.

Greg shook his head. "Jill, why don't you go wait for me at the table. I've ordered an appetizer."

I felt like I had been caught cheating on a test. "Crystal, if you ever want to talk—" I ignored the glare coming from Greg. She knew where to find me.

Greg sat down in my place—waiting for me to leave.

"Be sure to tell him about what Mary said," I called out to Crystal.

Greg pointed to the dining room.

"Fine," I said to no one as I walked toward the tables. We were the only couple in the restaurant, so finding our table wasn't rocket science. A baked crab dip steamed on the table, a loaf of fresh bread next to it, and a large iced tea rested beside my plate. I sat down and listened, trying to overhear Crystal and Greg's conversation, but the Muzak version of "Tie a Yellow Ribbon" filled the silence.

I ripped off a piece of bread, dipping it into the crab mixture. The sweet creamy dip filled my mouth, and I quickly took another bite. It would serve him right if this dish from heaven was all gone by the time he got back to the table.

I only had time to scarf down half of the dip before Greg slipped into his chair across from me. He put his napkin on his lap and reached over for a piece of the bread. "You like the dip."

"I love it. Tell me what Crystal said." I leaned forward, the food temporarily forgotten.

"If this Mary is right, Crystal did have motive to kill Miss Emily. Especially after Jimmy Marcum visited and basically called her a con artist." Greg popped a piece of bread and dip into his mouth. Then he chuckled. "She's still hot about his visit."

"Do you think she could have . . ." I still couldn't say *killed*, and tears filled my eyes when I thought of poor Miss Emily lying so still in her bed.

"Not really, but if Jimmy turns up dead, she'd be first on my list of suspects." Greg chuckled, using the last of the bread to clean off the edges of the crab dip. "She felt hurt Miss Emily didn't take the time to get to know Annie. Now it's too late."

I leaned back in my chair. We still didn't know any more than we had last week. In fact, things were worse. Miss Emily was dead. Amy had gone missing. My windfall inheritance might be Annie's. And now I was at dinner with a great-looking guy who seemed to be into me—except for the fact that he was married. I had become a walking, talking country song.

The waiter showed up at the table and set a large bowl of clam chowder in front of me. The creamy, fat-filled kind rather than that tomato broth stuff. And he brought a new mini loaf of bread that smelled like it had just come out of the oven. I grabbed my spoon and took a bite. I made some sort of growl of happiness. Greg started laughing.

"I told you the food here was great." He ripped a piece of bread off the new loaf and handed it to me. Looking into his eyes, I felt like I'd fallen into a deep pool, warm and comforting.

What the heck? I thought as I took the offered bread. Even country songs need to eat once in a while.

Chapter 12

The sun shone blindingly through the windshield as Greg drove toward the highway. Our dinner had been amazing except for the silence between us. Every time I'd think of something to say, I'd realize it came back to the investigation. Or his family life. Two subjects that I was trying to stay away from. I knew our time together wasn't anything more than him either just being nice to the potential murder suspect or victim, depending on the day.

I'd watch him suck the crabmeat out of shells and wondered what thoughts were running through his mind. Was it Crystal, Amy, or even just Miss Emily and the whole inheritance thing? I think the death threats actually took me off the suspect list—at least for now.

I leaned back in my seat, the warm sun mixing with the effects of my full belly. I didn't realize I had fallen asleep until a hand gently shook my shoulder.

"We're here." Greg's warm voice broke through my slumber.

"Wow, I didn't think I'd been asleep that long. Sorry." I peeked through my sunglasses and saw the looming store in front of me. "Wait, where's here? This isn't South Cove."

"Can't pull anything over on you, now, can I?" Greg laughed. "Come on, get out. I told you I'd buy you a housewarming present."

"I thought you were joking," I dangled my legs over the side of the truck seat and slid out to the pavement below. At five-six, I'd never felt short, until today. I shut the truck door and hurried to catch up with him. Men at hardware stores are like women at a bridal sale: You have to keep up or try to stay out of the way.

Greg's eyes gleamed as we entered the store. We stopped at a planter display right inside the door. "I know you're having Kevin do your fence, but you might want to look at some decorative plant hangers next spring. It will make that new cedar pop with a few hanging baskets. I can come over and help you with a landscaping blueprint for the backyard." He kept walking, talking about the future of a house that might not even be mine in the spring.

The thought brought me up short. I stopped walking. Greg finally realized I wasn't next to him.

"What's up?" He came back and stood in front of me. "You don't like landscaping?"

"What if I don't get to keep the house? I mean, with Crystal and Annie and the council and the mayor and the threats?" My breaths came short and fast.

Greg walked me over to a bench display and sat me down. "Calm down. Breathe slower."

"I love—love the house—and what if it gets taken from me, or if . . ." My eyes widened as I realized that maybe I would be the one who went away. I grabbed Greg by both arms. "You don't think that someone would try to kill me, do you? I know you're staying with me to keep me safe, but I'm not in any real danger. Right?"

My thoughts rambled faster than my words. Tears streamed down my face.

"Jill—Stop." Greg's hands tightened on my arms. "You're fine. No one's going to hurt you. I won't let them." He sat next to me and folded me into his arms. "Now just breathe. Slowly, breathe." He stroked the back of my head.

Breathe, breathe. I heard the words and followed. My tears slowed. I was having a breakdown in the middle of House Heaven. An old black-and-white film reel ran through my head, but instead of the heroine being escorted to the old-fashioned ambulance by men in white coats, the salespeople in their orange House Heaven vests were dragging me out of the building. I started giggling. Soon my body shook.

"Jill, it's all right." Greg's comforting voice only made the giggles stronger. He pulled me away from his chest. "Are you laughing?"

"I'm sorry. I just started thinking about how crazy this all is, and then I got the *they're coming to take you away* thing in my head." I pulled a tissue out of my purse and wiped away the tears. I took a deep breath, then asked the question that had been bothering me all morning. "Do you think someone's trying to get me out of the house?"

"The thought had crossed my mind. But I don't want you to worry about that." He stood and held his hand out. "Are you ready to go pick out your gift?"

I let him pull me off of the bench to a standing position. "I guess."

"Don't be so excited." Greg put his arm around my shoulders. "I promise we are going to figure this out."

That was a promise I hoped he would keep. I kept quiet as we walked through the long aisle of the store. I could see Greg looking at the shelves and wanting to talk about how great the water fountain or the magic ball would look in my backyard, but he kept the thoughts to himself. I just wanted to get home. Home to my kitchen, where I could heat up water for a cup of tea and curl up on the couch with one of the many books I had started. I wanted to read about someone else's life in shambles, not live my own. We stopped.

The aisle consisted of one thing—rows of grills—shiny silver ones, black ones, tiny ones, and one large enough to use in a restaurant. We stood in front of a silver grill with a propane tank attached.

"What do you think? Is it too small?" Greg pulled the lid to the grill open. "It's got three burners inside and one on the outside where you can heat up your sauce or chili or anything in a pan."

"It's nice." I didn't know what he wanted out of me. I didn't know the proper response to evaluating a grill—just like all the other grills. Awareness finally broke through. "This is my gift?"

"What did you think?" Greg leaned down to check the boxes next to the displays. "Here it is." He pulled out the box and leaned it up against the shelves. "Some assembly required, but I'm sure I could put it together quick. We might even be able to use it tomorrow."

I watched him study the box. "I can't accept that. I mean, it's too much."

Greg stood up. "Jill, until we close Miss Emily's murder investigation and figure out who's threatening you, I'm going to be spending a lot of time with you. I could assign Toby overtime to sit outside your house, but your aunt has already hired him to make low-fat mocha drinks. And having a grill will make our evenings out on the porch more convenient."

He grinned and picked up the box. "So, let's get back to South Cove and see if this puppy is easy to assemble."

I watched him walk away. Although I bought the it's-not-you-it's-the-job line, one nagging thought kept rolling through my head. *What about his wife?* I sighed. At least I'd have a grill as a parting gift worth more than what I usually got from doomed relationships.

Greg had the phone up to his ear when I caught up to him in the line. He grinned at me and pointed to an addition to the box. A square galvanized watering tub for farm animals sat on top of the box. It was either a planter or his idea of a cooler for the porch.

Greg was turning out to be more outdoor living space designer than tough robot, unlike cops I'd worked with in the city. Or maybe those guys had a soft spot, too, just not one they showed on the job. I don't think Greg realized how different his life would have been if he had lived up to his original dreams of working in a major metropolis. Or how lucky he was to work in South Cove.

He pushed the box to the girl at the counter without missing a beat on the cell phone. Pulling out his plastic, he ran it though the machine and quickly finished the transaction. He handed me the tub. "Cooler," he mouthed and moved the grill box off to the side.

"Look, I've got to go. I'll call you when I get back into town." He rolled his eyes at me and listened again. "If it's that bad, call Jim. He can fix the drain."

Again, silence as he listened to the person on the other end. "Seriously, Sherry. I'll call you later." He flipped the phone closed and put it in his carrier like a revolver to a gun holster.

Sherry? That must be his wife.

"Something wrong?" I asked, not wanting to know. Even with spending time questioning the murder suspect and my emotional breakdown in House Heaven, the evening had been the closest thing to a date I'd had in five years. One I didn't want to end.

"I just want to know when I became Mr. Fix-It." Greg lifted the box again and, this time, placed it on a low, flat cart. It landed with a bang. "Sorry, that woman can get under my skin even in a five-minute phone call."

He took off for the parking lot and the truck.

Following behind with the tub, I did the math. This was the point in the discussion where he told me all about how she didn't understand him. The script I'd read before. Bad boyfriend number three or four, I forgot.

Mentally, I practiced my line.

I'm not interested in getting involved with a happily or unhappily married man.

And my own mantra, *I'm worth more than to be someone's second choice*, even if he had arms the size of tree limbs.

Greg had the box loaded by the time I reached the truck. He grabbed the tub from me and flashed a smile. "This will work great with a bag of ice and a six-pack of beer."

Not the response I'd expected. Now, I had a choice. Play along and pretend I didn't know, or confront him, making the rest of our conversations uncomfortable and awkward. Maybe I read too much into his attention. He had never once been unprofessional or anything but nice and caring. I could be the one seeing stars because of my reactions, not because of his intentions. I shrugged off my doubt. Until I was convinced that his intentions were anything more than your local friendly law enforcement protecting the damsel in distress, I'd keep my mouth shut.

My phone rang. Leaning against the truck soaking in the last of the evening sun, hot on my face, I flipped the phone open. "Hello?"

"Jill . . ." Amy's voice crackled from a distance.

"Amy? Is that you? Where are you?" I waved Greg over to my side of the truck and stood rigid. I pressed the phone closer to my ear, trying to hear.

"I'm down in . . ." The crackle became worse and cut off the rest of Amy's words.

"Are you all right? Where are you?" I talked louder, hoping that my words were getting through the bad connection.

"I'm trying to tell you, I'm at . . ." Again, the poor connection cut out any hope of hearing Amy's words. Her voice came through again. "I need . . ."

"The place, Amy, just say the place," I screamed into the phone. Greg reached around me and took the cell phone from my hand.

"Miss Newman—are you there?" Greg's voice was calm. "Hello? Is anyone there?"

He handed me back the phone. "She's gone."

I stared at Greg. "Gone? What do you mean, gone?" A cold chill encased me.

Greg pulled me into his arms. "I meant the call disconnected. Sorry, didn't mean to scare you. You're shaking."

Amy was alive. I hadn't wanted to hope. But she was alive somewhere, and maybe she'd stay that way. Tears fell down my cheeks.

Greg stepped back warily. I'd fallen apart on him twice in less than an hour. His eyes showed concern—probably didn't want to explain to the authorities how the woman he'd been protecting had just disintegrated in front of his eyes. "Are you okay?"

I grinned. "She's alive. I don't know where she is or who's she's with, but she's alive." I jumped up and down in a circle, my form of a victory dance. One that no man I'd ever been involved with had seen. I stopped bouncing, realizing people walking into the store were staring. Then I gave one last circle for good luck. What did I care if people stared?

"I'm glad you're happy. Ready to head home?" Greg opened the truck door for me and helped me climb inside. "I've got a grill to put together."

"Hey, do you think they could trace the call? I know we didn't talk very long, but at least they should be able to find what number called me, right?" My mind raced.

"I'll call my buddy on our way home and see what he can do. It's a weekend, so don't get your hopes up." Greg shut the truck door.

I sat stunned in the cab of the truck, barely noticing the heat radiating off the windshield. Not get my hopes up? This was the first time I had dared to hope since Amy had disappeared. Maybe the mayor had been right. Maybe this was all about catching a good wave. I hoped so. And when I did get to talk to her, I'd give her a piece of my mind. After a great big hug, that is.

Greg completed putting together the grill by reading the directions after a few false starts and a couple of Band-Aids. The grill fit quite nicely on the back porch, like I owned the home, not was just some squatter. I had a small tabletop grill on the floor of the balcony at my apartment, but I had to pull up a chair and sit inside the apartment to watch the chicken so it didn't burn. And every time I used it, smoke filled the living room, reminding me of burnt chicken for weeks. I still felt a little guilty for letting Greg pay for the grill and the country cooler.

According to Jimmy Marcum, tomorrow I would be a pretty wealthy girl. By my standards, at least. My thoughts went back to Crystal. Working full-time, going to school, and trying to raise a baby. If Annie was related to Miss Emily, Crystal should be sitting here on the back porch watching the sun set over the ocean. A quiet sigh slipped through my lips. How did the world get so complicated?

"What's up, buttercup?" Greg walked over and handed me a beer out of the new cooler. He sat next to me on the wooden steps leading down to the grass. The backyard had been filled with pallets of new siding, cedar fence planks, and lumber. In the driveway stood the biggest Dumpster I'd ever seen. Todd had explained that all of the contractors would be using the same Dumpster so I was saving money. I think he'd just heard the rumors about my inheritance. But the time schedule the council had set didn't leave room for arguments. I had thirty days . . . well, twenty-six days now, to get the house up to code. Looking around, I wasn't sure we'd make it.

"There's just so much happening, it's hard to keep up." I wasn't going to start crying for the third time that day in front of this man. And he wasn't in any hurry to leave.

"I know things are a little crazy right now . . ." Greg used his calming voice, probably afraid of what was coming next.

"A little? My best friend is missing, Miss Emily left me with this house that's apparently worth more bulldozed than standing, someone else may actually be entitled to all of this, I'm getting slammed all over town by the greedy nephew, my aunt is messing with my business, and I'm getting death threats. Does that about sum it up?"

"You forgot one thing." Greg took a sip of his beer, pulling at the label on the longneck bottle.

"What, what did I forget? The fact that all three contractors I'm working with see money signs every time they look at me?"

"There's that. But what I was thinking about was how you have a new grill." He peeked up at me, watching my reaction. He held his hand up with the Band-Aids. "One I spilled blood to give to you."

"Only because you refused to read the directions first." I pulled his hand toward me and kissed the Band-Aids. "There, the boo-boos are all better."

"That helps." Greg's voice sounded deep and husky.

And his voice made my breath catch in my throat. My playfulness had crossed over to something else. My body reacted to the thought of kissing this man sitting next to me. Whoa, Nellie. Slow down.

Greg ran his hand up my bare arm. His fingers were hard and callused against my skin, making the gesture both soft and demanding at the same time. His hand reached my shoulder and then up my neck, where he traced the outline of my chin. I parted my lips, waiting for his lips to meet mine. My body was frozen from his touch.

A noise from the driveway turned my attention away from the man sitting next to me. Greg stood—he had heard it, too.

"Who's there?" he called out to the gathering darkness.

A man's body turned the corner of the driveway and came around the back porch. "I thought I'd find you here." The voice wasn't friendly, but there was something familiar about it. I just couldn't place where I had heard it before.

"Jim? What are you doing here?" Greg went down the steps to greet his brother. He bear-hugged him and then turned around and swung an arm my way. "Jill, meet my little brother, Jim King."

I stood, conscious of the beer bottle in my hand. "We've met. Jim is my painting contractor." After I had just whined to Greg about how much my contractors were gouging me for money, then I went and told him that his brother was one of the grifters.

Greg regarded his brother with a cool stare. "It's a little late for painting, isn't it?" He stepped back toward me.

"I didn't come to see her. I came to see you. Sherry called me. I had to go over and fix that drain of hers, again." Jim glared at me while he talked.

"I told her to call you." Greg put his arms out to his sides. "I was busy, and she made it seem like it couldn't wait."

"I can see you were real busy." Jim nodded toward me. "Ignoring her won't make her go away, you know."

"It's not like that and you know it." Greg sighed and finished off the rest of the longneck. He pulled his brother back toward the driveway. "Let's go talk."

"I'm not the one you should be talking to," Jim responded.

"Hold on," he hissed at his brother. "I'll be right back," he called over his shoulder to me.

"Don't bother," I said, loud enough for both men to hear me. "I'm going to head in to bed. Call me if you hear from Amy. Good night, Jim," I added as an afterthought.

The brothers could fight it out somewhere else. I wasn't going to be the Jezebel keeping Greg away and causing Jim to have to work his brother's honey-do list tonight. And besides, I needed a level head about me from both of them. I couldn't afford to make either man an enemy. And I sure didn't want to come between brothers.

One man I needed to paint my house—before the council's deadline. And the other man I needed to keep me safe—and find Amy. I locked the kitchen door behind me, closing out both brothers.

I went into my soon-to-be office and realized I should have picked up more paint while we were at House Heaven. Another thing for my to-do list tomorrow. I grabbed a can of spackle and a putty knife from my pile of painting supplies and walked around the room filling in cracks and nail holes. I needed to work off some of the tension that filled my body. There was no doubt I wanted Greg to kiss me, married or not. Did that make me a bad person?

What else would you call it? my other side responded to my question.

Looking around the room, I made sure I'd hit all the repair spots. I took the spackle can and the rest of the painting supplies and moved them out to the crowded living room so I could sweep and then lay down drop cloths. If I got the room prepped tonight, all I had to do in the morning was take a run to Bakerstown and pick up the paint.

Twenty minutes later, I closed the door to the office, the room ready to paint. And I was still wound tight, my thoughts churning. I sat at Miss Emily's desk, imagining my new room. I wanted a brown chocolate or caramel color, but maybe I'd do a focal wall in a color that popped. Electric blue? Fuscia? Yellow? Maybe I'd just stay with the brown. One of Miss Emily's paintings would match my mood for the room.

Thinking about the paintings got me wondering again why she'd left them in the shed. Which led me to the question of who had sold the paintings to the gallery. Too many questions—no way would I get to sleep tonight, not with my mind running in twenty different directions.

I considered the sturdy wooden rolltop desk in front of me. Might as well clean it out. It would be the first thing I'd place in the office once the paint dried. Then I'd figure out where the bookshelves would go. I imagined an overstuffed chair and ottoman, also in the room. I could just see myself curled up under a cotton throw deep into a book. Unless the stalker decided to force his hand to get me to sell. The thought made me shiver.

I grabbed a handful of files and took them over to the couch to sort. Before I started, I headed to the kitchen.

As I waited for the water to boil for tea, I grabbed two boxes out of the pile in my mudroom. Jimmy Marcum had told me that he would handle all the taxes for Miss Emily as part of the estate filing. He'd e-mailed me a list of what papers to keep, so I labeled one box with Jimmy's name. The other box I planned to use for personal letters or photos or anything else that Annie and Crystal might like to have.

George and Sabrina had left the family Bible and photo album when they stalked out of the will reading. Jimmy Marcum had retrieved the items and told me if they didn't come back for them, he'd turn them over to me, as well. If Annie was Miss Emily's true heir, I'd be handing the box along with the money and the house to the sweet baby in the picture. And my office/reading room would be turned into a playroom, complete with duck and mother goose wallpaper.

The whistle of the teakettle brought me back to the kitchen. No need to worry about what was coming; there was enough to worry about right here. Miss Emily's words echoed in my ears. "You gave me enough to keep me busy for a few 'todays'." I aimed the words at the landscape hanging in the kitchen. As I poured the water over my tea bag, I swore I heard gentle laughter.

I headed back into the living room with my list of tax papers, the boxes, and a steaming cup of tea. Maybe a few hours of going through files would dull my mind enough for sleep to become a possibility.

I had gone through two drawers of grocery receipts, utility bills, and letters from the city by midnight. One more, I thought, and then I'd head to bed. The next file was stuffed with letters. Handwritten in a man's large script and yellowed with age, there must have been a hundred of them. I flipped through the first one and found the signature, *Love, Robert*. These must have been from Miss Emily's husband. I took a sip of the now ice-cold tea and scooted back in the couch, my feet curled up beside me, settling in to read.

My Darling Emily, I pray that this letter finds you exactly as I left you, your hair disheveled—your mind wandering as you stand in front of your latest creation. Oh, how I miss waking up to the sight of you in your white gown, lost in your work . . .

I stopped, wondering what I was doing, reaching into a couple's private moments, but I soothed my guilt away with the thought that maybe if I learned a little more about my friend's past, I could help solve her murder or determine Annie's parentage. Besides, this Robert knew how to write a letter. I could no more put the letters down and head to bed than an alcoholic could turn down that second sip. Pandora's box had been opened; it was time to delve for the secrets.

The morning light streamed through the living room window right in my face. My contacts clung to my eyes, a side effect of not removing the thin plastic before falling asleep. I hadn't meant to stay on the couch, I'd just wanted to rest my eyes for a second. I glanced at my watch: eight-thirty. If Amy had been on a long weekend surfing jaunt, she'd be at work by now. I put the unread letters in a separate pile on the coffee table.

I'd learned almost nothing that would help, except how a man showed a woman he loved her. I had never even gotten a phone call from any of the men in my life that had conveyed so much emotion. So much love. Miss Emily had been a lucky woman to be loved the way Robert had loved her. And she'd known it. Amy had to read these letters.

I walked into the kitchen and started a pot of coffee. Brushing my teeth, I studied my reflection in the mirror. Dark circles under my eyes and a rat's nest for hair, not my best look. Maybe a shower first? That way if Amy was running late, I wouldn't call too early. Even the mirror reflection knew I was stalling. I cleaned up the sink, pulled my hair into a ponytail, and headed back to the kitchen and my cell phone. I poured coffee from the half-brewed pot and sat down. Steeling myself with a couple of sips, I stared at the phone.

Please Amy—answer the phone. Be there.

I reached for the phone and it rang. My hand jumped back like the phone was a snake curling to strike. I barked a short laugh. My nerves were shot. Picking up the phone, I answered, "Hello?"

"Miss Gardner, so nice to talk to you this morning." Eric Ammond's voice came over the line like butter on hot bread.

"Mr. Ammond, what can I do for you?" Man, this guy didn't take no for an answer. I thought back to our last conversation. I was pretty sure I had told him no. But when someone offers you more than a million dollars, it's hard to keep the facts straight.

"I am outside your lovely coffee shop. You are not open on Mondays? What a shame. I looked forward to seeing your lovely aunt this morning." I heard cars passing in the background. "Maybe you would consider coming down and opening the shop for us? My treat, of course."

"I'm sorry, I'm very busy this morning."

"I shouldn't have presumed. Of course you're busy. You probably need to find your lovely friend of yours with that cop person."

The hairs on the back of my neck flared. "What do you know about Amy?"

"Such a waste for such a pretty girl to go missing. But it happens every day, now, doesn't it? Women going missing and never being seen again?"

"Do you know where she is?" My voice cracked with fear. "Tell me where she is!"

"Miss Gardner, I'm afraid you misunderstood. I have no knowledge of the whereabouts of the beautiful Miss Newman. I am just a concerned citizen wondering about the safety of the innocents in this town." He paused, taking a breath. "Like your lovely aunt. It would be such a shame for her to come to harm, especially when it seems so random and senseless."

"If you hurt her . . ." My voice cracked, but I didn't know what else to add.

"Again, you're misunderstanding me. Maybe we should continue this conversation in person. I don't seem to be able to make you understand me over the phone."

"I don't want to see you. Stay away from me . . . and my aunt . . . and Amy," I added as an afterthought. I hung up the cell phone. Had that just happened? Had Eric Ammond actually threatened Aunt Jackie? I hesitated on whom to call first. If I called Amy and she wasn't there, I'd be devastated. But if I called Greg and Amy wasn't there, he'd feel bad about being the one to break the news. I decided to let him feel bad.

Chapter 13

"Are you sure he threatened your aunt? Tell me again what he said." Greg asked me about the phone call for the third time. We sat at the kitchen table. He'd been on his way over to give me the bad news. Amy hadn't shown up for work today. And except for a garbled message on the mayor's voice mail left sometime over the weekend, no one had heard from her since her brief call to me on Sunday.

"It was a threat, believe me." I repeated Eric's words again, a chill hitting my back. "Can't you tell him to stay away or something?"

"I can stop and have a chat with him." Greg leaned back in his chair. "But you don't even know if he was outside the coffee shop, he just said he was."

"You tell him to leave me alone," I babbled. I jabbed my finger at the table. "You tell him—"

Greg interrupted me. "Jill, I said I'd talk to him. I don't have any power or authority to be telling him anything."

"But—" I didn't even get the second word out before Greg put out his hand.

"No more. I'll see if I can get more out of him about his intentions for the house—that is, if you come to your senses and actually sell him the option to buy the house. Money's money, and that much doesn't come along often in our lives."

I was just about to argue that money didn't buy happiness, when Greg's cell phone went off. He went into the living room to take the call. I went to rinse out the cups in the sink and tried not to eavesdrop on Greg's conversation. For all I knew, the call was from Sherry, needing him home, this time not just wanting his handyman skills to fix a leaky sink—if you know what I mean.

I sat back down at the table and reviewed my to-do list for the day. Visiting Amy's apartment had to be first on the list. That is, if I could get the hunky local police detective who seemed way too comfortable in my kitchen to leave me alone for a few minutes.

Greg ambled back into the kitchen and refilled his coffee cup. "The district attorney. We have the warrant to search Amy's apartment." He sat down at the table.

"So, why are you still here?" Maybe I had waited too long to search Amy's apartment. But I swore this man was made of molasses.

"The crime scene techs won't be here from Bakerstown for an hour. I'm meeting them at the apartment."

"Why are the crime scene techs going to Amy's apartment? You have to find clues to where she's gone. There's no crime scene." Amy would not be happy with strangers traipsing through her apartment.

"The judge thinks there's enough evidence to show a threat, especially with your statement that she was hiding under her desk. And the district attorney feels the mayor has been less than forthcoming."

"You told them about that?" I'd misjudged his concern. Maybe this was all business.

"Jill, I've had a so-called natural death that turned into a murder, a possible kidnapping, and a threat on your life in the last two weeks. I've never handled anything like this. I'm pulling in all the big guns, no matter who doesn't like it." Greg's face was hard with determination.

"You mean the mayor." I read between the lines. First Greg had been told that he shouldn't see me as a suspect—without any proof—and now the mayor appeared to have an interest in the plot to gain access to Miss Emily's, correction, my house.

"I don't know what or who I mean." Greg ran his hand through his sandy blond hair. "I just know that things are out of control, and it feels like we're running out of time."

"You think something is going to happen to Amy?" My blood ran cold. What would I do if Amy died?

Greg stared at me. "You're the one I'm worried about."

The words rocked me. What did he mean? The threat was just part of the mayor and Eric's ploy to get me to sell the house, wasn't it? Before I could ask, Greg's phone rang again.

"The crime scene guys must be here already, looking for the apartment." He answered the phone without looking at the number. "Hello." He paused. "Sherry, I'm busy." Another long pause as he listened.

I could hear a woman's voice on the other end, and she didn't sound happy. "I thought Jim took care of that yesterday?"

Another pause. "I'll be there in five." He hung up the phone.

"Sorry, I have to take care of something before the lab rats get in town." He took his cup to the sink. "What are your plans today? Working on the house?"

"I have to pick up some paint, so I'm heading into Bakerstown." I left off my plan to get to Amy's apartment before they started searching. I didn't know what to look for, but maybe I could piece together something.

"I'll stop by later with some fried chicken from Lille's." Greg headed out to the front door.

I pulled out my key ring to check for Amy's apartment key— yep, still there. When I didn't hear the front door shut, I walked into the living room. Greg stood in the living room, reading one of Robert's letters to Miss Emily. Guilt flashed across his face when he realized I'd caught him.

"Sorry, I couldn't resist." He set the letter back down. "My grandma had all the letters Gramps sent her during the war. I read them last summer after she passed. The letters felt like they came from a different world."

I walked over and picked up the one he had been reading. "I spent last night reading. I couldn't put them down." I hesitated. "Reading them felt like looking into their lives. Almost like I was there."

"Yeah. I get that. My mom saved all my dad's letters from his tour in Vietnam, as well. But she won't let us boys read them, at least not yet." He shrugged. "I think she saved every letter that Jim and I sent her when we did our four years. And we never left the country. Maybe it's just an army thing."

"Or a mother thing," I responded, my mind whirling. Maybe there were other letters somewhere—letters from a son to his mother. Or to his pregnant girlfriend? My visit to Bakerstown now had another stop. I needed to find out more about Crystal's boyfriend. Maybe the proof existed in letters from long ago. Letters that Miss Emily might have kept.

Amy lived over the bike rental shop. The apartment took the entire second floor, with only four rooms carved out in the tiny square footage—but Amy didn't care. She was rarely there, usually spending her free time on some beach or another. This wasn't the first time she had taken off to chase a wave, if that was where she was. I parked my Jeep behind the building for a quick getaway in case Greg or the crime lab boys showed up early.

I climbed up the back stairs and slipped the key into the lock. The door creaked open. I walked into Amy's kitchen—spotlessly clean. Amy's cleaning lady, Maria, came every two weeks. I opened her refrigerator: nothing but bottled water and a leftover box from Tuscany Garden, probably from our trip after the reading of the will.

I wandered into the living room. Magazines were stacked neatly on the coffee table, books were lying opened on the table, stacked on the floor, and filling her bookcase. Amy was one of my better customers. In fact, we'd met at my store. She'd been coming in at least three days a week, looking for a book or two she had heard about from Internet buddies. I still usually had at least three to four books on order for her each week to place with my order with the book distributor. After the first couple of weeks, we started doing lunch, and over food and discussions about books, our friendship blossomed.

Nothing seemed out of place, that I could tell at least. Maria cleaned the dirt but she didn't handle the clutter. Amy said she always cleaned up before Maria got there so that she wouldn't feel like a complete slob. I walked into the bedroom, wondering if this trip had been just a waste of time. I wasn't an investigator. I didn't know the first thing about what to look for. I just hoped Amy wasn't in the same place I'd found Miss Emily, dead in bed.

I peeked around the corner. Light streamed into the bedroom. Amy's sleigh bed had been neatly made, another clue Maria had been there. I don't think Amy knew how to make a bed, even if she had wanted to. I examined her closet. The racks were filled. The girl had more pairs of jeans stacked in her closet organizer than I'd ever seen. The left of the closet flowed over with casual business clothes—khakis, dress shirts, cotton blazers, what she wore to work. The other side of the closet had what Amy called her "bar clothes." Sequined shirts, dresses, and skirts—short, sassy, and fun clothes. Both sides of the closet were packed—if she had gone on a vacation, wouldn't she have taken some of her party clothes? I turned to leave when I saw it.

Amy's wet suit hung over the back of the closet door.

Now I knew she wasn't surfing. She might have left her board behind, but there was no way she'd leave without her wet suit. She'd paid a month's salary on that custom-made suit.

Tears filled my eyes and I stumbled over to sit on the ottoman at the edge of Amy's bed. Something had happened to my friend. So, was her call yesterday a call for help? I tried to think about what I had heard, playing the tape over and over in my mind. I almost didn't hear the downstairs door bang open and Greg's voice coming up the stairs. The lab boys had arrived. I wiped away my tears just in time to see the front door open. Busted.

Frantic, I sought another escape route since the real investigators blocked my path to the kitchen door. My eyes fell on the bedroom window. I ran to the window, thinking hiding in the closet would only get me caught later than sooner. An old fire escape sat outside the window. Amy had called it her private balcony and had planted a mini garden out there. I opened the window and, climbing over the sash, stepped out onto the metal grate. I slid the window shut and caught a glimpse of Greg coming into the bedroom. He leaned down by the bed and picked something up.

I tucked behind the brick wall, out of eyesight, I hoped. I tested out the first step for sounds. No creaking or banging. Stepping lightly but quickly down the stairs, I headed for my Jeep and the long drive to Bakerstown. I needed to think, and the drive to get paint for my new office would do the trick. Besides, I had a feeling Greg's casual question that morning had been less than casual, so I wanted to be knee-deep in painting that room by the time he showed up with dinner.

I pulled away from the street and noticed a paper flying around the cab of the Jeep. I grabbed it, cussing the winery and its viral paper advertising campaign. At the stop sign, I noticed the crime lab van and Greg's truck, parked in front of the bike shop. Parking in the back had saved my tail.

I glanced down at the paper. It wasn't a winery advertisement at all. In fact, the words were handwritten. On the page was a message that chilled my blood.

Get out of that house before we carry you out.

Where had this come from? I racked my brain to remember. The paper had been part of the trash in my Jeep for a while.

It had been on my windshield the morning I picked up the Jeep at Lille's after Aunt Jackie had driven me home. The same night that we almost got hit by that car. So the call on Saturday hadn't been the first threat.

The call had been threat number two.

My superstitious side reminded me that bad things came in threes.

Going to Amy's apartment had only deepened the worry I felt about my friend. Knowing she wasn't just surfing made it all the worse. My thoughts turned to the mayor's claim that some girl had left a message. It just didn't ring true. Amy wasn't the type to avoid conflict or her job. She loved the freedom working for the city gave her to stay in her field as well as take off time for surfing.

Two months ago she had received an offer from a planning firm one of her college friends had started. It had been a great offer. We talked about how much more money she could make in the city.

"Why do I need that kind of money?" Amy had been sitting across from me, sipping a mocha on a Tuesday. She'd been on her way in to the office but had stopped by to request I order a new paranormal romance, one supposed to be hot. I'd ordered two copies, one for her and one for research.

"You could buy your own house and build up a nest egg so you could work consultations only in five to ten years." My shop had been my reward for the years working in the city. Some people might say I got the bad end of the deal, but I loved my little creation.

"And I'd be too old to surf by the time I had any free time." Amy finished off the mocha and stood up. "I love my life now. No pressure. Except I have to beat the mayor in to the office." She glanced up at the clock. "And even with him usually late, I'm pushing that today. Gotta go."

"Think about what I said," I called after her, even though I knew she had her mind made up.

Now I wished I'd pushed her harder. If she'd taken a job in the city, she wouldn't have gotten messed up with whatever this was. And she wouldn't be missing.

Chapter 14

I dug through my purse one more time, slowly moving my wallet, two paperbacks, two checkbooks—one for the shop—mints, keys, and pens. Crap, no purple notebook. I'd left my combo to-do and shopping list sitting on the kitchen table. I grabbed a receipt from my bag and a pen and stopped to think. I needed two cans of paint—chocolate brown and a can of a different color for an accent wall. More fine sandpaper, rollers, and a new set of paintbrushes should keep me from driving the fifty miles to the store again tomorrow. Oh, and more spackle.

The bank officer, John, had called me on the drive to let me know that my deposit of five hundred thousand dollars or so had been successful. He thanked me for using Bank of California for my business. Funny, he'd never called to personally thank me for my business when my deposits ran in the hundreds. Not even that one time when I deposited over ninety thousand from the sale of my cozy San Fran condo. Now we were suddenly best friends.

I guess he hadn't heard about my track record with friends. I wouldn't be surprised if my bad luck wore off on him and the bank was robbed tomorrow. I'd laughed for miles thinking about my bad luck transferring to the insincere manager.

Now just thinking about the bank being robbed because John had been sucking up gave me the giggles. Maybe I was hysterical.

"Jill, are you okay?" A young woman's voice broke through my haze. Crystal stood in front of me. She pushed a cart holding Annie, who played with a stuffed animal.

"Crystal, it's nice to see you." I walked over to get my first glimpse at Annie. She'd be a heartbreaker when she grew up. Her blue eyes reminded me of Miss Emily's. She had a shock of blond curly hair and a toothy smile. She grinned at me when I made eye contact.

"Puppy." She thrust the stuffed animal at me. When I didn't respond, she repeated, "Puppy!"

"Yes—that's a puppy." I took the offered toy, thinking about Miss Emily's order for me to get a dog. Greg and I still had to go visit the litter. "She's adorable."

"I'm pretty taken with her." Crystal scanned my empty cart. "Shopping?"

"I'm painting and needed some supplies."

"Miss Emily's house?"

I'd forgotten Crystal had visited Miss Emily at home. "Does that bother you?"

Crystal ran her hand through Annie's curls, and the girl actually cooed at her mother. "I don't care that she left you the house. I just wish Miss Emily had had time to get to know Annie. She never even knew about Joshua before the accident. Before I told her."

I could tell there was something else bothering Crystal. If it wasn't being left out of the will, I wondered what it was. "I'm sorry that she didn't believe you."

"Oh, she believed me, all right. After that creep Jimmy Marcum came by to call me a scammer and pay me off, she phoned me."

My mind raced. Had Jimmy paid her off? Thinking it was inappropriate to ask the going price of blackmail, I asked my second question, "Miss Emily called you?"

"Yeah. She was nice. She invited me and Annie over for iced tea the next week, but then I heard she died." Crystal pulled a bag of Cheerios out of her purse and gave it to the babbling Annie. "You don't think that the stress of finding out about Annie was too much for her, I mean, could that have killed her?"

"No, she didn't have a heart attack." I wondered how much to tell this young woman whom I liked more and more. "I think the day she found out about Annie and Joshua was probably the happiest day of her life."

"Well, we've got a ton of errands to run today. I feel like I haven't had a day off for months." Crystal started to push her cart away.

"Wait." I paused, wondering how to ask. "Could you give me Joshua's mom's name and address?"

Crystal's pretty face turned hard. "I'm not asking for anything from the estate, so you don't have to worry. We'll be just fine." She put her hand protectively on her daughter's shoulders.

"Don't get mad. I'm just trying to clear up some things. I'd like to know more about Miss Emily's life for my own piece of mind." I hoped that sounded vague enough, yet would get me the info I needed.

"Mary's dead. Cancer. She passed just after Joshua's accident." She looked toward the bathroom fixtures aisle but she saw something else. "Henry's a nice guy. He sent me money each month right after I lost Joshua. Not much, but it kept the lights on. I don't want you to upset him."

"Did he know that Joshua wasn't his kid?"

"Oh yeah. But he didn't care." Crystal started crying. "A few months after Joshua died, Henry came over to see me. He's the one who told me that Joshua had a different biological dad. He said that no one could have loved Joshua more. And he said that I'd find that kind of dad for Annie, as well."

"It must have been hard for him to bring up the past like that." I pulled a tissue out of my bag, but Crystal had already found one in her large purse.

"He said I needed to know that Joshua would want Annie to have a good life. And that it was okay to love again. He said he had been Mary's second choice, but that didn't matter. He'd been the one who raised Joshua, who had a family, not Bob."

Now Crystal sobbed. She grabbed a pink notebook out of her purse and wrote something down. She put the paper in my hand.

"I can't talk about this. I've got to go." She pushed her cart with Annie down the aisle. Annie waved bye-bye as she peeked around her mother back at me.

I opened the crumpled sheet of paper in my hand. *Henry Williams, Santa Maria*—written on the page. I hoped he was in the phone book. I'd hate to have to ask Greg for another favor.

I headed to the paint aisle, my excitement dwindling on painting the room I'd planned to be my new office. The office that would be Annie's playroom instead. I looked at the scrap of paper. I could just throw the paper away. Crystal didn't expect anything from the estate. Miss Emily had given me the house, not Crystal. But I just couldn't leave it like that. I put the paper into my purse and made a mental note to call when I got home.

I needed to know.

I had finished with the brown paint and started to roll out the blue accent paint. The color was bold. And I might hate it later. I'd set aside the perfect painting from Miss Emily's stash to finish the room. The rolltop desk would add a touch of history. Now, if I could find some old lawyers' bookcases with the glass shelves for one wall and a small love seat for the other, the room would be complete. Even if I wasn't here for long, I wanted the room to be complete before I gave up possession to a two-year-old.

The doorbell rang as I swept on the first coat of blue. I'd forgotten Greg said he was bringing over dinner. I didn't think Miss Emily's killer would walk through the doors and murder me even if the hunky detective wasn't sitting in my kitchen eating chicken. But at least I had company and didn't feel guilty about him being here. Okay, well, not too guilty. I pushed my hair out of my eyes and carried the roller and pan to the front door with me.

"I'm so glad you're here, I'm starving," I said as I swung open the door to let Greg in. Eric Ammond stood on the porch instead.

"If I had known, I would have brought you dinner." The side of his lip curled up in what I assumed he thought was a charming smile. I thought it made him look snake-like.

"What do you want, Eric?" I didn't have time for this. I had paint drying.

"You didn't call me back this morning." He leaned over me to see what I held. "You're painting? That's so disappointing."

I brought the edge of the screen closer to block the doorway, although I knew if he pushed, I'd be no match for him. "I told you yesterday that I'm not interested in selling. Now, if you don't mind . . ."

"I thought maybe your aunt would help you change your mind. You know she's on the verge of being homeless, don't you? You could use some of the money to help her golden years be more comfortable. And it's not like I want the property today. You'd still have your five years, rent free." Eric leaned up against the doorway, rubbing his hand up the doorframe. "The workmen you hired are doing a very good job. They must be expensive. Such a waste."

Fear gripped my heart. Could Aunt Jackie be in trouble she hadn't told me about? *Calm down*, I thought. *This guy probably thinks living from paycheck to paycheck is equal to poverty.* "You don't know what you're talking about." My voice didn't back up my bravado.

Eric chuckled. "I know more than you, apparently. Call your aunt. Then call me back when you're ready to deal." He reached for my hair.

I jerked back from his hand.

He held up a cobweb. "You don't trust me? Now, that will have to be remedied." His eyes searched my face. "You will learn to trust me. Give me time."

A chill ran through my body. I thought of all the men in my life who had seen my weakness and had preyed on it. Fed on the fact that I'd been insecure. Eric was a power seeker, I could tell. But he'd never win his way into my trust. Not this time. This time I'd be strong. For Miss Emily, for Amy, and for me. I gathered up myself and closed the screen door on my unwelcome guest. "Not in this lifetime. Good-bye, Eric."

I shut the door on his surprised face. I guess Bambi didn't talk back to the man. He needed to get used to it.

I headed back to my mostly painted office after engaging the lock on the front door and checking the lock on the back. Then I sat down on the one chair in the room and started laughing. I'd vanquished the bully. For the first time in my life, outside the courtroom, I had said what I wanted and ended the conversation. My body shook with laughter until the tears started flowing.

Miss Emily would be proud of me. Today I'd been strong.

I poured more blue paint into the roller pan. Determined, I set off to finish the wall before Greg brought over dinner. And then I'd call Aunt Jackie. We needed to talk.

The blue wall was complete and the painting supplies were cleaned, all before Greg rang the doorbell. I even had time to change into clean shorts and a summer tee—one without beer logos or paint. I pulled my hair back into a ponytail and put on mascara, telling the woman in the mirror that it wasn't a date.

It had been a good day, even discounting the impromptu meeting with Eric. I wanted to talk to Greg and see if he could get any information about Henry Williams. I had tried finding his address, but there were too many Henry Williamses in the phone book for me to find him based on just a name. I didn't want to ask, but I'd come to the end of my investigative skills. The mystery books made finding people seem so easy. I guess in real life, it was harder.

Searching through the kitchen drawers for my missing notebook, I stopped when a knock came on the back door. This time, I peeked out the window before opening the door, a habit I had lost during my South Cove life. Greg stood outside, holding two bags. My stomach grumbled at the thought of Lille's chicken. I hadn't stopped painting for lunch, so my last meal had been the Cheerios I'd eaten before leaving for Bakerstown.

"Come on in." I swung the door open. "Do you want a beer?" I headed to the fridge.

"I'll have a soda." Greg's cop voice echoed through the room.

Uh–oh, what's happened now?

He set the bags down on the table. The smell of fried chicken filled the kitchen.

I set two Cokes down on the table and went to grab plates from the cupboard. I froze. Maybe they had found something out about Amy. Adding silverware to the two plates, I walked back to the table. Greg still hadn't sat. Maybe he was just being polite and waiting for me. "Ready to eat? I'm starving."

Greg started unloading the bags, chicken, mashed potatoes, gravy, coleslaw, and biscuits, all still steaming. And then he pulled out my purple notebook and set it down next to my plate.

"Hey, I've been looking for that all day." I opened the notebook to check my last list, comparing it to the things I'd actually completed for the day. I had done pretty well by memory. But how did Greg have my book? "Did you accidentally pick it up when you left this morning?"

"Nope." Greg sat down in the chair and started filling up his plate. He handed me the box of biscuits.

Popping one of Lille's biscuits on my plate, I got up and got the butter from the refrigerator. Spreading the butter and watching it melt in front of my eyes, I took a bite. *Mmmmm.*

"So, where did you get it?"

He handed me the chicken box and I picked out my two favorite pieces, a wing and a breast.

Greg made a mound of mashed potatoes with a crater in the top for the gravy before he answered. "On the floor." He took a bite of the potatoes, then asked, "So, why were you in Amy's apartment?"

Chapter 15

I choked on the piece of biscuit I'd just swallowed. The notebook must have fallen out of my purse when I sat on Amy's bed. Taking a sip from my soda, I frantically thought of a plausible explanation. "I must have left it there the last time I visited her."

"So, why does it have a to-do list for today?" Greg opened the book and read aloud. "Pick up brown paint for office, make decision on accent wall, need rollers." He cocked his head.

"I could have written any of that days ago." I grabbed my chicken and took a big bite, avoiding his eyes.

"I'm not done." He continued reading, "Call bank and see if deposit hit . . . and my favorite, tell Greg about Eric's call and threat." He set the book down. "Didn't he just call this morning?"

Busted. I have never been able to get a handle on the art of lying. I swallowed. "Yeah, okay, I was in her apartment this morning. I wanted to see if I could tell if anything was out of whack."

"And?" Greg leaned back in his chair.

"Besides her plants needing water, which I need to do, nothing much—except her wet suit." I leaned closer. "You might be able to convince her to leave on a surfing trip without her board, which is doubtful, but she'd never leave the wet suit. She had it custom-made." Tears filled my eyes as I pondered the fate of my friend.

Greg handed me a napkin. "You're getting upset over a wet suit?"

My laugh came out as a bark. "You don't get Amy. She's fanatical about her gear. We had to drive back two hours on our last trip to Mexico because she forgot her wax for the board."

Greg sat silent for a moment. "You think there's no way she's off surfing?"

"Not unless she bought all new stuff, and she doesn't make that kind of money at City Hall." I pushed my plate away. I'd lost my appetite.

"Did you give her money?"

"No. I mean, why would she ask me for money? I'm not rich."

"You are now." Greg's voice was calm.

"If this was all about money, why hasn't anyone called?"

"Maybe she tried Sunday night and the call got garbled."

I froze. I hadn't considered a different reason behind the call. To get money for her release? Had I blown the ransom call?

"Listen, Jill, you have got to stop getting involved in the investigation. You're starting to mess around in things that don't concern you."

"What about Amy disappearing doesn't concern me?" I pounded my fork on the table. "I would have thought you would be thankful for what I found. You haven't found out anything else about her disappearance, have you?"

Greg jerked his head back. He pushed his plate aside. "These could be dangerous people. Stop looking for answers, Nancy Drew!"

"I bet you didn't know Joshua's stepdad's name."

"Who's Joshua?"

"Miss Emily's grandson."

"So says Crystal."

"Yeah, so says Crystal. And Henry Williams of Santa Maria." How dare he question my sources? I had found out more about Miss Emily's past in the last two days than during my entire time visiting with her.

"So, let me get this straight. You think Bob, Miss Emily's son, who's been dead for over twenty years, had a secret baby by a woman who's also now dead. Joshua, the secret baby, who's also dead, by the way, fathered a baby who's the real heir of all this." Greg held his hands up, sweeping the room. "Pretty convenient that no one's alive who can vouch for the story. Sounds like one of your books. Crystal is scamming you, just like she tried on Miss Emily."

"She wouldn't do that."

"She was arrested last year for blackmailing her professor." Greg paused and let the words sink in. "She told him he fathered Annie."

The wind completely left me. "Arrested?"

"For blackmailing her professor," Greg repeated. "The charges were dropped because the man didn't want to drag his infidelity through the court system. But they ran DNA tests on all three before the charges were dropped."

"And is he the father?"

"The professor was ruled out as being a possibility as the father. But that doesn't mean the whole secret baby thing is right."

"But it doesn't rule it out." I stopped and thought. "Can they prove family relationships by testing Miss Emily?" I didn't know how all this scientific stuff worked, but Greg would.

"They can definitely rule out Bob's being the grandfather. That's why I've already asked Doc Ames to order the tests." Greg ran his fork through his mashed potatoes. "I figured you needed proof to satisfy you about Miss Emily's inheritance. The estate is going to pay for the costs, and they aren't cheap."

"I don't care what it costs. If it proves that Annie is Miss Emily's great-granddaughter, well, that changes everything."

"It doesn't have to. You have no legal responsibility to explore this."

"But what about a moral one?" No longer hungry, I picked up my almost-full plate and set it in the kitchen sink.

"Jill, you need to let me do my job. First, I find out you're sneaking into Amy's apartment, now this thing with Crystal." Greg picked up the flyer that had been in my car and started reading. "What's this?"

I'd planned on showing him the threat, but not after this discussion. Now he'd think I'd hidden this, as well. "I found it in my car this morning. I mean, I found it last week, but I didn't read it until this morning."

"It's another threat," Greg stated the obvious.

"Yeah, but it was left on my car before the funeral, the day Aunt Jackie came." I leaned against the sink, hoping he wouldn't blow.

"How many threats do you have to get before you see this as a problem?" Greg sighed. "Give me a plastic baggie."

I grabbed a quart-sized one. "Will this work?"

He took the bag and slid the threat into it. "I assume your prints are on file at City Hall with your business license?"

"Why?"

"Because I'm going to send this off to those crime scene boys and see if we can get anyone's prints besides yours and mine." He stood up, leaving his full plate behind, as well. "If it's not been too long. You need to be taking these things seriously."

"I told you, I didn't find it until today. I planned on giving it to you tonight." I wasn't going to run to him like a scared little girl. I already had him almost living at my house.

A voice called from the living room. "Jilly, are you in the kitchen?" Aunt Jackie popped up in the doorway, a pie in her hands. "Sadie Michaels dropped this off at the apartment, and I have a gift for you."

Greg headed to the door. "I'd better get going. I'm sending Toby over to watch the house tonight, so if you need him, call."

"Detective King, I'm glad you're here." Aunt Jackie set the pie down on the table. "Stay for a piece of pie. I have something to show you."

"I have police business, ma'am." He tried to duck around her.

"But this is police business." Aunt Jackie set her floral bag on the table and started going through it. "Wait, it's right here," she said as she continued to dig.

Greg stopped and looked over at me, his shoulders rising in an unasked question.

I shook my head. I had no clue what my crazy aunt was up to.

"Ma'am, I have to go." Greg started walking back to the kitchen door.

"Wait, here it is." She handed a flyer to Greg.

"What is that?" I crossed the room and tried to see over Greg's shoulders. I could have used a stepladder.

"That, my love, is the gallery where they are selling Miss Emily's paintings. I talked to the owner today, and he has five more that were delivered last week. So, we know it wasn't Miss Emily doing the delivery." Aunt Jackie went to the cupboard and pulled out three plates. "Now, who's up for some apple pie?"

"Did he say who delivered them?" Greg asked.

"He said his acquisitions manager, Shelia, took this delivery. She's out of town now, but is supposed to be back late this week." Aunt Jackie started cutting the pie. "I left him your number, and he promised to have her call the moment she gets back. John Paul is such a nice man."

"John Paul?" I asked, watching the apple slices fall out of the flaky crust as she moved a piece onto one of the plates. My stomach growled. Suddenly, I was starving.

"The gallery owner, dear." She nodded to the cabinet. "Get us three forks."

"None for me." Greg glanced at the pie. "Sadie makes great pies." He shook his head and started to the door. "Make sure you lock up when I leave. Toby will be over as soon as it gets dark. If you need me before that, call my cell. I'll be at City Hall."

I was sure that this evening hadn't gone the way Greg had planned. I know it wasn't the way I'd planned for the evening to end, either, but at least I got apple pie to appease my desire. Greg got to go back to work. I followed him to the door.

"You don't have to have Toby watch me," I said to his retreating back.

He turned and looked down at me, emotions running behind his eyes, emotions I couldn't decipher. "You may not take two death threats seriously, but I, I mean, the South Cove Police Department does." He reached down and pushed my hair out of my eyes.

I leaned into his touch automatically. I closed my eyes, waiting for the feel of his lips on mine. When nothing came, I glanced up at him. He grinned at me and touched the end of my nose.

"Lock the door." He waited for me to obey before he left the porch, a smile on his face. Twice he'd pulled that almost kiss joke on me, and twice I'd fallen for it. There wouldn't be a third time. I returned to the kitchen, my aunt, and the pie.

"That man is sure fine. A cool drink of water, I'd say." Aunt Jackie patted the table next to her. "Come sit down and tell me about these death threats. I'd say you've been holding out a little on your old aunt."

I walked over to the sink and filled up the teakettle, my thoughts on Greg. Yes, he was something else, but he was also someone else's. Where did I get the idea that he had been going to kiss me? I could feel the heat on my face, probably beet-red from embarrassment. I so totally read him wrong. From now on it would just be business. I could do that. Just treat him like one of the contractors, here to do a job for me. I suspected that hiding my feelings would be harder than I thought.

"Jilly?" Aunt Jackie called from the table. "Are you all right?"

Squaring my shoulders, I turned and put the kettle on the stove to warm. I pulled out two cups and a box of orange spice holiday tea. I sat down to wait, avoiding the question. I didn't know if I was all right, not yet. I started talking out my fears about Crystal and the house and Annie and if I was even supposed to be here. Our tea had grown cold by the time I finished.

"Well, you sure have been carrying a load of worry on your shoulders." Aunt Jackie got up and turned the heat back on under the kettle. She took the pie off the table and covered it with plastic before popping it into the fridge.

"What, you think I'm overreacting? Do you see Amy sitting here with us?" Had she heard anything I had just said?

She sat back down. "That's not what I'm saying. Listen, is there anything you can do about Amy being missing? Did you take her or pay someone to take her?"

"No, but if she hadn't been looking into the council and Miss Emily's house for me, maybe she . . ."

"Exactly, *maybe*. You don't know that she was kidnapped because she was looking into this house. Hell, you don't know she was kidnapped at all. She could have run into one of those drug gangs that are always picking up women to sell for the slave trade. She could have found an ex-boyfriend who swept her away for an impromptu trip." Jackie took my cup back to the counter to make a fresh cup of tea. "The fact is, you are worrying about things that are completely out of your control."

"So, what should I worry about?" I laid my head on the table. I felt dead-tired.

"Things you can control, like finding out more about this Joshua kid and if he was related to Miss Emily." She set the cup of tea near my head. "You said you found letters from her husband she kept. Have you found any Bob wrote while overseas? If he knew his girlfriend was pregnant, wouldn't he have let Miss Emily know?"

I lifted my head. I'd forgotten to check for more letters. "I have a box of letters and bills and stuff from her desk that I still need to look through."

"Well, bring it in. I don't have plans for tonight, and the town has already rolled up the sidewalks."

"I'll be right back." I left the kitchen to grab the box. Two sets of eyes would make this an easy chore. Besides, it would give me time to ask Aunt Jackie about the state of her financial affairs. Was my globe-trotting aunt broke?

An hour later, we had gone through all the boxes where I'd stashed the papers from Miss Emily's desk. Aunt Jackie dropped the last of the paper into a box on the floor and sighed. "Nothing. I went through everything from the last ten years of that woman's life, and nothing. Electric bills, grocery receipts, letters from congressmen and people running for Congress. Didn't she ever throw anything away?" She stretched. "How about we grab a glass of chardonnay before we call it a night?"

"Sounds good." Frankly I had come up with a big fat nothing in my pile, as well. Something Aunt Jackie had said was tickling the back of my mind, though . . . congressmen? Letters? All I knew was I was knee-deep in paper. Besides confirming Miss Emily's pack rat obsession, I didn't know anything more that would lead me to believe Crystal's story about Joshua's parentage. I didn't have anything to disprove it, either. Maybe waiting for the DNA tests was the best idea. If my stalker didn't follow up on his threats, that is.

I went to a side window. I could just see Toby's aging Dakota truck parked on the street. I poured the last of the coffee. "I'm taking this out to Toby. The wine's in the fridge and the glasses are—"

Aunt Jackie cut me off. "I can find wineglasses. Just hurry back. I'll watch you from the window."

"I don't think anyone is going to grab me in the driveway." I pulled on my sweat jacket that had found a new home on a hook behind the kitchen door. The house had been making me feel at home one room at a time. Whenever I finished painting and moving out Miss Emily's stuff, the room seemed to welcome me. One room after another, the house was becoming my home. If I could just stay alive long enough to finish the renovations, I might be able to stop calling it Miss Emily's house.

The night air felt chilled from the breeze coming off the ocean.

Once the sun set, the California night air, though still warm, had a feeling of wetness to it. I had heard once that the fog that blanketed the coast around San Francisco watered the gigantic redwoods upland on the mountains. I never considered the morning fog a bother on my commute again. The fog had a purpose. I pulled my jacket closer and watched the steam from the coffee waft through the air as I walked.

I could barely see the truck as I zigzagged through the piles of wood for the fence and siding stacked in my driveway. I wished I'd turned on the front light before I had stepped outside. Or grabbed a flashlight. Navigating through this mess was like trying to walk through a junkyard, not the effect I wanted for the house.

Kevin needed to finish up the fence tomorrow so that I could show some progress on the restoration. I had less than three weeks left before the court date and I wanted the council off my back. I was passing by the front fence when I noticed that the fence wasn't there anymore. The rails were there, but the planks that had crisscrossed the front of the house were missing.

What the hell? I walked closer and found the missing planks. They were broken in two, lying on the ground next to the fence. I picked up one of the broken halves and walked over to the truck. How could Toby have let this happen? I rapped on his window with the jagged piece of wood.

"Toby! Do you see this? I thought you were supposed to be watching out for me?"

No answer. I opened the truck door; the dome light illuminated the empty cab. No Toby. I glanced inside the truck. His keys hung in the ignition, and a bag with what smelled like one of Lille's burgers and fries sat on the bench seat. No Toby.

A chill ran up my spine. First Amy, then Toby? Could he be chasing down whoever ripped up my fence? I let the door shut quietly and glanced around the empty street. No one, no cars, nothing. South Cove's business district closed at five on weeknights, with Lille's staying open until seven. But Lille's sat at the other end of town. None of the shops on this side had even a flicker of light shining from the inside of their buildings. I set the coffee on the top of Toby's truck and sprinted back to the house, dodging construction materials as I went.

A light encircled me. "Stop right there," a male voice boomed out.

I could see the back porch, but reaching it would be impossible. I turned to the voice.

"Miss Gardner? What are you doing out here?" The light lowered, and I could see Toby coming up the driveway.

Relief flooded through my body and my knees almost gave out. "I came to give you coffee. But my fence?" I pointed over to the front of the house.

"Yeah, I saw it. I dozed off for a moment. Lille's cheeseburgers do that to me." Toby walked over next to me, a sheepish grin on his face. "When I woke up, there he was just tearing off planks. I tried to stop him, but he's quick."

"Someone did that on purpose?" Tears threatened. It was bad enough that I only had three weeks to fix this place, now I had someone undoing what was already completed. I'd never win.

Greg's truck flew into the driveway, coming to a stop just in front of the Dumpster. He jumped out. "What the heck, Toby? Can't you handle one stakeout without screwing up?" Greg walked toward us. "And what are you doing out of the house?" He took me by the arm and started toward the back door. "I'll be back to talk to you in a second," he growled at Toby.

"I can walk." I tried to shrug my arm out of his death grip. Geesh, never make this guy mad.

He opened the back door and pushed me inside. He stayed in the doorway. "Are the rest of the doors and windows locked?"

Aunt Jackie jumped up from the table, nearly knocking over her glass of wine. "I'll go check."

"Wait," I called after the retreating body of my aunt, but if she heard me she ignored me. I straightened my posture, shooting an icy stare Greg's way. "I'm not an idiot. All of the doors and windows were locked."

"And yet I find you outside and this door completely unlocked when we came in." Greg leaned up against the doorway.

"I was taking Toby some coffee. Sue me for trying to be nice."

"Jill, did you ever think that what happened to your fence could have really been aimed at you? That someone could be trying to change the outcome of the will and what happens to this house?"

"I didn't."

"You didn't think. I'm not an idiot, either. I know the council has eyes on this house for some new development, but, Jill, if you are going to stay safe, you have to listen to me. A help-me-help-you sort of thing."

Greg seemed tired, but I had to know. "You think the council had something to do with this?"

"The council, the mayor, that developer, Crystal, or even George Jones, the list of suspects isn't shrinking as the investigation goes on, it's growing." Greg shook his head. "I'm tired, and I've got to go knock some sense into Toby. Lock the door behind me and stay inside." He shut the door but stayed right outside looking at me through the window until I came over and locked the door and the dead bolt.

"Everything's still locked up, Detective King." Aunt Jackie came into the kitchen. Her face fell when she saw I was alone in the room. "He's gone?"

"For now." I went to dump my wine out into the sink and rinsed the glass. "Hey, why don't you bunk with me tonight? There's a spare room upstairs."

"I have to be up early to open the shop."

"Not a problem." I figured I wouldn't get much sleep tonight, but knowing Aunt Jackie would be safe with me would help. Although I wasn't sure if either one of us was totally safe here, at least Greg knew where to find us.

Chapter 16

After watching Aunt Jackie drive off to open the store the next morning, I turned back to the overstuffed living room. I'd already called Kevin, the fence guy, to come give me an estimate for the insurance company and repair the fence. I didn't have time to wait around for the bureaucracy to approve the estimates. I'd just have to take my chances I'd be at least partially reimbursed. Time to finish off the new study and start on the living room. The harder I worked, the less likely I would fret about the vandalism and the threats. No one would scare me away from my house.

I walked into the study. The colors glowed, warm and inviting. I could just see the love seat with a tall marble end table on one side, a green droopy plant taking up most of the table. Miss Emily's desk would go next to the window. All I needed to do was scrub down the floor and move in what furniture I did have. Then time to go shopping.

The clock struck noon by the time I had stripped away the paint cloths, cleaned the floor, and gone over it with a sealant that should help protect the wood. I was done with the room until the floor dried. I went into the kitchen to make a sandwich, and Miss Emily's painting caught my eye. I needed to bring in another one for the study before my art thief cleaned out the rest of my supply. I wasn't sure getting back stolen art was as easy as it seemed in the spy novels I read. I quickly made up a PB and J and took the sandwich out with me to the shed, grabbing the shed key from the basket on the kitchen counter.

A beautiful fall day greeted me; the birds were singing in the trees. But all I heard as I walked out was the hammering of siding being replaced on the front of the house. I saw Kevin's crew had already cleaned up the wreckage of the fence and had a few new boards on. He saw me in the backyard and raced over to meet me.

"I guess you noticed we're starting to replace the damaged section. I've got guys in the back finishing up there, as well. If your friends leave you alone, I should be out of here today." Kevin gave me one of his giant smiles that always came with a larger bill or an extension-of-time request. Today was no exception. "I left the estimate for the damage on the front porch for you. I knocked but you had that stereo rocking."

"Yeah, I've been working on the study." I glanced down at my outfit. An oversized man's shirt I'd kept when I threw my husband out and a pair of capris that had seen better days. Not a go-to-town outfit by far.

"You heading out back?" Kevin nodded to the shed.

"I'm looking for something."

"Can I walk with you? I want to show you something."

I couldn't imagine what he wanted to show me, unless the vandal had torn down fencing in the back, as well. We walked in silence toward the small creek that ran through the back of the property behind the shed. I'd never been this far back in the field and the ground sloped downward a few feet past the creek. It was like I had my own forest back here. A dirt path disappeared back into the trees.

"Where is the property line?" I glanced back, toward the house, but all I could see was the top of the roof.

"About ten feet that way. It looks bigger than it is." Kevin pointed toward the dirt path. "Come on, it's this way."

"What's this way?" I asked Kevin, but he had already gone into the trees. My guard went up. "Kevin?" I called. No answer. "Bad idea, Jill. Very, very bad idea," I whispered as I headed through the trees. Following the path for a few feet, I broke through the tree stand and saw Kevin, sitting on a four-foot-tall rock wall, grinning.

"Okay, what did you want to show me?" I was tired of the games.

"This!" Kevin patted the wall. "I had heard rumors when we were kids, but no one was brave enough to sneak back here. I can't believe I didn't come back here when I measured out the fence line."

I glanced around the area. All I saw was the wall and what seemed to be a crumbling fireplace up next to the tree stand. The wall appeared to have been whitewashed, like, a thousand years ago. "Was this an old homestead?"

"Girl, you don't know anything about South Cove, do you?" Kevin hopped off the wall and walked the broken outline of the old house.

"I know enough. Like the fact my shop is in the original bank building built in 1860." Now I sounded like one of the council's promotional flyers.

"Nah, I mean the original South Cove. The one before the city was built out there." Kevin stopped to gaze over the area.

"I'm confused. The town before the town?" I sat down on the rock wall. The area around me consisted of a small meadow surrounded on all sides by a forest of trees. My house was on the east side of town away from the ocean. But on clear days from my bedroom, I could glimpse the Pacific shimmering in the distance. Anywhere in town was within biking distance to the public shore on the highway. Another good fact for my tourist trade, not that I've ever personally taken the bike ride.

Kevin turned, his eyes gleaming. "A mission existed before the town. A Spanish mission tied to the Spanish crown. As a kid, I heard stories about how the mission became the hiding place for Aztec gold Cortez stole from Mexico."

"And why wouldn't they just send it back to Spain? Your story has a few holes. And seriously, like the lost city of gold even existed." I tried to remember my California history, but fourth grade had been a long time ago.

"They couldn't take a chance on shipping the gold because of the Barbary pirates." Kevin's voice went up in pitch when he got excited. Right now, he was a soprano. "Whether or not the Aztec's lost city existed, this wall is proof that the mission existed. You are standing on a piece of California's history." Kevin sat down on the wall, out of breath.

The wall area looked kind of pretty. I wondered if I could set up a patio out here, a place to hide in plain sight with a book or two. I could put a fridge in the shed for cool drinks. The birds gently chirping in the background and the air a mixed smell of salt air and the pine trees surrounding the spot. For a second, I felt happy. Then I remembered the council's thirty-day summons. Putting my landscaping daydreams aside, I asked, "You think you can get this all done by the end of next week?" I would have liked to get at least one local contractor off my personal payroll.

Kevin shook his head. Inwardly, I groaned. This would not be good news. "We're going to have to get the historical commission out here to verify the site and give us permission to finish up the fence."

Another delay. No way would I meet the council's deadline. I'd have to get a lawyer and appeal for more time. "How long is that going to take? I'm on a deadline here."

"Two, maybe three weeks. They'll send someone out to do an initial survey, but if this is the lost mission, you'll have people in your backyard for months, maybe years. I'm sure once they verify the site, they will want to have the fencing completed as soon as possible. Maybe even do an upgrade." Kevin had a gleam in his eyes.

I wasn't sure if the gleam came from finding missing treasure or a possible increase in the fencing contract. I'd bet on the latter being the source of his joy, but I'd become cynical around my contractors lately. I sat down on the rock wall and ran my hand over the rough edges of the stone. "It doesn't look big enough to be a mission. Not like the one I visited in Santa Barbara."

"My high school history teacher was an expert on the mission period. She said that when the measles epidemic wiped out most of the Native American tribe, the chief decided that the mission had been cursed. They tore down the mission and carried off the stones, scattering the pieces over miles so the mission could never be rebuilt. Most of the friars were killed, but a few escaped and headed to the San Luis Obispo de Tolosa Mission down the coast." Kevin recited the history like high school had been last week rather than more than fifteen years ago.

"You remember all that from a class?" In all the time he'd worked on the house, I'd never heard him talk anything but fencing products and sports. He was an ESPN junkie.

Kevin grinned. "It's the only thing I remember from high school except for the basketball season our team took state. Miss Kelly was closer to our age and hot. She used our class more for research for her master's degree in the local legends about the mission. Everyone had at least one story to tell that his or her family has passed down through the generations. At least the locals."

"Sounds like a fun class." Cost estimates on a new, higher fence were running through my head. "The delay will push me past the council's deadline. I guess I'd been a fool to ever think I could save the house." I glanced around the area, my dreams of a secluded patio slipping away before my eyes.

Kevin stared at me. "You don't get it, do you? If this is the mission, and I think it is, the historical society is going to want to preserve this find. If not, they still will take months to determine the site's historical value. Either way, the council is going to have to give you more time. It's rare to find something like this that hasn't already been destroyed or poached for any historical value at all. This mission has to be preserved."

Hope seeped into my bones. "Do you want to make the call to the historical commission or should I?"

After being transferred six times, I finally reached someone who promised a surveyor out to the house on Friday. When I asked if they would call the council, the woman had been vague. "The surveyor will make a determination of future commitments for the site within two weeks of the visit." In bureaucratic code, don't get your hopes up.

I made a second call to Jimmy Marcum and scheduled an appointment for nine on Wednesday. I wasn't going to wait for fate to intervene. This time I would force the council to back off, even if it cost me all the money Miss Emily left me to do it. I didn't have the money last week, so if I didn't have it tomorrow, it would be no big deal.

Kevin had taken off after the first call but promised his crew would have everything done except what he now called the mission site tomorrow. "I'll be here on Friday when the history guy shows up. Do you mind if I bring my camera? This is going to be South Cove history I can show my kids when they're older."

"Knock yourself out." I watched as he danced a modified version of the electric slide on his way out of the kitchen. You would have thought I'd just promised him a million dollars the way he acted. I glanced at the clock. Three o'clock. If I hurried, I could get changed and head over to Bakerstown to pick out furniture for my new study. I headed upstairs.

After showering, I pulled on a blue flowered sundress I'd found in my closet and some cute but sturdy sandals. I had to either do laundry tomorrow or stop by my apartment for more clothes. The sundress had been my only option.

I locked the front door when I heard a voice behind me. "Going somewhere?"

I knew that voice. "Heading into town for some shopping and dinner." I turned and almost fell over.

Greg sat on the rails of the fence surrounding my front porch. His crisp white button-down shirt was tucked into black jeans that hugged black cowboy boots. I could feel the way the cool cotton would touch my skin as I ran my hands down his chest, the heat of his body matching mine and heating up the cotton as I pushed harder, making contact.

"Jill?"

God, I had to stop that. This man could make me think, well, think. I put my keys into my straw bag. "What?"

"Where were you? I asked if I could come along." His grin said he knew what I was thinking.

Blushing, I headed to the truck parked in front of my house. "If you drive." I felt the heat of his body as I walked by. I had to be imagining this. I should have said no. I wasn't quite sure I'd be able to keep my hands from following my thoughts, especially on the road trip to Bakerstown. I whirled around. "Why do you want to come, anyway?"

His eyes met mine. "Do I need to tell you?" He paused. "Who else is going to keep you out of trouble? Until we determine who's been threatening you, we're joined at the hip."

My heart sank. The job, nothing more. "I guess I should say thanks." I took a deep breath. "I'll fill you in on the latest episode of the soap opera that has become my life on the way to the furniture store."

"Now what?" Greg called after me, but I was already sprinting to the truck. He wouldn't have to open my door or help me in if I could help it.

I waited for him to climb in and start up the truck before I filled him in on the rock wall that Kevin swore was the old mission. Greg's eyes stayed on the road while I went through Kevin's logic. When I got to the part about the mission hiding Aztec gold, he snorted. I stopped talking and turned to watch him. With his eyes hidden behind his sunglasses, the only thing I could see on his face was an enormous smile.

"Why are you laughing?"

"Kevin's wrong about the mission being Cortez's hiding place. Unless Cortez lived for at least two hundred years, his body had already turned to dust before the first rock was laid to build the mission." Greg sped up and went around a slow-moving minivan with Texas plates.

"Tourists," he mumbled under his breath.

"How come you know so much about local history?" This man had more layers than a Vidalia onion.

"I majored in history." Greg glanced at me. "What, cops can't know anything except how to catch bad guys?"

I'd assumed he had a criminal justice degree if he had even gone to college. But I wasn't going to admit my error to him. "I never see you in the shop, so how would I know your tastes in reading?"

Greg's face turned pink. "If I tell you this, you can't hate me." He paused, waiting for a response. When I stayed silent, he continued, "I buy my books online."

I swatted him with my notebook. I couldn't believe him. "I'm trying to build a business here. Online might be a little cheaper, but you can't replace real expertise."

"I know. I'm sorry. It's just that once I get off shift, the last thing I want to do is go shopping."

"And yet, here you are, driving me to the furniture store. Is it all stores you target for destruction or just mine?" I turned my head, staring out the window at the ocean. Seagulls played in the gentle breeze, and I could hear their calls.

"If I'd realized what I'd been missing, I would have been your best customer."

The tone of his voice made me stop watching the birds hunt for a quick fish dinner and turn. He stared straight ahead. Had I imagined the words or at least the feeling behind them?

"You'd better stock up your history section," he said quietly. "I'm not going to make that mistake again."

I didn't know how to answer, so I didn't. The rest of the ride to Country Collections, we listened to the country ballads coming out of the radio. Greg had turned the volume up after the first five miles of silence. Thoughts kept flying through my head, but by the time I sorted through something to say that wouldn't make me sound like a schoolgirl or worse, desperate, Greg had pulled the truck into the parking lot.

"Here we are." All I could come up with.

"Yep," came the response from the other side of the truck.

I opened my door and slid to the ground, knowing if I just sat there, I'd wind up kissing him. And once I tasted those solid, totally soft lips, I wouldn't stop.

My cell phone rang as soon as we walked in the door back home. Greg followed right behind me, carrying the shaggy rug I'd picked out to go under the love seat being delivered tomorrow. I shifted the potted fern I held into one hand and pulled the cell out of my purse.

"Hello?" I hadn't had time to check caller ID. At the worse it was a telemarketer or another threat. Either way, I had Greg for backup today.

"Jill Gardner?"

Telemarketer. "This is Jill." Half-listening, I followed Greg into the study and set the plant down on a chair.

"Miss Gardner, this is Henry Williams. Crystal told me that you were asking about Mary."

I sat down at the desk, pulling out a notebook. "I'm glad you called. Did Crystal fill you in on everything?"

"She said that you were trying to settle an estate. So, Bob's mom passed?" The man didn't say anything for a few seconds, then added, "She was a great lady."

Shock went through my body. "You knew Miss Emily?"

"Bob and I were on the football team together. Then, when he shipped out to Vietnam, I followed three months later. We were assigned to the same platoon once we were in country. What a coincidence, huh? Two boys from the same small town together in that hellhole."

Greg glanced at me as he unwrapped the rug. "Mr. Williams, I guess I don't know how to ask this delicately."

"You want to know if Joshua is my son or Bob's." The voice on the line seemed to pause.

"That about sums it up, yes." I paused, waiting for the answer. This man must have been an actor during some part of his life, because he knew all about the dramatic pause.

"See that's the thing. I don't know. Mary and I were dating after Bob left, but we both got leave at the same time. As soon as we got off the plane, I knew where her heart belonged, but I made her go out that night just one more time. I'm not proud of what I did, but I played the pity card. It had been a while and we weren't going to be home long."

"And you had sex."

"Now don't you go labeling Mary a bad girl or anything. She was nice and kind and sweet. I pushed that night. And I spent the rest of my life making up for it."

"But you broke up?"

"Mary confessed she was still in love with Bob. After that night, I didn't see either of them again until we boarded the plane to go back. Bob told me he'd asked her to marry him."

"So Joshua could have been your son." I put the pen down.

"I always hoped so. Bob stepped on a land mine out on patrol a few months later. I kept seeing that grin on his face when he got on that plane. Sometimes I saw the same grin on Joshua's face."

The phone line went silent. I thought I'd lost the connection when I heard, "I've mailed you a package. I found them when I went through Mary's things." His voice cracked. "I guess she kept them all these years. I couldn't read them, but maybe they can help you."

"What can help me, Mr. Williams?" But this time the line had gone dead. He had hung up on me. Greg had unwrapped the rug and sat on the floor, running his hands through the light blue shag.

"Did you get your answers?" He didn't look up as he continued to finger the soft cotton fibers.

I sighed. "I think I just got more questions." I leaned back into the chair and took in the office that would be filled with new furniture tomorrow, marking my territory. The paint smell still lingered, giving me a headache. "He's not sure if he's Joshua's dad or not. But he's sending something over that could explain."

Or not, I thought. He hadn't been able to read whatever he found. A journal? Letters? Either way, I hoped it helped settle the uneasy feeling I had that all the work I'd done on my house would be enjoyed by a new family.

"Some women cheat." Greg's voice sounded muffled, his head tilted downward.

"It's more complicated than that. It sounds like Henry had always been Mary's second choice." I paused. I wasn't helping Mary's cause out here.

Greg raised his head and stared at me. "It's always complicated," he said with a sarcastic tone. His eyes were tight.

"I guess I'll have to see what he sends me and wait for the DNA tests before I do anything or make any decisions." The room felt chilly, like the temperature had dropped ten degrees.

Greg walked the few steps to my chair. He reached for my hand and pulled me to a standing position. "Let's head to Lille's and get some dinner. You look beat."

I was too tired to fight, and my stomach was growling at the thought of a plate covered with mashed potatoes and gravy. I didn't even care what meat came with it. Maybe some food would help knock me out of the slump that my conversation with Henry Williams had caused. I hadn't asked Greg what he had found out about the art gallery selling Miss Emily's paintings. Which reminded me, I had never got to the shed for the ocean seascape I wanted for the office. "Can you help me with something first?"

"As long as it's not more shopping. I'm starving."

"I need you to come out to the shed with me. I'll just be a minute, but I'd feel better if we moved the rest of Miss Emily's paintings into the house where I can keep an eye on them."

"Not a bad idea." Greg pointed to the door. "After you."

We headed out the kitchen door. The backyard was quiet; the setting sun had sent the chirping birds in search of their nests. Plenty of light played in the open areas but the shed would be dark and gloomy. I'd grabbed a couple of flashlights and the shed keys from the kitchen cabinet. I handed a flashlight to Greg.

"How many paintings are still out there?" Greg played with the flashlight, twirling it in his hands.

"Maybe twenty? I haven't ventured up into the loft yet."

"Did I mention I was hungry?" Greg growled.

"It shouldn't take very long." I glanced over at him. Ever since the phone call, Greg had seemed distant. "I'll buy dinner?"

"Let's just get this done." Greg grabbed the keys from me and unlocked the door. He turned on the flashlight and slowly lit up the entire room, moving from one side to the other. "You head up to the loft and make sure there's no more canvases stuffed up there. I'll stack these together and start taking them up to the porch."

I walked through the shed room to the loft ladder. I switched on my flashlight and started to climb up the steps, my hands gripping the straight ladder rungs tightly, or as tightly as I could with the flashlight in one hand. "A gentleman would have offered to do this for me . . ." I mumbled under my breath. It was official—heights scared the crap out of me. I didn't even like riding the little roller coasters at the pier.

One step, both feet, two steps, both feet, this would take a while. I was about halfway up when Greg came back into the shed after his first trip back to the porch with an arm full of paintings.

"You still haven't gotten up there yet?" Now I heard humor in his voice, which just ticked me off.

"Nothing wrong with taking things slow," I called back, taking another step up as proof I would make it.

"Again, I say, I'm hungry," Greg called out as he picked up more paintings and headed back out the door.

"Whatever," I mumbled and took another step. Two more and I'd be able to see the loft's content. I took the stairs quicker and stopped. I could see. I shone the flashlight over the dusty floor to check for more paintings. No reason to keep going if the loft was empty.

Dust and, ugh, a dead mouse, littered the floor. Then the light found a trunk tucked in the back under the small spyglass window straight ahead. I scanned the rest of the loft, but there was nothing there except the trunk. I could have stopped and gone back down to the safe floor, putting *Check the trunk out* on my list, but then I'd have to climb this stupid ladder again. I might as well finish the job now.

I put the flashlight down on the floor and pulled my body up the last few steps. I sat down on the floor and swung my legs around, scooting away from the edge. My legs were going to be filthy from this dust. Grabbing the flashlight, I headed to the trunk. It was one of those old steamer trunks that I saw at the local antiques stores for hundreds of dollars, but this one seemed to be in better shape. I'd have to have Greg bring it down. I'd put the antique dealer off from his original appointment. Maybe he'd be interested in this, too.

I opened the trunk. Brightly colored clothes, a children's pirate hat, plastic swords—this must have been Bob's dress-up trunk. I wondered if Miss Emily had even remembered it was here. She would have gotten a kick out of the old toys. I pulled out one of the vests, gold and purple. I jumped as I heard a footstep on the floor behind me.

"What's that?" Greg's voice came from behind the gleam of the flashlight.

"Bob's pirate chest. Miss Emily told me how he loved to play pirate." I thought back to our conversation late last summer on the front porch, sipping a glass of tea and watching the sunset over the ocean. Somehow going through the junk in the pirate dress-up chest made me miss her even more. There would be no more peaceful evenings sipping tea and chatting about the day's activities. My chest hurt as I held the child's vest that Miss Emily had sewn for her son.

Greg knelt beside me. "This is cool. I would have loved to have had a pirate's chest as a kid." He dug through the chest. "Look, there are even fake gold coins for your buried treasure." He pulled out a coin and shone the flashlight toward it. "This is pretty heavy."

"Toys were better made in the sixties." I dusted off my pants. "Any chance I could get you to move the chest down to the shed floor?"

"Planning on getting on your pirate groove?"

"No, I'm planning on getting an antiques dealer over here to look at some of this stuff I don't need." I thought about the ladder. "I'd rather not have to come up here again."

"Chicken." He closed the trunk, lifting it to test the weight. "I should be able to move this down if you help me."

"Maybe I can get a couple of the construction guys to move it tomorrow." I didn't know how I would get down the ladder myself. How would I help him move a trunk?

"Don't freak out, it will be easy. I just need you to slide the trunk down to me when I get farther down the ladder." He picked the trunk up and moved it to the side of the ladder. "Now let me get down and you'll just slide the trunk over the edge."

This was not going to turn out well. I knew it. But Greg had been forewarned. If he thought he was strong enough to move the trunk with what little help I would provide, let the man prove it. I watched as he disappeared down to the bottom floor.

"Okay, now just slide the trunk over the edge a few inches."

I pushed the trunk slowly over the edge, holding on to the handle. I hoped it wouldn't drag me over the side with it.

"Stop right there," Greg called from below.

The trunk teetered halfway over the edge. I leaned over and could see Greg standing below, reaching up his arms, but the chest remained just out of reach. He stepped over to the ladder and went up a step. This time his fingers just brushed the edge of the trunk.

"Now tilt it up on your end so I can grab this end."

Really a bad idea, I thought but I followed directions, leaning back so I could counter the trunk's slide with my weight. Or so I thought. I tilted the trunk up and heard Greg's whispered "Gotcha," before the trunk started sliding.

I tried to hold it back and fell backward on my butt. The trunk's handle slipped through my fingers. I hoped Greg wouldn't be flat on the ground under the trunk when I made my slow descent from the loft.

"I lost it," I called down, leaning forward to see what damage I'd caused. I heard the trunk hit the floor with a bang. "Greg, are you okay?" No answer.

I scooted forward to see over the edge, my heart beating hard in my chest. He had to be dead, I'd killed him, and I knew it. Peeking over the edge, Greg kneeled by the trunk, very much alive.

"Greg?"

He glanced up at me, a grin covering his face. "Get down here. You've gotta see this."

"See what?" The trunk might be broken, but at least I didn't hurt him. Or maybe I had hit his head with the falling trunk. I couldn't be sure.

Greg held up his cupped hands full of the play pirate gold from the chest. "This."

I didn't understand why he would get so excited about some old painted coins, but I ungracefully made my way down the ladder. Not a pretty sight, but Greg wasn't watching me anyway. When I finally hit the floor, his attention focused on the gold coins in his hands.

I grabbed one and glanced at it. "So, what's so exciting?" I turned the coin over and saw a portrait of a long-dead king. "Boy, these look real."

Greg grinned at me. "I think they are."

"Are what?" I said crossly. Dirty and hungry, I was tired of playing games. I brushed the dirt off my sundress and my knees.

"Jill, I think this is the treasure hidden at the mission."

"The Aztec gold? I thought you said the history didn't match the rumors."

"It's not Aztec gold, it's Spanish coins—sent from the crown to assure that California would be taken for the king. There was a theory, rumor mostly, that the missions were used as staging grounds for the military's attacks on the natives." He fingered the coins.

"Are you sure?" I kneeled down beside him, unwilling to touch the coins. It might have been superstition, but I didn't believe in found money. And my life had been blessed with way too many gifts lately. I remembered a story I'd read in freshman English about the gifts of the monkey's paw and the consequences for asking for your desire. Now I lived the legend, one of my friends dead and the other missing, even though I hadn't asked for the money. Adding in more wealth to the mix might just trigger another tragedy.

"Well, as sure as I can be." Greg grabbed his handkerchief from his pocket. "Do you mind if I take a few of these? I'll run to the university tomorrow and see what my old professor thinks." He grabbed up the coins and put them in the middle of the white linen square. Separating out two, he tied a knot in the cloth and slid them in his front pocket.

"Do you think Miss Emily knew they were here?" The trunk seemed to have a fake bottom that had broken when it dropped to the floor.

"I'm pretty sure Bob knew. I'm sure when he told his mom she just racked it up to an active imagination. Most of these pirate clothes are hand-sewn. She probably just thought he was playing with her." Greg scooted the chest over to the side of the room. "I bet if we had someone date this chest it would bring us back to the mission again."

"All roads lead to that damn wall in my backyard." My stomach growled. "Can we go eat now?" I needed to leave all the mystery behind for a while. I wanted fat. Fried fish, fried mushrooms, fried anything. And a beer.

"Let's drop these off in the house and move the paintings inside, then we can go." He ran into my shoulder as we were walking. "You're buying, right?"

"I guess I can, why?"

"If I'm right, the offer that creep Ammond made you on the house is chump change compared to your new net worth." Greg locked the shed as we left. "And I'm just a poor city employee."

Visions of the monkey's paw scratching at the kitchen door shook me to the core. This was not good. Not good at all.

Chapter 17

I'd barely slept. I dreamed of pirates chasing Amy and monks in full black robes with ropes tied around their waists running around my backyard. I woke to the sound of the construction guys nailing on the new siding at 5 a.m. Who works at five in the morning? Bleary-eyed, I grabbed another sundress and headed to the bathroom for a quick shower. I needed to do some laundry today, otherwise I'd be down to a little black date dress or the blue business suit I saved for bank meetings—neither of which was suitable for painting the living room. Right after one or two pots of coffee.

I had just sat down at the kitchen table, one load of laundry in the washer, and my third cup of coffee in front of me, when I heard a knock at the door. I peeked out the window to see Kevin.

"Good news," he said as I opened the door. He walked inside the kitchen and pointed to my coffee. "Got any more in the pot?"

"Sure, cups are over there." I sat back down at the table. I didn't think this was going to be a quick conversation.

"The commission called me back, and they'll be out here this morning to evaluate the site. They said they couldn't reach you." Kevin pulled out a chair and turned it backward toward the table. He leaned into the back of the chair and set his coffee on the table. "I'm meeting the guy in a few minutes. Want to come watch?"

I glanced at my phone, sure enough, three missed calls from yesterday. I considered my to-do list. Even without the laundry, I had furniture being delivered, and I didn't even have a path cleared through the living room yet. And standing around watching some guy look at a rock wall wasn't what I wanted to do. "Just tell me the results. I've got a lot to get done." Too bad Kevin couldn't help me with my list. "Hey, you don't have a guy who can help me move some furniture for a few hours today, do you?"

"I bet Todd does. Hold on, I'll ask." When Kevin returned, he had a tall teenager with him.

"Derek, this is Jill. Help her out today, okay?" Kevin slapped the kid on the back. "I'm going to check out by the wall before the commission guy gets here." He swallowed the remainder of his coffee in two gulps and put the cup in the sink. Someone had trained him well.

"So, what do you want me to do?" Derek asked, looking around the kitchen filled with paintings that Greg and I had just brought in from the shed.

I had him move all the paintings into one of the spare bedrooms upstairs, and while he kept busy, I started marking boxes with Miss Emily's china and other personal effects. The boxes would go into the shed, and when I finished, I'd call the antiques dealer over to give me some evaluations. No use making a plan now. There was plenty of room in the shed now that I'd moved out all of Miss Emily's paintings.

Two hours later, the kitchen looked back to normal, and all the boxes were out of the living room. The study would be completed as soon as the furniture was delivered. Time to focus on the living room. I had Derek help me take measurements of the living room, the bathroom, and all the bedrooms upstairs. Derek took off to grab some lunch with the rest of the construction crew, and I sat down on the worn couch to make decisions on what living room furniture to keep. If I planned this right, I'd have the entire house cleared by the end of the day.

The doorbell rang. I slapped a stickie on the recliner, a sign to Derek to move it to the shed, and went to answer the door. This having-an-assistant thing was working out for me. I might have to keep Toby on once I reclaimed the coffee shop from Aunt Jackie . . . if I ever did.

I opened the door to a deliveryman in brown. At least it wasn't another summons from the city. I signed for the envelope and walked back into the kitchen. I needed food.

I threw the envelope on the table, planning on getting to it after eating a sandwich or two. I ate my tuna on white over the sink watching the backyard. Kevin and the commission guy were finally done and coming up the grass, deep in conversation. I could see Kevin throwing his arms around. Either they'd determined the wall was just that, a wall, or Kevin was telling a story about looking for the pirate gold as a kid. I wasn't sure which outcome I wanted. I mean, having a piece of history on your land is pretty intense and probably needs a lot of attention. I kind of liked the late-evening-barbeques and sitting-on-my-back-deck version of the future for this house. Especially if the version included a certain cute detective.

I brushed the crumbs off my face and headed out the kitchen door to meet them.

"So, what's the verdict?" I asked as soon as the men were close enough to hear me.

"Frank, this is Jill Gardner, the home owner. Jill, Frank Gleason, the commission inspector." Kevin did the formalities. "Frank was just going over the preliminary results with me."

"Which are?" I waited for Frank to respond. He clearly spent a lot more time researching in a darkly lit library than outside in the real world. His pasty white skin jarred against the black suit he wore. Not a typical California outfit, even over at the college.

"Debatable," Frank whined. "I'm not comfortable talking about my conclusions until I'm certain. I thought I made that clear." He shot a look at Kevin that should have brought the man to his knees, but Kevin ignored it.

"He thinks the wall is part of the mission," Kevin crowed.

"Now, I told you, I can't be certain until we complete tests on the wall. I took soil samples and samples of the wall and grout to age the materials. It's hard to tell, the wall's been painted recently." He glared at me.

"I don't think Miss Emily's painted anything around here in the last fifty years," I responded.

"I didn't say yesterday. The wall's been painted in the last hundred or so years. Which makes it almost impossible to determine age without doing lab work." The man peered at me through his round glasses and then back down at his notepad. "Who's this Miss Emily? I thought you were the owner of record?"

"I am the owner of record. Miss Emily left the house to me." I didn't know why I felt I had to explain to this little bureaucrat. *Be nice,* my rational side said.

"Tragic." The man kept writing on his notepad.

I wasn't sure if he meant Miss Emily's death or my inheritance. But if this man was the key to my stopping the council from condemning the property, I would have to at least pretend to be nice. "Mr. Gleason, can your office contact the city and put a hold on the condemnation proceedings? Or maybe write a letter?"

"We can't say for sure if this is a historical site." Frank glanced at the back of the yard, even though the wall wasn't visible from where we stood. He paused and appeared to be weighing his next words. "However, I feel that there are ample questions on the origin of the wall, so my office could file a cease-and-desist order with the City of South Cove."

I wrapped my arms around the little man and hugged him. "Thank you so much!" I squeezed him and then moved over to Kevin. Kevin and I hugged and jumped around in circles.

"Miss Gardner, I didn't say the wall was part of the mission," Frank called over our celebration. "And my filing will only hold the council off while we investigate. If I were you, I'd handle the other issues on the property as quickly as possible."

I stopped jumping with Kevin. "I will, Mr. Gleason. I promise." I skipped back to the kitchen door. I had a lot of items still on my to-do list, but I felt like I'd been given the get-out-of-jail-free card. And first on my list, while Derek moved the extra stuff out of the house, was to finish laundry so I could head over to Lille's to meet Aunt Jackie for dinner. Fried shrimp night—time to celebrate.

"I've set up your books on a computer accounting system. Don't look at me that way, it's easy." Aunt Jackie pointed at me with her fork. "It's time you were brought up to date. And the program even links up with your suppliers and will alert you when you need to place an order for coffee or supplies or even books. Of course, I had to purchase some new equipment."

I groaned. I had priced setting up a system last fall, but the cost had been out of my reach. I wasn't sure I wanted to know but asked anyway, "How much did it cost?"

"Don't you worry about it. If foot traffic stays up like it's been the last two weeks, we should have the system paid off in less than a year." Aunt Jackie took a sip of her wine. "This is good. Did I tell you I talked to the winery owner about doing a joint event? Maybe a murder mystery dinner? Donna's such a sweetheart."

"Darla, the owner's name is Darla, not Donna." I sank back in my chair. I guess the money didn't matter. I had plenty in my account now. But that wasn't the point. I wanted the store to be successful on its own. Not just because I poured the money Miss Emily left me into new accounting systems. I couldn't pull away from the house project just yet. Frank Gleason had bought me some time, but as soon as he lost interest in the four-foot section of rock wall, the council would be pushing for the house to be up to standards. And right now, the only standard the house could meet was for a training video for newly hired construction workers on how not to remodel a house.

"What's wrong, honey? Did I overstep?" Aunt Jackie refilled my glass of wine.

"No. I planned on installing a system, so I guess now is as good a time as any." Tiny pity party over. I'd invited her to help with the coffee shop, and I had to accept Aunt Jackie's take-over style. I swallowed. "I want to thank you for stepping in like this. I couldn't have done everything on the house and handled the shop."

"I'm glad to help. I was going to wait a couple of weeks, but since you brought up the subject, I'll ask now." She leaned closer over the table.

God, now what? Did she want to start an adult section in the basement? I plastered a smile on my face and asked, "What did you want to ask?"

"You know I've been traveling a lot since I retired. And I love it, I do. But living in San Francisco's so overwhelming. There were three break-ins on my block last week. And you are so happy in the new house. So I wondered . . ." She took a sip of wine.

"I don't understand." I didn't know where this conversation was going, but I had a bad feeling I wouldn't like it.

"Well, you don't have to work anymore, and I just need a little pin money, so it works out perfect." Jackie sat back, waiting for an answer.

"Wait? You want to stay on at the store? After I get the house done?" My mind reeled. I loved my aunt. Especially in small doses. But to have her in the same town, working for me at the shop? I'd probably have to kill her. "But you love to travel."

"And I still would. Just not as much." Jackie leaned forward. "Jill, I've loved running the shop. I didn't want to tell you, but they are selling my building. Refurbishing it for new condos. They offered to sell me my apartment, but I don't have that kind of money. Not since the Wall Street thing. Since I have to move anyway, why not move here and do something I love?"

This was the first time Jackie had ever mentioned a money problem. Uncle Ted had left her well off. I mean the wealthy kind of well off. If she couldn't afford to buy her apartment, her money situation had gone further south than I'd realized.

"What about the money Uncle Ted left you?" As long as we were talking, it was time to get it all on the table.

Aunt Jackie wiggled in her chair and wouldn't meet my eyes. "They told me it was a sure investment. That everyone was raking in cash from this guy. I guess I was just one of the last ones to be fooled."

"It's all gone?" For the first time ever, my aunt looked her age, a small, defeated seventy-year-old.

"Not all, I didn't put all my eggs in one basket. But the other investments went down, too, so now I'm just trying to hold on while they build back up. And living in the city is just so expensive." She pleaded. "Please, Jill? Let me move into the apartment? I'd pay rent."

"Of course you can stay." I might not like it, but I wasn't going to let her live on the street. "I've moved out most of Miss Emily's extra furniture that I'm not keeping. I'll hire movers to get my stuff out of the apartment so you can move in."

"Thank you." Aunt Jackie finished her wine. "Shall we have some dessert to celebrate our new arrangement?"

"Why not?" I chirped. I wasn't great at hiding my feelings, but I did a better job with a piece of chocolate mud cake in front of me. I had gained a business partner for the shop and lost my apartment in the last two hours. I'd better make Miss Emily's house meet council standards or I was going to be the one homeless.

* * *

As soon as I got in the door, I knew I was too keyed up to sleep. When had my life gotten this crazy? Before Miss Emily's death, my biggest worry had been how much coffee to order or which book to read. Now I juggled construction, worrying about Amy, trying to make the house my home, and now, figuring out how to work with my aunt without killing her or myself in the process. And, oh yeah, trying to solve Miss Emily's murder before my own personal stalker made good on his threats.

At least I didn't have to deal with Greg today. He'd been oddly absent, not even a phone call to check on me. I checked the answering machine I had just set up in the den, no messages. My gut wrenched just a little. I wasn't missing him; I had no claim on the detective. But a message would have been nice.

I powered up my computer, deciding to work on my business plan and how adding a partner would change the goals of the business. I'd already planned out the projections for the coffee shop for the next five years, so it would take a while to rework the document. But having it done would make me feel better.

I headed to the kitchen to put the kettle on to heat. Herbal tea, something calming, definitely not coffee or I'd never get to sleep tonight. While I waited for the kettle to whistle, I noticed the envelope I had thrown on the table that afternoon. Sealed super-tight with a double roll of packing tape surrounding the clasp. I'd need scissors to open that bad boy.

I carried the unopened envelope back to the office with my cup of orange zest tea; probably not the best choice to help me sleep, but I liked it. Digging in the desk drawer, I found the scissors and sliced open the packet. A bundle of letters still in their original envelopes had been banded together with several rubber bands. A single sheet of paper slid out with the bundle.

Miss Gardner,
Here are the letters we discussed over the phone. I can't tell you what you'll find because I could never bring myself to read them. I want to remember Mary as the woman who loved me, not just her second choice. I leave the disposition of the letters in your hands. I do not wish to have them returned. If you feel that Crystal should have them for Annie,

*please forward them on. Otherwise, you are free to destroy
them.*
    Henry Williams

I'd forgotten that Henry was sending me something. Letters, the
only way at the time to communicate between California and the
army camps in Vietnam. Letters were a way to stay in touch that
wouldn't be erased by deleting a quick e-mail or video chat. As
much as I loved my computer, I wondered if I would ever know the
joy of getting a letter from someone I loved, being able to pour over
its contents time and time again, to feel the paper that he touched,
and to know he took the time to share his day.

I quickly sorted through the envelopes and stacked them according to postmark, the oldest one first. Feeling like a voyeur, I folded
open the first letter and began to read.

    Mary,
    *It's been less than twenty-four hours since we parted, and
the taste of your kiss is still on my lips. Last week was honestly the best week of my life. I had thought I'd lost you when
I left the last time, me being a jerk and telling you to date
other people because I would be dating. Then I realized I
didn't want to date other girls. I only wanted to be with you.
But by the time I'd gotten out of boot camp and had five minutes to think about what I wanted my life after this hell to
look like, you were gone.*
    *Now, don't get me wrong, Henry's a great guy. I know he
took care of you when I didn't. But, Mary, you and I are des-
tiny. You are the Juliet to my Romeo. And you thought I never
listened during Miss Hastings's class. And I'm so happy and
proud you chose me.*
    *I'm signing off now to write my mom and tell her all about
you. She was kind of upset that I didn't spend more time with
her at the house while I was home. But she'll understand
when I tell her our news.*
    Hold me close to your heart and wish me home.
    Love always,
    Bob

No wonder Mary kept these letters for all these years. And in a way, I was glad Henry never read them. This was a part of Mary that she held private. And I could respect that. Are we destined to be with only one person? Is there a soul mate out there for each of us? I didn't know. What I did know was in all the relationships I had been in, no one had ever moved me the way this letter had tonight. Maybe I settled too easily, wanting love at any cost.

Miss Emily's words from our first chat on the porch came back to me: *"You have to find yourself before you find the one."*

The clock on the computer screen showed it was after midnight. Time to call it a day. I turned off the computer and the downstairs lights. Checking the locks on the front door and the kitchen door, I headed up the stairs, alone. Tonight I wanted a companion. If I was going to follow Miss Emily's advice and find myself, I needed a dog to help me through the long nights waiting for the time to be right to find my Romeo. She'd been a smart woman.

The sounds of nail guns and men shouting woke me the next morning.

Just a few more weeks and the construction would be done. I hoped. Today, I was heading back to the home supply store for paint for the living room. I'd stop at the furniture store, as well. The room screamed for new furniture. And after last night, I knew if I didn't spend the money Miss Emily left me, Aunt Jackie was more than willing to take on the task.

Once the living room was done, I'd be moving upstairs. The bathroom on the main floor needed more attention than I and my do-it-yourself remodel skills could provide. And the thought of having a remodel team inside the house as well as outside made my head spin. I'd tackle the bathroom some other time.

I hurried and dressed in capris and a tank, Slipping on my sandals, I grabbed my bag and notebook with the room measurements Derek and I had spent yesterday afternoon getting down. I locked the back door and was just about to walk out the front to my Jeep when a knock on the door surprised me. I swung open the door to find Greg.

"Hey, there you are. I thought you'd given up on protecting me," I joked. "I'm on my way to Bakerstown. Want to tag along?"

Greg was quiet. Too quiet. "Jill, the tox screens came back from Miss Emily. She was poisoned."

The weight of his words hung on me. I walked over to the rockers on the porch and sat down, dropping my purse to the wooden slats. "I knew she didn't just die." Tears fell down my face.

"I'm sorry." Greg sat down in the rocker next to me. He put his hand on my shoulder. "Doc Ames got the results yesterday, and I've been running between here and Bakerstown since. Miss Emily didn't have any history of heart problems or physical evidence during autopsy. In fact, Doc Ames said she was too healthy to be dead on his table. That's what convinced him to run the tox screen."

I only half-listened. It was funny that the news was affecting me so hard, since I had been the one to press Greg into looking more deeply into her cause of death. I had known, deep down, I had always known. "So, what happened?"

"She had an extremely high dosage of an herbal supplement called ma huang. Or ephedra. They haven't nailed the exact source down. But the lab guys think it was served in her evening tea."

"Miss Emily didn't believe in supplements. Called them new wave hooey. I don't think she even took vitamins."

"I have the entire contents of her medicine cabinet back at the office. We've been going through everything to find a match. So far, nothing."

"Do you have any leads? Any suspects?"

"I checked out Crystal's alibi yesterday. She was working at the time Miss Emily would have taken the final dose, according to Doc Ames. Her boss confirmed the date and time. And so was her new boyfriend. We've ruled them out." Greg put his forearms on his legs and leaned forward.

"What about Eric or Bambi or the mayor?" Crystal might have been the number-one suspect on Greg's list, but she had already been removed from mine. "Where were they?"

"We're checking their stories, but right now, I need to ask you to come with me." Greg held out his hand.

"Come with you where?" I didn't like the sound of this. "I have to get to Bakerstown and pick up the paint for the living room."

"You have to come down to City Hall and answer a few questions." Greg's face contorted. "Look, it's not my decision. Mayor

Baylor threatened to turn the investigation over to the state cops if I don't bring you in."

Anger flooded my body. "Really? You and your friend the mayor think I killed Miss Emily? Someone you didn't even know existed before she wound up dead and ruined your weekend fishing trip?"

"Don't make this hard." Greg's voice got cold.

I stared up at him. I suspected he was mad. But I didn't care. Rather than find out who killed Miss Emily, he was dragging me down to the station for questioning. I slung my purse over my shoulder. My eyes welled with tears. I couldn't believe this was even happening. I motioned for him to leave and I'd follow. I didn't trust my voice.

"You'll be done in no time. And then this stupid idea that you killed her will be put to rest." Greg put his hand on my back as we walked to his truck.

I wasn't sure that this would ever be done. Innocent people went to jail all the time.

Chapter 18

My first thought was I should call Jimmy Marcum and have him meet me at the police station. My second thought was how much I hated Greg King right now.

Greg opened the truck door and helped me in. "Seriously, Jill, it's going to be all right. Don't look so scared."

I wasn't going to talk until we got to the station.

I wanted some sort of record of my words so I could have proof I didn't confess. I couldn't believe Greg would do this to me. After all the time we spent together, he was still a cop. And I was his suspect.

Greg kept glancing at me while we drove. Finally he gave up trying to say anything and turned up the music.

When we reached City Hall, I got out of the truck on my own and headed to the side door, where the police office was located.

"Hold on, we're going in here." Greg pointed to the front doors that led directly to the mayor's office. I hadn't been there since Amy had disappeared. Bambi sat at Amy's desk, reading the most recent *Smithsonian* magazine.

"Hey, it's the coffee lady." Bambi tucked the magazine under a copy of *Vogue*. Proper office attire for Bambi seemed to be a low-cut passion pink jumper with leopard print stiletto heels. I wouldn't be surprised if the shoes had been real leopard skin. "Your aunt's ordering supplements just for my lattes. I can't wait until we get back to civilization."

"We have an appointment to see the mayor," Greg announced. "Is he ready?"

"You know that Esmeralda always gets the first appointment of the day. I'm sure they'll be done soon." Bambi scanned Greg's body like it was a three-course dinner. "Now, don't you look especially yummy today? When are you going to come over to the hotel and see me?"

Greg glanced at me and shifted his shoulders. "That's not going to happen."

"Why not, sugar pie?" Bambi broke off a piece of blueberry muffin and hand-fed it to Precious, who sat on top of Amy's desk. When Amy got back, if she came back, she would have to disinfect this entire office. Greg's face turned beet red.

"Yeah, why not?" I chided. From the casualness of their banter, Greg and Bambi had been spending some quality time together. My gut tightened.

"Because I don't want to become shark bait if your boyfriend found out." He glanced at me. "I'm kind of seeing someone anyway."

"Well, isn't that a shame. Any time you change your mind, though, you just let Bambi know. I bet we'd have a real good time." The sound of the mayor's office door opening cut off Bambi's offer of companionship and other things.

Esmeralda floated out of the office, her black cat cuddled in her arms. City Hall was becoming pet central. The fortune-teller stopped short when she saw me. "Jill, my dear, how have you been? Oh, that was a silly question coming from me. I see you're with your match." She pointed toward Greg.

"What do you mean, my match?"

Esmeralda put her free hand on my arm. "Trust in the process. The sun will rise tomorrow. And you will be happy. I've seen this in my visions."

The sun will rise tomorrow? What was she now, a weather girl? "Well, thanks, I guess. We have to go now." I shot a pleading look at Greg, and he took my arm.

"The mayor's waiting for us." He walked me into the office and closed the door. Just before the door closed, I heard Bambi ask if Esmeralda could do a reading for Precious.

His chair was turned, and the mayor talked to someone on the phone. I could overhear his part of the conversation as Greg motioned for me to sit down.

"She just left." The mayor paused. "No, she didn't give me any more direction. She just said the winds of change were about to run through our lives."

Greg took the chair next to me. I pointed to the mayor and raised my shoulders, silently asking what was going on. Greg just shook his head.

"How the heck am I supposed to know? Honey, look, I've got people here. I've got to go." The mayor turned the chair around and hung up his phone. He glared at Greg.

"Bambi told us to come in," Greg apologized. "Should we come back later?"

"No, it's fine. That girl has no business sense. I'll be glad when Amy's back." The mayor fingered through the files on his desk.

Hope shot through my body. Maybe this was why he wanted to see me. "Have you heard from Amy? Where is she? Is she okay?"

"Oh, I was just making a comment. I'm sure Miss Newman is fine and will be returning to her job at any moment. At least I hope so. I don't know how much more of Bambi's attitude I can take." He leaned forward on his desk. "Did you know not only does she bring that mangy mutt into the office, she takes him for five walks a day? Five! Who does she think answers the phone when she's not at the desk? Me. That's who."

I didn't know what to say after that. I sank back into my chair, hoping that Amy was off on some cruise or vacation somewhere. I missed having someone to talk to, especially now that Greg had gone all police detective commando on me. Maybe a cloud of radioactive gas had hit the town and was slowly turning people into comic book characters of themselves. We already had a Malibu Barbie answering phones at City Hall. But to be fair, I was pretty sure Bambi had been that way for her entire life.

"Back to business. I wanted to clear up this art theft ring. Now that we've determined that Miss Emily was murdered, we have to find her killer. The City of South Cove doesn't take kindly to one of our own being murdered in her own bed. It's just not good for the tourist trade." The mayor twirled a pen in his hand.

"And why did you need to see me?" I managed politely through gritted teeth. He was thinking about the town's image? I tried to control my rage, but every time I talked to the little weasel, I got angry.

"We have a visitor from the city coming in. I wanted him to meet you." The mayor buzzed Bambi. "Ask Mr. Hunter to come in now, please."

"All righty then. And just to let you know, Precious and I are stepping out for a second." Bambi's chipper voice came over the intercom.

"See what I mean?" He nodded to Greg. "This will happen all day long. Maybe Esmeralda could help with phone duties?"

"Sir, Esmeralda is swamped—" Greg started but was interrupted by the door opening.

"We'll talk about this later." The mayor waved his hand at Greg, quieting him. "Mr. Hunter, please come in."

I turned to look at the new arrival to Circus City Hall. He was tall, dark, and handsome, and he knew it. His clothes were California casual, pricey but appeared to be just thrown together. I'd dated a real estate developer who had the same style, so I knew the man raked in some serious dough to pull off looking that laid-back.

"Mayor Baylor, I still don't understand what was so important that I had to drive all the way down here so early in the morning." The man pushed his sunglasses farther up on his head and adjusted the sweater tied around his neck before he sat down.

"Introductions first. John Paul Hunter, this is Greg King, our police detective."

"Nice to meet you." Greg stood and reached over me to shake hands.

"And this is . . ." The mayor pointed at me and waited.

For a few seconds, no one said anything. Then Mr. Hunter spoke up.

"This is who? I've told you, I'm a busy man. If you want me to meet these people for some reason, please let's get on with it. I'm opening a new show this weekend."

"I thought you might know her."

"Why would I know her?" The man almost sneered at my outfit. Now, I admit, it wasn't couture, but it was clean and comfortable. At least I'd finished laundry last night and it wasn't the little black dress. I was headed out shopping when Greg had ambushed me into this meeting.

"This isn't the woman who sold you the paintings? The ones we talked about?" Mayor Baylor's face fell. "Look again. Are you sure? This is Jill Gardner."

"Look, Mayor, I told you I've never seen this woman before. And if you remember, I distinctly told you over the phone that the woman who sold me the paintings was quite overweight."

"She's fat." Mayor Baylor pointed his finger at me.

"Hey, I'm not fat. I'm not a size one like Malibu Bambi out there, but I'm not fat. I'm curvy." My face felt hot. I'd been pleased when I checked myself out in the mirror this morning, seeing the results of losing weight since my world went topsy-turvy. Perfect weight-loss diet: turn everything on its ear and you'll be too upset to eat.

The mayor had a way of getting down to the core of my insecurities. I'd never left this office feeling anything more positive than annoyance. I wondered how he managed to get elected year after year. It couldn't be on charm.

"Seriously, you thought Jill was the one selling Miss Emily's artwork?" Greg stood up. "This is why you had me drag her down here?"

"Well, yes." Mayor Baylor sneered. "She fit the description of the woman, and you know the city is committed to finding Miss Emily's killer. And now she has full access to all the paintings she wants to sell."

"And if it gets me out of that house so your friends can finish the little development they have planned for my home, more the better, right?" I stood and glanced at Greg. "Are we done here? I have work to do."

"Wait, you have the rest of the paintings? Can I see them? I've got several buyers who are interested in acquiring anything she did. Especially now that she's deceased." John Paul's eyes gleamed as he leaned closer to me. Apparently my lack of fashion sense had been forgiven now that I had become important to him.

"I'm not sure what I'm doing with the paintings yet. But I would like to see what you still have at the gallery and pictures of what you've already sold." I wanted to gauge the value of the artwork. I didn't know if John Paul Hunter's gallery deserved to sell the rest of the lot. He'd been selling the stolen paintings for months before we accidentally found them.

"Call me any time and I'll be glad to drive down and give you an estimate. I'll have my assistant send you a portfolio of the paintings we've handled so far. I assure you, we've been very successful in procuring high-dollar amounts for the sales." John Paul handed me a card embossed with *Hunter Gallery*.

"Have your assistant send that portfolio thing to me. What exactly did you do with the artist's share of those funds?" Greg moved in between the two of us.

"As I told the officer who came to interview me, the woman came by weekly to pick up the funds from any sales."

"The checks were made out to what name?"

John Paul glanced around the room, his eyes landing on Greg sizing up the effect his next words would have. "I gave her cash."

"You what? Isn't it standard bookkeeping procedure to use checks to track sales and purchases? Did you get a receipt?"

Now the man was sweating. Literally. I wondered what other shady deals we would find if someone opened the books on this guy.

"Look, she told me she needed the money. Artists are always strapped for cash. So I discounted her cut by a little and fronted the cash. All galleries do it." John Paul played with the tie in his sweater.

"So there is no paper trail for these paintings. Please tell me that your shop has a video security system."

"We do. Except it doesn't work right now. I planned on having it fixed, but the fact that it's there, well, that works just as well."

"Unless a crime really happens." Greg glanced at me. "I'm going to need to talk with Mr. Hunter for a few more minutes. Do you want to wait and I'll drive you home?"

"I can walk. Besides, I need to stop by the coffee shop and check in with my aunt." I wasn't hanging around City Hall with Bambi and the mayor any longer than I had to.

"You will call me, though, right?" John Paul called after me as I headed to the door.

"Miss Gardner, I'm not done with you," Mayor Baylor's voice chimed in.

"Yes, you are," Greg growled. He nodded toward me. "I'll stop by tonight."

I took that for permission to leave before the mayor opened his mouth again. Glancing around the empty reception area, I realized that Bambi was still outside with Precious. Sadness filled my body as I touched Amy's desk. I glanced at the closed door of the mayor's office and the glass door outside—nobody was in sight.

I slipped into Amy's chair and pulled open the side drawer. Bambi had filled this one with dog biscuits, toys, and a book on California history. The second drawer had makeup and more brushes, combs, and hair clips than I'd owned in my entire life.

The bottom drawer had Amy's possessions crammed inside. Bambi apparently needed the room for more important stuff. My friend's life was reduced to this one drawer. I moved past the framed pictures of Amy and her surfing friends and only paused a second when I found the one of the two of us at last year's Renaissance Faire, decked out in medieval costumes. Amy's smile twisted my heart.

Will I ever see my friend again?

Digging deeper, I found her day planner. Bingo. I heard voices from the mayor's office coming closer to the door. Slamming the drawer shut, I stuffed the day planner to the bottom of my purse and sprinted for the door. Watching behind me for the office door to open, I ran straight into Bambi leading Precious back into the office.

"Hey, watch it." Bambi teetered on stacked stilettos. Precious growled.

"Sorry," I called back. I wasn't stopping until I could lock myself up in the supply closet at Coffee, Books, and More and see what I could find in Amy's planner.

The shop was half-filled with customers when I walked through the door. It seemed like forever since I had been at my own shop. Conversation stopped at most tables as they watched me approach Toby at the counter. The scent of chocolate and coffee wafted through the store.

"Hey, how are you doing?" Toby had been stocking the paper coffee cups I designed for the store.

"Good." I nodded toward the display of coffee for sale, both whole bean and ground. "This is new."

"Jackie just started selling the packets. They are going like hotcakes, and we have several new flavors that we only feature in the shop. Then we sell them the next month out on the retail rack.

Pretty neat, huh? Jackie says it builds up demand when we limit the supply." Toby nodded like he was committing Jackie's words of marketing wisdom to memory.

"Where is the marketing maven?" I took inventory of the other changes my aunt had made without my approval. I was relieved to see the bookshelves were still on the south wall. But what was that sign? I leaned closer to read.

Local author signings welcome.

"She's upstairs. She takes over at noon. That way I can get some sleep before I head over to the police station at eight." Toby twisted the dish towel in his hands. "I hope you can figure out a way to keep me on, once you start managing the place again. I've learned so much, and I like working with people who aren't mad at me or drunk."

The sign my aunt had put up advertising author signings distracted me. Why hadn't I thought of that? Amy's planner burned a hole in my purse—I had to sit down and search it for any clue of her whereabouts. "Sorry, I was woolgathering. I'm sure we can work out something. Can you pour me a cup of carmalotto blend? I'm going to head to the back to check out something."

Toby threw the dish towel over his shoulder and poured a mug full. "Do you want a slice of pie or cheesecake with that?"

Tempting . . . I shook my head. "Just the coffee. And if my aunt comes down, let her know I'm in the back?" I headed to the supply room, where I stored my boxes, books, and other supplies. As I went through the door, I heard the voices from the dining area start back up. Gossip about me was my bet. Sitting down, I pulled Amy's planner out of my purse along with my purple notebook. There had to be something here. If I could just find it.

An hour later, I'd gone through her entire planner, and except for finding out my friend highlighted her pretty blond hair during the winter, I came up blank on finding a reason for her disappearance. Except for one note two days before she vanished—*Meeting with TA*. Who was TA? She had written in Miss Emily's funeral with a doodle of a crying face, dripping a tear. So she had planned on being there.

I doodled in my own notebook. TA. Texas Authors. Teen Angst. Terrible Angina. This wasn't getting me anywhere. I tried to see TA through her eyes. Trouble Amy? Surfing? A type of wave? An urban planning term? I threw the pen on the notebook. Nothing. I leaned back in my chair and closed my eyes.

"Don't you think if there had been something, I would have followed up on it? Or at least taken the planner for evidence?" Greg stood in the doorway, leaning up against the door frame, watching me.

Jerking up, I tried to cover the planner with my notebook. Then, as Greg's words sank in, I realized hiding it was like shutting the dog pound door after the escape had occurred. Too little and too late.

"Toby told me you were back here." Greg came and sat down. "I'm sorry about the ambush this morning. I didn't know what he was up to."

"It's okay. I mean, I knew I could be considered a suspect. I just didn't think it would be because our honorable mayor thought I was the fat girl who sold the paintings."

"I thought you were going to jump over the desk and throttle him." Greg chuckled at the image.

"Not funny. You don't know how hard it is to lose weight. And I kind of like the shape I'm in. I know I'm not skinny like most of the girls who hang out on the beach, but sue me, I like food."

"I think you look fine. More than fine, you look amazing."

Something in Greg's voice made me look up. His glaze smoldered, and if I didn't know better, I would think there was a hint of what, passion? Desire? Lust? My stomach lurched as my girl parts twisted. My glance moved down to his lips. Full, husky, with a five-o'clock shadow on his chin. I lightly bit my bottom lip, wanting to jump over the table for the second time that day, but for a totally different reason.

Stop. Just stop.

My reasonable side chimed in. *There's an entire shop full of people just on the other side of the door.*

And they were probably waiting for Greg to bring me out of the room in chains. I sighed and pushed the planner across the table toward him.

"The only thing I can find is this meeting with TA. Did you find out who she was meeting?" My voice came out too husky, and heat flashed on my face.

"The mayor said it was probably one of the office suppliers.

After the fiasco today, I'll check that out a little more closely. I'm not sure our mayor is playing with a full deck."

"That's the understatement of the millennium."

"Nothing else jumped out at you? I should have asked you to look at this before." Greg leaned back in his chair. "You have a good eye for seeing missing pieces."

A compliment? He sets me up for an ambush with the mayor, and then he compliments my investigative techniques? "I thought you said I should let the professionals handle this."

Greg leaned over the table and sighed. "After the fiasco today, I'd rather have you on my side than the professionals I'm dealing with. Come on, spill. I know you found something in the day planner that just seemed off."

I slid the book back toward me and glanced at the week of Amy's disappearance. Nothing. Then I turned the pages forward. Maybe there was something else. The page covering this week had a note. Schedule time for Jill at council meeting.

I hadn't been planning on speaking to the council. Did Amy know something about the zoning committee or the threat on the house? I pointed the notation out to Greg.

"Look at this. She planned on me presenting to the next city council meeting."

"About Miss Emily's house?"

"That's the thing. She never talked to me about presenting anything." I pulled out the folded letter that Amy and I had found in Miss Emily's desk. "The last thing we discussed was why the council used an out-of-town attorney to send these threatening letters. Amy was going to check out who had hired this guy. But I never heard anything back."

"Why didn't you ask me about it?" Greg read the letter silently while he waited for my answer.

"I didn't at first because, well, I thought you might be part of the whole thing." My face flushed, this time not because of the ultra-hunkiness of the man sitting across from me. "And then when Amy disappeared and I started getting those calls, I didn't know who to trust and it just seemed too late."

"Someday you're going to have to trust someone." Greg stood and walked toward the door. "I'll go call this guy. What are you doing this afternoon?"

"Home Heaven in Bakerstown. Then I'll be home painting the living room."

"I'll bring dinner by around six." Greg walked out into the shop area.

"I guess I'll see you then," I said to the closed door. I stared at the door for several minutes before I noticed that Amy's planner was gone. Greg must have picked it up on the way out. I stuffed my notebook back into my purse and headed back out to the front of the shop. Time to buy paint and pretend that my life was normal, for just a few hours.

Blue, I think I'll paint the ceiling blue. My mind kept running over that old joke about wives and lovemaking as I rolled sapphire blue paint over the beige living room walls. All the walls in the house had been beige. Miss Emily must have gotten a great deal from a local painter who needed to use up his office remodel left-over paint.

Already planning my bedroom, I'd decided on peach walls, leaving the hardwood floors and adding a thick floral area rug to give it some warmth. The living room would be my television and entertaining room, focusing on the television part of that. I couldn't remember the last time I had invited anyone over for dinner.

Except Greg.

And that didn't count since he was just doing his sworn duty to serve and protect. The logical side of my brain chirped in. *He's just doing his job.* Yep, the living room would focus on a new flat-screen television on this wall to mirror the fireplace on the opposite wall. I could imagine being curled up with a dog at my feet, music playing in the background, a roaring fire in the hearth, a good book in my hand, and Greg watching sports on the television.

Wait—what?

My imagination was getting the best of me. I set the roller down in the pan and surveyed what I'd accomplished that day. Half a wall left and I'd be done. I glanced at my watch. Four-thirty. If I hurried, I'd have time to grab a quick shower and change of clothes before Greg got there with dinner. I ran to the kitchen to grab a soda from the fridge. Looking out on the construction mania in my backyard, I froze.

Greg's brother, Jim, stood in the driveway talking to Todd. Apparently enough of the base work was done and soon the painting crew would replace the siding and roofing crews I'd been living with. Todd saw me through the window and waved at me to come outside.

Dread filled every pore of my body as I walked out the door. One, I wasn't looking forward to seeing Jim King again after he'd caught Greg and me sipping beer together on the porch. And two, the only reason contractors wanted to talk to me lately was to get my approval on cost overruns or show me the termite/water/fairy dust damage in the wood that would run me a few thousand more dollars.

I crossed over the yard and braced myself for the bad news. "Hey, guys, what's up?" I said in a tone that I hoped sounded more cheerful than grumpy.

"Good news," Todd chirped. "I just told Jim here that I'd be out of the way by Friday and he could start the painting on Monday."

Hope filled my soul. "So, we could be done by the end of the month?" If everything fell right into place, I could take pictures of the house for next week's council meeting. And maybe they'd get off my back.

"One problem," Jim barked.

I glanced at him. Great, now he was going to turn down the job on moral grounds? What, he thought I'd corrupt him while his crews painted the house? "What problem?"

"I haven't received the color approval letter from the city. I called last week, and they said the city planner was on an extended leave. Didn't know when I'd get my approval." Jim seemed almost cheerful about the delay.

Frustrated, tears filled my eyes. "Amy's not on leave, she's disappeared. Did they say if anyone else could approve the color choice?" South Cove was very concerned that the building colors, especially the buildings on Main Street, stayed true to historical color tones. I lucked out with the shop since the facing wall was brick, but I still had only a few choices when I'd painted the back of the building.

"The girl who answered said the mayor was handling all those requests."

"The mayor, of course." I spat out the words. I could almost see the finish line, and fate had thrown me another hill to climb.

"Do you want me to call back?" Jim seemed like he was trying to be helpful. "I can't start the job until the city has approved the color choice. I'd be removed from the approved contractor list if I took that kind of risk."

"You call and I'll call. Between the two of us, maybe we can get that approval by the end of the week." By the end of the year was more like it, especially after my run-in with the mayor today. I was sure he'd love to help me thwart his plans to condemn the property and sell it to Eric. Jimmy Marcum's face came to the front of my mind. I had a meeting scheduled for next week. Hiring a lawyer just might help my chances of ever getting the clearance.

"I need to make a call. Anything else I can do for you guys?" I glanced back at Todd, hoping he'd say no. So far, this conversation had only cost me time, not more in materials or labor.

"A cold beer would be nice." Todd grinned. "Other than that, we're fine."

"I'll check back in on Friday. I can hold the crew off until then, but if we don't have clearance Friday, we'll have to start on another house and I won't be able to get you back on the rotation for a week. Later." Jim slapped Todd on the back and headed to his truck.

"Mr. Sunshine," I commented, nodding to Jim's retreating back.

"He's an acquired taste." Todd watched the painting contractor get into his truck. "I've never seen him act this way around a pretty, single gal. Did the two of you date?"

"Nope." I spun around and headed to the house, but Todd's voice stopped me and I turned back.

"Hey, that history guy came back this morning taking pictures. I let him go back behind the shed. That's okay, right?" Todd's face looked like he'd been caught with his hands in the cookie jar. "I mean, I walked back with him and all, but he didn't seem in too much of a hurry. I've never seen someone take so many pictures of a broken-down wall."

"Mr. Gleason's working on a project for me." A project that might just save my butt and this house.

"So, the rumors are true?"

"What rumors?"

Todd kicked at a dirt clod lying on the driveway. "That the wall is part of the old mission? You know there's a story about a chest full of pirates' gold being buried around the mission."

I didn't miss the gleam in Todd's eyes. What was it with stories of pirates that made grown men act like little boys? "I'm sure it's just a story."

"You might want to get that fence done sooner than later. Once the rumor gets out, I'd be on the watch for fortune hunters. You don't want your lawn dug up in the middle of the night."

I sighed. I knew Todd was right. I'd already had to lock up the shed to keep the art thief out. Now I needed to know—and soon—if those coins Greg and I found in the play chest were real or fake. If they were real and word got out, I'd have people all over this property. I was never going to get the house up to code for the council meeting at this rate. I needed to talk to Jimmy Marcum—now.

I waved good-bye to Todd, headed back to the house, and picked up my cell. Maybe I should put the coins in a safety deposit box at the bank. I hadn't thought much about them since I'd shoved them into a kitchen drawer yesterday. I glanced at the clock. Ten to five. No answer at the law office and the bank would be closed before I could get there. Two more items for tomorrow's to-do list.

I climbed the stairs to shower and change before Greg arrived with dinner. It might just be take-out on the porch, but I didn't have to look like I worked on his brother's painting crew.

Chapter 19

My hair was still wet when the doorbell rang. But at least I wasn't covered in blue polka dots from my painting. I'd be glad when the house was finished and I could concentrate on other disaster areas in my life, like my business and nonexistent love life. I felt totally pathetic for leaning on Greg the way I'd been, but like Scarlett, I'd think about that tomorrow. Tonight, he was bringing me dinner.

"Hey, you're early." I swung open the door. And stopped. Greg wasn't standing in front of me.

Sabrina Jones filled my porch in a hot pink pantsuit that strained at the buttons. She barreled through the open door. "Well, it looks like you've been busy."

"Why don't you come in?" I said to her back as I closed the door. Gritting my teeth, I decided to find out why she had appeared on my doorstep. Maybe I'd even be able to trick her into saying she took the paintings. Sabrina had to be the fat woman John Paul Hunter had described. Too bad Greg would believe that he needed actual proof to arrest her.

Sabrina gazed around the room and then stuck her head into my new study. "What have you done with her furniture? You know most of those items were antiques. Valuable pieces that have been in the family for years. Please tell me you haven't destroyed them."

"I'm not sure it's any of your business since Miss Emily gave them to me, not you or your husband, but no, I'm waiting for an an-

tiques dealer to come and appraise the furniture I'm not keeping."
Stay calm, Jill. Keep her talking until Greg gets here.

"I still don't understand why she left everything to you. After all George and I did for that old bat. All the times I made her tea. He's devastated that his aunt treated him so shabbily." Sabrina nodded to the study. "I see you're keeping her old desk. Is there any paperwork in there about the history of the house and the property? George should keep that kind of family heirloom, and you'd see that if you had any sort of decency at all."

I wanted to strangle the woman in front of me, but I was pretty sure my hands wouldn't fit around her neck. "After I look through the papers, I'll be glad to give any family keepsakes to your husband."

"We'll see." Sabrina's beady eyes glanced toward the kitchen. "Aren't you going to offer me a drink? It's very warm in here. You should invest in some fans."

"Sure, what would you like?" I pointed to the kitchen. "We can sit in there, away from the paint fumes."

"Pepsi, if you have it." Sabrina barely fit through the arched door frame leading to the kitchen. She plopped down into one of the chairs at the table. "I think we have some business to discuss."

"Really? I can't think of anything we need to talk about." I opened the fridge door and grabbed two Cokes, nudging the lone can of Pepsi farther back in the fridge. "All I have is this, unless you want some ice water."

"I guess it will have to do." Sabrina sighed. She flicked the pop tab with a long, polished nail and drank down half the can.

I opened my soda and waited. Sabrina's eyes kept glancing at the painting by Miss Emily that I had hung in the breakfast nook. I decided to jump in the fray. "Nice painting, isn't it? Did you know Miss Emily was such an artist?"

Sabrina's cheeks turned as pink as her jacket. "I didn't know. The painting is beautiful."

"She even had a studio back in the shed. Of course, some paintings were stolen before we moved them to a more secure location." I watched her face. "I'm surprised with all the times you came over, Miss Emily never mentioned she painted."

Sabrina stared down at the soda can. "That's terrible about the break-in. South Cove seems such a quiet place to live, not like the bigger cities." She twirled the can. "Where did you move the paintings?"

Sure, like I would tell her. I'd wake up one night with my throat slashed and she'd have the paintings ready to sell to the Hunter Gallery or some other willing dealer. I didn't trust John Paul as far as I could swing him by his carefully tied sweater. "Somewhere safe. So, why did you stop by?"

Sabrina's eyes scanned the kitchen. I swear she was counting the amount of money I'd spent on the remodel. "Just wanted to see how you were getting along. The contractors must be costing you a fortune. Are you sure this old house is worth the money? You probably could have bought a nice little condo in Bakerstown for half of what you are spending just to get this house up to code."

I wanted to say it was my money and I'd spend it any way I saw fit, but that would have been rubbing her nose in the fact that Miss Emily left it to me, rather than her and her creepy husband. Several answers crossed my mind, and I filtered them out for good taste. "But I love this house," was what I finally came up with. Tears came unbidden when I added, "and it reminds me of Miss Emily."

"I would have sold it to that developer and gone on with my life." Sabrina sniffed.

Had Eric approached her, as well? "So, you've met Eric and Bambi?"

"They might have stopped by the house to pay their respects to George after Miss Emily passed. Most people thought she would have left this dump to family, not some stranger."

Now we were getting down to the reason Sabrina had come by. I glanced at the clock, five-thirty. Greg would be showing up in thirty minutes. No reason to get her ticked off too soon. "Bambi's working at City Hall, helping out since Amy's disappearance."

"I heard about that. You and Amy were friends, right?" Sabrina finished off her soda.

"We are friends." I corrected her tense. Man, this woman knew how to push buttons. I felt like I was in a boxing ring, dodging punches.

"Yes, of course. Have the police come up with any leads on where the poor girl might be?" Now Sabrina twirled the soda can.

Like she gave a rat's butt. "Not yet, but it's early."

"I read somewhere that if you don't find the missing person in forty-eight hours, you're more likely to find a body."

Okay, that was just mean. I was done. "What do you want, Sabrina?"

She grinned at me. "So we're done playing nice, huh? Okay then, I want you to split the inheritance with George. He deserves that money. You'll walk away with more than you deserve."

"And why would I do that?" The nerve of this woman.

"Let's just say it's good karma. The little roadblocks you've been running into may all suddenly disappear. Maybe your friend will even show back up."

"If you did anything to Amy—" My voice rose as I stood up.

"Who said I did anything to Amy? I might just know where she is, though." Sabrina leaned forward. "Maybe we can make a deal. You give George half of the inheritance money, before you went on the spending spree. And we'll call it even."

"Seriously, if you know where Amy is, you'd better tell me." My voice got louder.

"Or what? You'll throw that can of soda at me?" Sabrina laughed. "Sit down, girl, and think about this. You don't need all that money anyway. George was related to Miss Emily. That old bat never once listened when I'd explain why it would be better for estate taxes to give the money to us before she croaked. Even when I told her—"

"Told her what?" Greg's voice came through the open screen door. His body filled the space and I was never more glad to see anyone in my life.

"Hey, Greg, come in." I stood to unlock the screen. Taking the bags of take-out from his hands, I put them on the counter. "You know Sabrina, right?"

Greg's look told me all I needed to know. I was in big trouble. No matter that she came to see me, this was another one of my investigative shenanigans in his mind.

"What did you tell Miss Emily when you visited? And when was this? If I recall, when I talked to you, you said you hadn't seen her in months. Too busy with your own life to cater to some dried-up prune of an aunt? Wasn't that the answer?" Greg eased into a chair next to Sabrina and spun his cell phone on the table. "So, let's start over. When did you see your aunt last?"

"I don't like what you're implying, Detective King. I'm sure if I forgot to tell you anything, it was due to the shock and grief we went through when Miss Emily passed." Sabrina struggled to get out of her chair.

"You didn't answer my question. What did you tell her?" Greg leaned back, watching the woman struggle. He picked up the cell and seemed to be searching through his messages.

Sabrina's face turned redder than her jacket this time. "I told her that she owed it to George to pass on some of the family money. It was his grandfather's, and George had every right to it."

"According to Jimmy, George's dad got his share of his grandfather's estate and blew it before he died. So, how did you think that you had any right to Miss Emily's share?"

By this time Sabrina had managed to stand up. She adjusted her jacket. "She didn't have any kids—the money should have passed to George. If that's all, I'm sure my husband is expecting me."

"One more thing. I've been trying to reach you all day. I stopped by the house, but George said you were shopping." Greg didn't even look at the woman, staring at something on his cell phone screen instead. I couldn't read his expression. "How do you know John Paul Hunter?"

Sabrina's beet-red face lost all color at the mention of the gallery owner's name. "I don't. What makes you think I know this man?"

"Because he described a woman resembling you as the person who sold several paintings to the gallery. Miss Emily's paintings." Greg sounded cool.

"I didn't even know she painted until today. Maybe you should be asking your girlfriend about Mr. Hunter."

"Actually, Mr. Hunter met Jill this afternoon. He categorically stated she was not the person he bought the pictures from." Greg grinned up at me. If he mentioned the mayor thinking I was fat, I would slap him.

"Well, I don't know the man. I have to go." Sabrina headed out of the kitchen to the front door.

"I'll walk you to the door." Greg winked at me. "By the way, do me a favor and don't leave the area for a while. I might have some more questions for you."

Shaking, I sank down at the table. What was Greg thinking? Now Sabrina knew she was under investigation. I laid my head down and tried to focus. Sabrina had offered me Amy back if I transferred the money she wanted. Did she have Amy held somewhere? Or was she just playing with an emotion she knew would work?

"Ready for dinner?" Greg's voice brought me out of my funk. Startled, I jerked my head up to see him opening the cabinet drawers, looking for silverware.

"To the left of the dishwasher." I leaned back into the chair. It had been a long day, and I felt exhausted. When Greg didn't answer, I turned and pointed. "Right there, the next drawer."

"You're keeping these here, in the house? Are you crazy?" Greg held up the bag that held the pirate coins, his face hard, waiting for my answer.

"They were in the shed for years. Why is keeping them in the junk drawer an issue?" The smell of Lille's fish and chips was perking me up. All I wanted was to eat dinner and drink a couple of beers.

"The guy from the college called me back today. These are real, Jill. Real silver colonial coins from the mint in Mexico. He estimated if they were all in the same condition, you could probably get two to three hundred apiece, or more from the right collector." He threw the sack at me.

Catching it with two hands, the bag slipped almost to the floor. I hauled the bag to the table. Reaching in, I pulled out one of the coins. Turning it over, I whistled. "There must be over a hundred thousand dollars here, if he's right."

"He's right. So, please, move those to the bank tomorrow first thing. Too many rumors are floating around town about the mission for you to keep these here. While I was waiting at Lille's, three people asked me if the story about finding the mission was true." Greg pulled out forks from the silverware drawer and brought the bag of food over to the table.

I dropped the coin back into the sack. Laughter bubbled out of me. I tried to control the giggles. I started laughing out loud as I opened the Styrofoam container filled with fish and chips.

"Okay, I give. What's so funny?" Greg watched me as I tried to catch my breath.

"Sabrina would have died if she knew she sat that close to something worth that much money. She drooled over the painting I'd hung, and I don't think she was getting anywhere close to that for the ones she sold."

Greg shook his head. "That's what concerns me. I'm going to have Toby parked outside tonight, just in case. She doesn't seem like the type that gives up easy."

I pulled out the container from the bag with Greg's dinner and pushed it toward him. "Quit worrying and eat."

Greg's cell phone buzzed. He glanced at it and opened a text. "That's what I thought."

"What?" I didn't want to glance over at the phone. Okay, so I did. Shoot me.

"I sent a picture of Sabrina over to the gallery owner. He's just identified her as the one he bought the paintings from." Greg contemplated the food sitting in front of him.

"So, that's why you were playing with your phone."

"Yep." He sighed and closed up the container.

"You have to leave?"

"I need to get this over to the judge so I can get a search warrant for her house. Maybe this will be over sooner than we thought." He stuffed a couple of French fries in his mouth as he stood up.

"Do you think she killed Miss Emily?" My appetite was gone. Could this be finally over?

"Money's a strong motive for murder. Let's just take things one at a time." Greg closed up the container and headed to the door. "Toby won't be here until after nine. Stay inside!"

"Greg, stop." I hurried to catch up with him. "She said she could bring Amy home if I gave her the money. Maybe you should wait."

Greg studied my face. "You're not telling me you believed her. Are you? She'd say anything to try to get you to pay her off. Believe me, she didn't kidnap Amy. And even if she did, this is the best way to find out."

"But Amy . . ." Tears filled my eyes. "I'd give away all the money if Amy would just come back safe."

"I know. But we just have to have hope. The state police are working her disappearance. I'm going to call them to help me execute this warrant. We won't do anything that will put Amy in danger." Greg reached out and pulled me close. "Trust me."

I didn't want him to let go. I melted into his arms, tucking my head into his chest.

"Jill, I have to go."

I felt his words as they whispered through my hair. I heard his voice rumble in his chest. And I knew I had to step away. Taking a deep breath, I pulled away, even though every cell in my body cried out as I leaned against the hallway wall. "Be careful."

"That's my line." He touched my cheek and left. As the front door shut behind him, my fear stuck in my throat and I followed, locking the door behind him. Before I returned to the kitchen, I circled the house, closing windows and testing locks. Finally, in the kitchen, I double-checked the lock on the back door. Sinking into a chair at the table, I stared at Lille's fish and chips. For once, my mouth didn't water. I closed the container and put it into the fridge, grabbing a Coke instead.

"Amy," I whispered to my missing friend. "I hope I've done the right thing."

The dark gloomed around the house. The sun had set, and I sat in the living room, reading the same page over and over. In books, the good guys find who did it, the bad guys go to jail, and the hero saves the damsel in distress. No one ever tells you that being the damsel really sucks.

Click. Click. A noise came from the front of the house. Was someone on the porch? I leaned forward, laying the book down on the couch. *Click.* There it was again. I tiptoed to the door. Taking a deep breath, I steadied myself. Every fiber of my being screamed out: *Don't go in the basement.*

Giggling over my favorite line from the horror movies, a Friday night staple growing up, I put my hands on the lock. "One, two, three," I counted under my breath and pulled the door open. A hand on the other side reached for the doorknob.

Startled, I slammed the door shut, hoping I surprised the person standing on my porch more than they surprised me. The door easily shut and I snapped the lock secure.

I backed up, watching the door. Should I call Greg? Toby was supposed to be here soon, but someone was outside now. Before I reached the phone, a knock sounded on the door and a voice called out.

"Jill? Jill, it's me."

Was that my aunt's voice? She was the shape on the porch? I inched closer to the door.

"Who's there?" I called out, my voice shaky.

"Jackie. I brought over brownies from the store. Are you going to open the door or just slam it in my face again?"

It was my aunt. And from the sound of her voice, she wasn't happy. I opened the door a crack and peeked out to see her face before committing to letting her in. Just in case.

Aunt Jackie pushed past me. The smell of baked chocolate followed her into the house. "I swear, you almost gave me a heart attack. I knew you were flighty, but really, you need to calm down."

Flighty? She called *me* flighty? The woman who hadn't stayed with a man for more than three dates since my uncle died? My fear turned to annoyance as I asked, "Besides bringing over brownies, why are you here?"

"Well, isn't that nice? No 'great to see you'? Or 'thanks for coming over'?" Jackie walked back to the kitchen, clearly expecting me to follow.

Sighing, I locked the door, checking the front porch one more time, and did exactly that. Aunt Jackie already had plates out and placed large, frosted brownies on the center of each one.

"Good, you already have coffee going." She grabbed two cups from the cabinet.

"Again, why are you here?" I put the plates on the table while she finished with the coffee.

"To help you, of course. Greg called me and asked me to come by and wait for Toby. He's running a little late. I think he overslept."

Great, my watchdog was sleep-deprived. Now I felt safe. Especially since I had a seventy-plus-year-old woman here to protect me.

"Toby said you stopped by this morning. Why didn't you come see me?" Jackie brought the coffee cups over to the table.

"I had to check something out." I took a bite of the brownie. Heaven.

"He also said that Greg followed you into the back room? Is there something going on there? He seemed concerned about you when he called me." Jackie watched my face for a reaction I tried not to give her.

"We just talked about the art theft case. They tracked down the gallery owner and wanted to exclude me as a suspect." The mayor's words flashed in my mind. I took another large bite of the brownie just to shove them down.

"Greg thought you were a suspect?" Jackie's face went cold.

"No, but the mayor did." I took a long sip from the coffee to clear out the deep chocolate taste calling to me to grab one more brownie. "Now the gallery owner is panting over the other paintings. He wants me to let him sell the rest."

"Miss Emily didn't realize her paintings would be so sought after, now, did she?"

I stood in front of the sunny landscape hanging on the kitchen wall and thought about the other paintings she had long ago abandoned in the shed. Had she considered taking up painting again? Or was the desire lost to her after losing the ones she loved? I issued a short chuckle. "I think she would have found being an artist hilarious. I could just hear her now: *Why would anyone want to buy my pictures? Can't they make their own?*"

The cell phone rang. I answered the call on speakerphone mode. "Hello?"

"You should be happy now." The woman's voice filled the room.

"Why would I be happy? Who is this?" Fear gripped me as I glanced at Jackie, pulling out a notebook from her purse.

"The DNA tests came back. Annie's not related to Miss Emily. Her grandfather is Henry, not Bob." It took me a moment to place the voice. Crystal. I could hear emotion in her voice as she choked out the words, but I didn't know if it was happiness or sadness. Aunt Jackie stopped writing and laid down the pen.

"Crystal, are you all right?" There was a pause from the other end of the line.

"I'm just so happy for Henry. He wanted Josh to be his kid all along, but he was too afraid to hope. This might have been the best thing that's happened to him since Mary died." Crystal sniffed loudly.

"I'm glad for him, too. I'm sure Miss Emily would have loved to have had you and Annie as part of her family, though." I felt bad for putting her through this roller coaster, but getting the truth out there was all that mattered.

"I need to tell you something. When we thought Bob was Josh's father, I agreed to be part of a suit challenging the will. I've called the lawyer and told him I didn't want anything more to do with the lawsuit." Crystal paused. "He didn't seem very happy."

"Let me guess, Sabrina and George hired him?"

"I don't know who hired him. He came by the house that day I ran into you at Home Heaven."

The pieces were falling into place, and all roads were leading back to Sabrina. "You were just trying to do what was best for Annie."

"That's the thing. I'm afraid I was trying to do what was best for me. Knowing how easy things would be with the money that the lawyer promised me, that was all I wanted. For life to be easy, for once."

I didn't know what to say. Money seemed to be motivating a lot of people around here. For me, having the money just meant I could shop for furniture or remodel the house. For Crystal and Aunt Jackie, it had meant daily survival. Before I could collect my thoughts, Crystal's voice came over the speaker again.

"Jill, I just wanted to say I'm sorry."

The line clicked off and disconnected the call.

"Well, that was interesting." Jackie drummed the pen on the notebook. "I guess I didn't have to take notes. Now I'll have to start a new to-do list." I hadn't noticed that my notebook habit came from my aunt until tonight. She pulled the sheet with the notes she'd made from Crystal's call. At the top of the page was a list of five items. She recopied the list onto a clean sheet of paper when item number three jumped out at me. She started to put her notebook back in her purse.

"Wait, what's that?" I pointed to the third line.

"I told you, my to-do list. Don't tell me you don't use one. I've seen your notebook on the counter."

"No, I mean what does number three mean?"

"Call my travel agent? I told you that I had thought about taking a trip this summer. I'm just calling to cancel before I lose my deposit. I'm not going to leave you high and dry at the shop, I promise. Jeez." She stuffed the notebook back into her purse and finished off her brownie.

"No, it's not that. You wrote TA."

"Yeah, so, TA is my shorthand for travel agent." Jackie stared at me like I was crazy. "Do you need to get some sleep? I can stay up and watch for Toby."

"TA was the appointment Amy had before she disappeared. Maybe TA meant travel agent for her, too." The wheels in my head were spinning. If Amy was on a trip, why hadn't she called since that last cryptic message on Sunday? I went and pulled out the regional phone book and turned to the yellow pages. Fifteen travel agents were listed between here and Bakerstown. I glanced at the clock, and confirmed it was too late to call. Something to check on tomorrow. For the first time in days, I felt hope.

Pushing aside the phone book, I finished off my brownie and thought about Crystal's call.

"Who would have known Crystal might have grounds to challenge the will? Sabrina and George?" My thoughts were racing. Could the threats on my life, the fence vandalism, Amy's disappearance, and even Miss Emily's death all be about the same thing? Her money?

I went over to the cabinet. I grabbed my own to-do notebook and opened up to the page where I'd listed all the suspects I could think of that first day when I'd decided to inject myself into the investigation. I crossed Crystal's name off. There still were four names that I'd underlined. George, Sabrina, Eric Ammond, and Mayor Baylor.

Reluctantly I crossed the council off the suspect list. I didn't think that people who spent their free time arguing over the historical significance of a shade of house paint were viable threats. Especially since the current council was made up of a glass blower, a weaver, and Darla, who owned the local vineyard. None of them seemed like the mastermind for a murder.

As much as Sabrina's name screamed at me from the page, I left the other three names, as well. No use making assumptions until we found out more.

"What are you working on?" Aunt Jackie's voice cut through my thoughts.

I shut the notebook. "Nothing, just trying to keep all the players straight." I stretched my arms toward the ceiling. Glancing at the clock, I realized Toby should have been there by now. Looking out the side window, I saw his truck parked on the street in front of the house.

I grabbed one of the brownies and put it on a paper towel and poured coffee into a travel mug I found in the cupboard. "How does Toby take his coffee?"

"Black, just like us. He's here?" Aunt Jackie glanced out the window.

"That's his truck right there." I pointed to the truck becoming just a shape in the darkening night. "I'm going to take these out to him."

"Maybe you should stay in the house. Greg wasn't too happy with you the last time."

"Relax. This is over. Greg's at Sabrina's right now. No one's going to bother me. Lightning never strikes twice." Seeing the look on her face as I headed out the door, I added, "I'll be quick, I promise. Just in case, lock this after me."

"You're not making me feel better about this," Aunt Jackie called after me as I went down the porch steps, avoiding the Dumpster and the piles of construction materials. I'd be glad when this remodel was over and I could park my Jeep in the driveway. I was beginning to see a light at the end of the tunnel. I could put in flower beds parallel to the driveway, perennials that wouldn't grow too high. Still considering what flowers to choose, I realized I had reached Toby's truck. The cab of the truck was dark. Asleep. I couldn't believe it. Greg should have just let him off guard duty if he was this tired. I knocked on the window. He had put that dark shading on the windows, making it hard to see inside.

"Toby?"

No answer.

The last time he'd been on guard duty, my fence had been vandalized. Anger filled me. Here I stood, bringing him out coffee and dessert. I pulled open the door.

"Toby, wake . . ." I glanced around the empty truck cab. "Toby?" My voice came out as a whisper. I placed the brownie and coffee cup on the truck console. Shutting the door, I glanced around the empty street. No Toby.

I felt the hood of his truck. Cool. He'd been here for a while before I'd noticed the truck on the street. So where the heck was he?

An owl hooted down the street, and the hair on the back of my neck stood up. I'd been an idiot to come out here in the first place. I had one thought running through my head: *Get back to the house and call Greg.*

That option seemed logical, and I started trotting back to the house. Just a few more feet and I'd be at the back porch, where Aunt Jackie waited to unlock the door for me. Passing the Dumpster, I heard a moan.

Dodging through the first pallet of siding near the Dumpster, I saw a blue jean–clad leg sticking out of the darkness. I peeked around the pallet. Toby lay crumpled next to the Dumpster, in a half-sitting position, blood running down his face from a gash on his head. I glanced around. Nobody. Rushing over to Toby, I reached down for his hand, warm. I shook it.

"Toby," I whispered. "Toby, can you hear me?" No response. Everything I'd ever heard said to leave people the way they were until help arrived. But what if the person who did this came back?

I examined Toby again. He had one of those police walkie-talkie things on his pants. Maybe, just maybe, Greg or Esmeralda was still at the office listening, just in case. I pulled the black box off the clip on Toby's belt and found a button on the side. *Here goes nothing. . . .*

"Greg, are you there? We need help. Toby's been hurt. Hello, can you hear me?" I shook the stupid thing and then realized I needed to let go of the button on the side. The speaker crackled to life.

"Jill? Is that you?"

Relief flooded me as I realized my message hadn't just gone to a cosmic message machine.

"Help us. Toby's been hurt." A searing pain started at the back of my neck, and I found myself falling into Toby before the blackness took me.

Chapter 20

So many lights flashed I thought I'd fallen asleep at the carnival on the pier. I tried to sit up and found two sets of hands restraining me, one with latex gloves. The non-gloved pair was attached to my aunt. "Where am I?"

"Getting ready to be sent to Bakerstown Hospital. Are you all right?" Aunt Jackie's words came slowly through to my brain. I felt like I was processing a new language.

"Toby?" I could see Toby's face as I fell into him. Did the stack of siding fall in on me?

"Toby's already gone." Aunt Jackie stroked my face.

"Dead?" I fought to sit up, but the EMS guy had strapped me down while I talked to my aunt.

"No, honey, he's on the way to the hospital." Aunt Jackie put both hands on my shoulders and pushed me back down to the gurney. "You saved his life."

"Greg heard me?"

"He heard you, called me to lock up the house, and arrived with the rest of the cavalry in minutes. That boy certainly has a fast speed and a way of taking charge." Aunt Jackie sniffed. "Although why he thought I needed to lock myself in rather than come help you, I'll never know."

Thank God for Greg—otherwise my aunt could have been in the gurney next to me rather than sitting here sulking about not saving me. "He was probably just concerned for your safety. Who did this?"

"By the time Greg got here, there wasn't anyone around. Greg thinks it's the same person who's been writing you notes and tearing up your fence. You probably interrupted his plans to finish trashing the house to stop you from meeting the council's timeline."

"A vandal did this?" The world got fuzzy again. I lay back down on the gurney.

A man's face filled my view. A very cute face. "We're heading in to the hospital now." The EMT smiled over at my aunt. "I need to ask if you'll follow us. County rules don't allow any passengers."

Aunt Jackie sniffed. "Well, it's not like there's anywhere for me to sit anyway." She grabbed my hand. "Just relax and I'll see you at the hospital. I'll go lock up the house."

"A lot of good that will do," I mumbled to her retreating back. Gazing at the dark-haired, tanned paramedic, I asked, "So, what's wrong with me?"

"I'd say someone cracked you upside the back of your head. But I'm not a doctor, so I'm not allowed to give opinions." He grinned, showing off a mouthful of white teeth worthy of an actor on a corny television show. Or the cover of one of the romance books I stocked for several of the women in town.

"My head doesn't hurt at all." I thought maybe this was all a mistake.

"It will later, chica." He nodded at the tube attached to my arm. "We put some happy juice in your IV for the ride." He set the straps on the gurney to attach it to the side of the ambulance. "You're lucky. When I worked in the city, they didn't allow us to give out any pain drugs without prior approval from the trauma nurse. Here, they are a little more relaxed. Although if you are a serial drug seeker, you went a long way to get this dose."

My eyelids were getting heavy. "I don't understand." I could hear his words but they didn't make any sense.

"Don't worry about it, chica. Just close your eyes, and we'll be in Bakerstown before you know it." He slapped the cab of the ambulance. "Horace, we're all set back here."

I heard the engine start and thought about Toby crumpled against the Dumpster, lifeless. I whispered a prayer for his recovery, and like all good girls after prayer, promptly fell asleep.

* * *

I woke up in a hospital bed. A nurse stood by my side, checking out the array of machines now attached in some way or another to my body.

"Hey there." The nurse focused on me. "I was beginning to worry about you. Those ambulance jockeys tend to overdo it with their pain med dosage." She put her hand on my chest. "Lift up for me so I can check your dressing. The doctor got you stitched up as soon as you got here and you slept right through it."

I lifted a hand to my throbbing head and felt bandages. "I had a cut?"

"A gash, I'd call it." The nurse gently grabbed my hand and put it down by my side. "Seventeen stitches, from the chart. In a little while, we'll run you down to CT to get some pictures to make sure nothing's happening inside that cute little head of yours."

I glanced down at my shirt and found a hospital gown. "My clothes?"

"Honey, you were blood from head to foot when they got you here. I'm thinking you're going to want to throw those clothes away, especially since they cut you out of them."

"How long have I been here?" Light streamed in the window, and I could hear birds chirping outside.

"Just since last night. I sent your poor aunt home to get some sleep, but you have a visitor in the waiting room." The nurse checked on my IV drip and raised my bed. "I'll tell them to come on in while I call down to get you in to a scan."

I straightened the covers, not knowing who might be coming in. Call me a freak, but being naked except for a hospital gown and some sheets didn't make me feel like entertaining company. And with my luck it would be Mayor Baylor telling me that I'd missed my deadline on getting the house fixed up.

Greg peeked around the corner as he knocked on the door. "All right if I come in?"

Concern showed on his face. He wore the same clothes he'd had on when he left the house yesterday and the shadow of a beard had turned into the real thing.

I patted the bed beside me. "I have to tell you something. Come in."

"I think I have to tell you something first. I'm so sorry for leaving you last night. If I hadn't been so convinced that Sabrina was behind all this, I would have been there instead of Toby." Greg stood by the bed, his head drooping as he talked.

"Greg, look at me. This isn't your fault. You saved us." I paused. "Oh my God, is Toby dead? Is that what you have to tell me?"

Greg started. "What? No. Toby's fine. He's camped out in a room two doors down with both of his girlfriends fighting over who's going to fluff his pillow."

"Toby has two girlfriends? I didn't know that."

"Apparently neither did they. I thought I would have to haul both of them out of there, but I guess they came to some sort of an agreement, at least while he's here. After he gets released, I'm thinking there is going to be a come-to-Jesus meeting for Mr. Toby."

I started laughing until the pain shooting through my head stopped me. "Ouch, stop that. I can't be having fun in my condition."

Greg took my hand. "Sorry, only serious talk from now on. But you should have seen when they first got here."

"You're evil. Tell me all about it." I found the bed controls and inched myself into a seated position.

"Later. Right now I want to let you know that after John Paul identified the picture of Sabrina as the woman who sold him the paintings, we arrested her at her house. She's over at the station not talking and waiting for her lawyer to show up."

"I knew it. So, why did she kill Miss Emily? And where is Amy?" I paused for a second and put my hand to my bandaged head. "Oh my God, she did this, too?"

Greg pulled my hand away. "Hold on, Sabrina didn't attack you and Toby. That was George."

"George, skinny, no-balls George?"

"George with a two-by-four in his hand to give him courage. I caught him in the shed digging through the old furniture when I arrived."

"Aunt Jackie said the guy got away."

Greg's lips curled into a smile. "I didn't want her to kill him."

"So, why did he want the furniture?" I wasn't sure if it was the painkillers or my head injury, but none of this made much sense.

"He heard Jim talking down at the diner about the mission wall and the history guy you've got researching the place. George told me in the police car that Bob had insisted he had real pirate gold when they were kids. Then Sabrina told him you'd moved all the old furniture out to the shed."

"Money." It was all about money. I leaned back, feelings of sadness overwhelming me. Closing my eyes, I asked, "Why is it always all about the money?"

"Money can make people change. Look at you. Once you got the inheritance, you became a house restorer and everyone's target."

My eyes flew open. "You can't really be blaming me for inheriting the money?"

"Just seeing if you were still awake. So, both Sabrina and George have an alibi for the night Miss Emily was killed. I'd already checked it out. They were at a spa in Arizona for the entire week."

"So, they could have hired someone," I protested.

"I haven't ruled them out entirely, but it's looking like they just didn't do that. And they claim they had nothing to do with Amy's disappearance. Believe me, if one of them had dirt on the other, we'd be hearing about it. I've never met a couple so intent on throwing the other spouse under the bus."

I sank back into my pillow.

If it wasn't Sabrina, who else would it be? And where the heck was Amy?

Amy's name rolled around my brain a few times. There was something I needed to tell Greg about Amy, but I couldn't remember.

Sally, my nurse, hustled into the room. "You're up next for the scan. Your buddy was set for the slot, but there's been some kind of argument over who's going to accompany him?"

Greg chuckled and squeezed my hand before he stood up. "I guess I'd better get back over there and referee the girls. I'll check on you tonight. Rest—that's an order."

"You're not the boss of me." I watched Greg leaving the room and let Sally lower the bed down to set it up to wheel me through the halls.

"Don't bet on it." Greg waved as he left the room.

"Your boyfriend's cute," Sally commented as she started pushing me toward the hallway.

"He's not my boyfriend."

"Really? I guess I just got that vibe."

The bed slowed as we eased through the doorway and headed

down to the lower floor where the radiology department was housed.

"He's a police detective." Why was I explaining myself to my nurse?

"Well, if he's single, maybe I should be a little nicer next time when I see him?" Sally's voice echoed in the empty hallway. "And maybe then he'll look at me the way he looks at you."

My body tightened. Could Sally be right? Was there something happening between Greg and me? I knew I didn't want to go back to just nodding on the street when we ran into each other. My best memory of the house that was trying to kill me was of Greg and me sitting out on the porch, watching the sun set. Now that George and Sabrina were in custody, would this be over?

I couldn't think of a response. Sally was nice enough to leave me with my thoughts. A few turns and a short elevator ride and we were at radiology. Wheeling me into a room with a machine in the middle, Sally left, promising to have my lunch ready for me when I came back. Except for the pounding headache and the medical supplies all over the place, the hospital was the closest thing to a spa that I'd been at for a long time.

"I can't believe they sent you home after only one night," Jackie grumbled from the driver's seat as she negotiated the turns on the highway. I stared out the window, watching the ocean for random whale sightings. It was the wrong time of year, but maybe I'd get lucky. I needed some luck.

Turning toward her, I tried to calm her down. "I'm glad they did. My insurance is expensive enough as it is. I don't want them to jack up our policy. Especially now that I have employees to consider."

Jackie smiled, the first smile I'd seen on her face since waking up at the hospital. "I don't need much, just a supplement for my Medicare. I do appreciate you letting me stay on. Did I tell you I signed the papers letting them take over my lease?"

"No." I stared out at the waves again. The painkillers were wearing off, and my head throbbed.

"They cut me a nice little check to have my stuff out of there by the end of next week. So, I wondered if I could have the movers start with moving your stuff out of the apartment on Thursday and then they can bring my stuff on Friday."

"Wait, what?" All of a sudden, I felt I missed something.

"Dear, if I'm going to be living here, I need room for my own furniture. Not that what you have isn't nice," Aunt Jackie hedged.

"Yeah, that's fine." I went back to my ocean watch. I hadn't wanted to jinx my good fortune about keeping the house until I got the council's seal of approval on the remodel, but my aunt was right. It was time to jump into the fight. First thing on the agenda when I got home would be to call Jimmy Marcum. If they were going to throw lawyers and summons at me, I'd better play their game.

"Look, there's a whale." Jackie pointed toward the left.

Smiling, I watched the sea creature playing in the surf until he swam out of my sight. My luck was changing. Even if I had to make it change myself.

I must have dozed off, because the next thing I knew, Jackie was helping me out of the car and we were walking up the steps to the house.

"I brought over some clothes and stuff. I thought I'd stay here for a couple of nights." Jackie nodded toward the stairs. "Bed or couch?"

"There's a second bedroom upstairs for you." It was good to be home. Even if the living room was still a mess from painting and still had one wall to finish. Now, to get the room pulled together. I stepped too quickly toward the couch and almost fell face-first into the bookcase that I'd shoved into the middle of the room.

"Hold on, Speedy, you're not one hundred percent quite yet. Now, bed or couch for you? I need to set you down so I can get you some soup made for lunch."

"Couch, but I can make it myself." I tried to shake off my aunt's arm but didn't get more than an inch before I felt her hand tighten around my waist.

"Yeah, I can see that. Come on, let's get you settled." Jackie walked me over to the couch. She turned on the television and laid my purse on the coffee table. "Iced tea?"

I nodded and grabbed my purse. Digging into the bag, I found my notebook. I turned to the page where I'd written out my list of suspects. I clicked my pen several times then crossed George and Sabrina off my list. I turned to my to-do list and wrote down *Call travel agent* and *Call Jimmy*. Looking at the other items on my list, like shopping for furniture and cleaning the bathroom, I decided that maybe phone calls were more my speed, at least for today.

I found Jimmy Marcum's card in my purse and dialed the number. I should just program the number into my phone. I'd always handled my own legal business, part of the perks of three years of law school, but I knew I was too emotional about the house to be my best advocate in front of the council. Besides, I had to admit, Jimmy had more clout in the town than I did. Especially since most of Lille's regulars put me as the front-runner as Miss Emily's murderer.

His secretary patched me right through.

"Are you all right? I heard what happened. George had the nerve to call and ask me to represent him." Jimmy's voice sounded warm and concerned.

"Are you going to do it?" I hadn't thought about Jimmy representing George.

"I told him it was a conflict of interest since I handled your legal issues with the inheritance." He paused, then went on, "I wanted to tell him he was a weasel and to go jump in the lake."

I chuckled. "I'm glad because I need you to help me on something."

"What's up?" Jimmy's tone became serious.

I explained the ongoing issues with the house and the council, and Miss Emily's pile of correspondence I found with several lawyers, including the one letter Amy and I had found from the lawyer from San Francisco. "To make matters worse, now the historical commission doesn't know when they'll file their paperwork. And now, with Amy gone, the city won't approve the paint color, therefore, Jim King can't finish the outside work."

"And you won't meet your deadline," Jimmy Marcum finished the thought.

"It's just not fair. I've been working my butt off to get this house done by their guidelines. All I needed was a little luck from the gods, but did I get it? No way."

Jimmy's chuckle vibrated my phone. "Relax. I'm sure I can get you an extension. Although I don't know why you didn't just file one when you got the subpoena. It's standard real estate law stuff."

"I practiced family law. If there was property involved, one of the firm's other lawyers handled that part." I sighed. "You think you can get me an extension?"

"I know I can." Jimmy's voice became muffled. "My next appointment's here. I've got to go. Fax me a copy of the subpoena and the other letters."

"I'll get it done today. Thanks." I leaned back into the couch. Maybe I wouldn't be homeless after all.

"No problem. Take care of yourself. And be careful."

Clicking the cell off, I thought about Jimmy's words.

Be careful.

I thought I had been careful, but here I was, beat up and bandaged, sitting on my couch and having my elderly aunt fussing over me. As if on cue, Jackie appeared with a glass of iced tea and a bowl of chicken soup on a tray.

"You need to take it easy." Jackie frowned at the cell phone in my hand.

"Actually, I just handed off worrying about the house to Jimmy. He says he'll be able to get the council off my back." I set the phone down and grabbed the glass of iced tea.

"I don't understand why you didn't ask for help earlier." My aunt covered my lap with a blue cloth napkin I didn't recognize.

Groaning, I set the tea down and sipped a spoonful of the soup. "That's what he said."

"So listen, for once." Jackie flipped the television on. "Oh good, Judge Harry is on."

I suppressed this groan. Watching television with my aunt was close to visiting a retirement center. Boring! "Hey, before you get caught up in the case of the missing false teeth, can you grab me the phone book out of the office? It's on the bookshelf."

Jackie tore her attention away from the introduction of the plaintiff. "The phone book?"

"And the mystery that's on the desk. Unless you want me to get it myself?" I shifted like I planned on getting up, but Jackie popped up first.

"Stay there. You can rest for a few hours at least." Jackie headed to the study. "Stubborn as a mule . . ."

Grinning, I opened my notebook to a new page and wrote *Amy Newman* at the top.

Jackie came back with the phone book. "There were five of these on the bookshelf."

"I know, they just keep coming—and I usually don't even look at them." I pulled open the Yellow Pages to *travel agents*. Fifteen listed in the South Cove/Bakerstown area. I wrote down the name and phone number of the first one and punched the numbers in my cell phone.

After the first ten, Jackie now was watching her favorite soap opera. And I was no closer to finding out which travel agent was TA than I had been during the trial of the two ex-best friends/roommates who broke up when the one slept with the other's man. At least Jackie knew the soap was fiction, I hoped.

At agent number fifteen I finally caught a break. Not only did she remember meeting with Amy, she'd booked her a trip.

"Where did she go?"

"Hold on, I've got the file right here. I've been out of town on a cruise junket. I can't believe after all these years, I finally won a Carnival cruise to Alaska. I've got some great pictures if you're interested?"

"I'm in the middle of a remodel and can't get away, but thanks." I shrugged my shoulders at Jackie.

The doorbell rang as I waited on hold.

"If she's got a good deal going, maybe I should talk to her." Jackie turned down the volume on the television and went to answer the door.

"I'm back," the cheery voice chirped in my ear.

"So, Amy booked a trip? Do you remember where?"

"Here's the file. She didn't book this trip, she won it." I could hear pages turning.

"How did she win the trip?" My gut churned.

"I got a letter from CD Development saying that a Miss Amy Newman had won a trip to Baratonga and I was to contact her to make the arrangements."

"Baratonga? I've never heard of the place." Jackie still stood at the door, talking to the unexpected visitor on the other side. I saw her shake her head.

"It's a small private island near the Mexican coast. Known for excellent surfing. All the big names go there during their downtime for practice."

"And this letter had you set up a trip for Amy?"

"The weird thing was, we had to get her on a plane that same day because the offer ran out that Friday. The package included a new designer wardrobe provided on site, and new, top-of-the-line surfing gear. Man, you don't see prizes this inclusive anymore. When I called to get the credit card approval for the charges, the lady seemed very concerned that Amy not miss out on the opportunity."

"Did you get her name?"

"It should be on my credit approval memo, just a second." More rustling. "That's odd. I didn't get her name. But the charge went through with no problem. I checked it the next day just to make sure."

"Can you tell me anything about the woman? Was she old, young, accent, anything?"

"I'm sorry, it's been a while. The only thing I remember is she kept having to quiet down her dog. It just kept barking."

"Her dog?"

"Yeah, she called it Honey, or Sweetie, no, that's not right."

"Was it Precious?"

"That was it. All I could think of was the ugly Gollum character from *The Lord of the Rings.*"

As if the thought of Bambi had summoned her, I watched as she pushed past my aunt and stilettoed toward my couch.

Bambi had sent Amy on the trip. But why? Access to the mayor? This wasn't making any sense. And now the woman was standing in front of me.

"So, when was she supposed to be back?"

"It was a week's stay, all expenses paid."

"She's been gone three weeks!" Images of planes crashing into the ocean alternated with a vision of Amy, lying in a hospital bed, bandaged from head to toe.

"That's not right. She should have been back by now. Wait, here's a note from my assistant. Miss Newman called and cancelled her return flight." There was a pause. "That's odd. She didn't reschedule a new pickup date."

"What do you mean, a pickup date?"

"Baratonga only has air service one day a week. Even if she'd wanted to stay another week, we should have booked her for the next Thursday."

"Hang up the phone." Bambi held her hand out for my cell.

"Call the police," I yelled into the phone as Bambi ripped it from my hand.

"Hey, stop that." My aunt tried to squeeze in between me and Bambi. "You need to leave now."

Bambi shook her head and pulled out a small handgun from the bag that usually held Precious. "Sit down or I'll shoot you."

My aunt slipped down next to me. "I couldn't stop her from coming in. She had flowers."

"It's okay." I put my hand on my aunt's arm, trying to think of a way out of this. The beating I'd taken from George yesterday and the painkillers the hospital had given me made me feel like I was in slow motion. I said the first thing that popped into my head. "No Precious today?"

"He's back at the hotel. He's not fond of loud noises." Bambi glanced around the living room. "I like this blue much better than the tan the old lady had on the walls. Too bad you won't be around to enjoy it."

Of course, Bambi had been here before. She'd been trying to get Miss Emily to sell. But why? "You did this for Eric's development?"

Bambi laughed. "Actually, Eric did this for me. Of course, he couldn't know the real reason I wanted this run-down shack. So I convinced him that an upscale residential development would make him millions. Men are so easy. All they want are two things. Sex and money."

"And power," my aunt added.

I squeezed her arm, but Bambi just smiled.

"And power. Your mayor falls under all three of those vices." She shuddered. "Luckily, I didn't have to actually sleep with him to seduce him."

"So, why did you want the house?" I figured as long as Bambi was talking, she wasn't shooting.

"I think you know the answer to that." Bambi smiled. "Where did you hide the coins?"

"What coins?"

"Playing dumb isn't as easy as I make it look, sweetheart. And after teaching high school for a few years, I can tell a lie a mile away."

Kevin's story came back. "You taught history here. And had the kids tell you the town's secrets."

"Kids will tell a cute, flirty teacher anything. And, hey, they all got excellent grades, so what was the harm?" Bambi smiled. "Now, this gun is getting heavy, so can you just tell me where the coins are and I'll be leaving."

"And you'll let us live?" My heart leaped at the hope.

Bambi seemed to consider my question for a few seconds. While I watched her, the hope drained out of me. She was debating between lying or telling me the truth. Either way, Aunt Jackie and I were dead when she took her stilettos and left.

"Of course." Bambi had decided on the lie.

I pushed myself into a standing position.

"Jilly, you shouldn't move," my aunt protested.

I stared at Bambi as I answered, "I don't think it matters much right now."

Her lips turned into a slight grin. "I think under different circumstances, you and I could have been friends."

"I think you would have to grow a heart first in order to have a friend." I pointed to the kitchen.

"Now, that was cruel." Bambi waved the gun toward the kitchen. "After you."

I shuffled slowly into the kitchen, touching the blue wall I'd just painted, saying good-bye to the house as I walked. After Bambi shot Aunt Jackie and me, no one would ever live in the house again. Too many deaths, too close together. Tears filled my eyes when I walked into the sunny yellow kitchen.

"Now, this is nice. You should have been a decorator. Your store is precious, by the way." Bambi giggled at her wording.

"Thanks." Now, the world was surreal. I walked over to the cabinets and pulled open the drawer. I wished I'd gone to the bank days ago. Before everything went to hell. But instead, I'd been too busy tracking down Crystal and buying paint. My hand found the napkin and something else. I glanced down at the smooth cylinder. Was it what I thought?

I grabbed the makeshift bag, hoping that Jackie had taken advantage of Bambi's absence and run. I heard the door opening right at the same time Bambi had. Her face went gray.

"Here!" I held the bag in the air, trying to distract her from my aunt. "The coins are here."

"Put them on the table and untie that." Bambi's full attention focused on me.

Run, Jackie. Run.

I slowly walked toward the table, keeping my right hand covered by the bag. As I untied the handkerchief, the coins tumbled out on the table.

"Oh my," Bambi leaned closer and picked up a coin. When she did, I swung my other hand as close to her face as I could and sprayed her with the pepper spray I'd bought when I worked in the city. I hoped it didn't have an expiration date, or I'd be dead sooner than later.

Bambi screamed and dropped the gun and the coins. Her hands flew to her eyes.

I grabbed the gun off the table and stepped out of her reach. Now, where the hell was my phone?

"You bitch." Bambi tried to open her eyes wide enough to find me, but just then, my kitchen door burst open and Greg and Toby stood in the kitchen, guns drawn.

Greg nodded to Toby, who grabbed Bambi, pulling her hands behind her back. He walked over to me and gently removed the gun from my outstretched hands.

"It's over," he said gently.

"You're paying for that lock," I said before I fell into his arms.

Chapter 21

Greg had sent Toby off to get Bambi settled into the one South Cove jail cell and wait for the county sheriff to arrive. I'd told Greg about Amy; now all I could do was wait. Jackie kept trying to get me to eat or watch a movie, but I felt exhausted. My aunt had been a trooper, dialing 911 as soon as she hit the porch. Of course, Greg had already arrived after receiving a call from the state troopers who'd heard from the travel agent about my desperate plea.

I grabbed my laptop and keyed *Baratonga* into my search engine. All I got was a bed–and-breakfast website, an article about the surfing, and a Google map showing the island just off the Mexican coast. All I could think about when I thought of Mexico was the horrible drug wars and the fact that shooting Americans had become the new blood sport.

"Please, Amy, just hold on a little while longer," I kept whispering over and over. At least I knew my friend was somewhere, hopefully alive.

Night came and Jackie made pasta with artichoke hearts with a wine reduction white sauce. I barely touched the food. I was still twirling the noodles with my fork when a knock came to the back door. Jumping up, I almost knocked my plate off the table.

Swinging open the door, Greg walked in. I'd never been so glad to see anyone. The sight of him coming in the kitchen reminded me of his rescue earlier that day. The man played Prince Charming well. He gave me a quick hug before he said anything, rubbing his hands down my hair, probably trying to get it to stay out of his eyes.

"We have her."

Tears fell and I started sobbing.

"The Coast Guard went down to the island and picked her up, no worse for wear. She was mad as hell that the plane hadn't come for her, though." Greg smiled. He nodded at Aunt Jackie. "Got any more of that pasta? It smells amazing."

"Jill, let the man come through the door. I'll dish you up a plate since my niece seems to have lost her appetite." Jackie hurried over to the stove, but not before I saw her wipe tears from her eyes and grab her Saint Christopher medal.

"Sorry, come in." I held on to his arm for support, as I wasn't quite sure my legs would carry me back to my chair. "She's all right? Really?"

"She was in the kitchen with the bed-and-breakfast owner when the Coast Guard came up the beach. They were making muffins." Greg shook his head. "She had no idea we were looking for her. She thought her call on Sunday went through but then she realized she was talking to dead air."

"And Bambi? What did Bambi say?" Fire flashed through me as I waited to find out what excuse she had given for putting me and Amy through this hell.

"She's down at the station. She admitted sending Amy the trip. And more, she confessed to killing Miss Emily."

Greg sat down at the table and continued his story. "Apparently, before she met Eric, Bambi Kelly was a history teacher right here in South Cove. But you figured that much out already. She found enough in her research to make her believe that the missing mission story was more fact than fiction. She had been searching on Miss Emily's property, but had run into Sabrina stealing paintings. And when Eric couldn't talk Miss Emily into selling, she slipped into the house and snuck a healthy dose of ma huang into her tea. Which caused a heart attack, killing her."

"How did she? I mean, she doesn't look that strong."

"Miss Emily was poisoned, not strangled. The marks on her neck happened after death, according to Doc Ames. I guess Bambi wasn't sure the ma huang had worked." Greg smiled wearily at Jackie when she put a plate in front of him. "Thanks, this is the first food I've had since the sandwich at the hospital last night. Your aunt has been the main source of my meals the last few days."

I didn't understand. "Your wife doesn't cook?"

Greg choked on the bite of garlic bread he'd just taken. "My wife? Well, when we were married, she might have cooked once in a while. But now, Sherry's too busy dating the hospital staff to cook for me. You thought I was married?"

"Your brother said . . ." I stopped, not wanting to open a can of worms between the two men.

"Jim thinks marriage is forever. He lost his wife in a car accident and has been at me ever since to make it right with Sherry. He doesn't understand that there's too much water under the bridge for me to go back there." Pain crossed his face.

"I didn't mean to bring up bad memories."

"You didn't cheat. She did. End of story." Greg dug into the pasta.

I took a bite of the pasta on my plate. Amy was on her way home, Bambi was in jail along with George and Sabrina, Jimmy was fighting the council to save the house, and I had only one more loose end to tie up. I stood up.

"Where are you going?" Jackie asked.

"I need to make a quick phone call."

The house was filled with people. Half the town had to be in my backyard, some taking pictures of the mission wall, even though Frank Gleason was still undecided about the wall's origin. I had set up a display area with Miss Emily's paintings, letting the townsfolk view the talent of my friend. Sadie and the women from the Methodist Church had been the first to arrive, arms filled with covered dishes.

Greg had set up the galvanized tub on the deck and filled it with ice and a variety of soda and adult beverages. He'd been a regular on the back porch these last few months, and we'd gotten a lot closer, now that I wasn't having to worry about somebody coming up and knifing me from behind. He'd even come with me when I spoke in front of the council about the advantage of mixed use property codes. Apparently that had been Amy's grand plan all along, to convince the council that single family dwellings brought up everyone's property value over large apartment buildings. I had to admit, she'd done her homework on the subject. I was in the kitchen setting up another appetizer tray to take out to the backyard.

"The grill's ready anytime you want to start up the hot dogs and hamburgers." He put his arms around me and pulled me close. "Happy housewarming."

His lips found mine, and I melted into his kiss. Soft, warm, promising.

"Ahem," a woman's voice came from the kitchen door.

I broke away from Greg and handed him the tray to take outside. "Make yourself useful."

He grinned and headed out the door, nodding a greeting to the newcomer.

I studied the young woman in front of me with the baby in her arms. "Crystal! I'm so glad you could make it."

Annie pointed to the pile of yellow lying on the kitchen floor. "Puppy."

Emma's head popped up at the sound of the child's voice. Greg had brought the golden retriever over to the house the weekend after Amy came home. The dog stretched and skidded over to meet her new best friend.

"Annie, meet Emma." I put my hand on Emma's head, hoping that would calm her down just a bit.

Crystal put Annie down, and she toddled over to pet Emma.

"I wanted to thank you."

"No problem, I'm glad you agreed to come. We have lots of food and room. Did you see Miss Emily's paintings?" I kept my eye on Emma, but so far the dog was too busy giving Annie kisses to worry about the child's hands being a little too rough.

"That's not what I mean, Jill. You didn't have to set up those scholarship accounts for Annie and me." Tears glistened in Crystal's eyes.

"It wasn't much, just enough for you to get through school. Now, Annie's should be worth some cash when she's ready. Maybe she'll want to go to Harvard or Yale." I squeezed Crystal's shoulder.

"No one's ever done something that nice for me, ever."

"Then it's about time. Just study hard and make her a good life." My voice got raspy, but I wasn't going to cry. Jimmy Marcum had thought I was a fool for setting up the education accounts, but I viewed the gift as paying my good fortune forward. And I was sure Miss Emily would have agreed with me.

"We are all waiting for you outside. Greg wants to start up the grill." Amy's voice came through the screen door before she did. My friend was no worse for wear, but I still gave thanks every time I saw her.

"We're heading out now." I grabbed Crystal's hand. "Let's go eat."

Keep reading for more adventures
with Jill and the residents of South Cove.
Look for MISSION TO MURDER,
the next Tourist Trap Mystery,
available Summer 2014
from Lynn Cahoon
and
eKensington

Chapter 1

Some people like to hear their own voice. That jewel of wisdom hit me as I filled the coffee carafes for the third time. As chamber liaison, I'd volunteered my shop, Coffee, Books, and More, to serve as the semi-permanent host site for South Cove's Business Basics meeting. The early morning meeting was scheduled to run from seven to nine, but the clock over the coffee bar showed it was already twenty minutes past. With more items to cover on the agenda, we'd be ordering lunch, maybe dinner, before the end.

All because the newest committee member, Josh Thomas, owner of the new antiques store down the street, had issues. He didn't like the agenda, the city's promotion plan, and he especially didn't like the fact that the city didn't have a formal animal control office. These subjects were not part of the regular list of discussion topics for the eclectic mix of owners of gift shops, art galleries, inns, and restaurants. I usually loved feeling the creative energy and listening to the wacky ideas members brought to the table. Today, the meeting droned on, and I couldn't wait for it to end.

"I wonder why he even moved here," Aunt Jackie fake-whispered to me as she sliced a second cheesecake. "He hates everything."

"Hush." I elbowed my aunt, trying to quiet her.

"Jill Gardner, don't tell me you weren't thinking the same thing." She started plating out the cheesecake.

A couple of the council members snickered, and Josh's face

turned a deeper red than normal. His wide girth barely fit into the black suit he wore. From what I could tell, he wore the same thread-bare suit every day. Watching the buttons on his off-white shirt, I worried one would pop off each time he took a labored breath.

"As I was saying, we must press the police department to deal with felonious teenagers running the streets." Josh didn't acknowl-edge he'd heard Jackie, a tactic I've often used with my aunt. She's overbearing, opinionated, speaks her mind, and I love her to death.

"There's no problem," Sadie Michaels replied, the words harsh and clipped. "There's not a lot for kids to do around here, so they hang out at the park. They don't cause problems for local busi-nesses. We've raised them better than that."

"I beg to differ. Craig Morgan, the manager over at The Castle, has caught kids breaking in after-hours. They've been having drink-ing parties, swimming in the pools, and he's even caught a few cou-ples in the mansion's bedrooms, doing heavens knows what." Snickers from the rest of the members floated around the room as Josh wheezed in another breath. "We must stop these criminals be-fore there's real trouble. The antiques housed at The Castle are priceless."

"My son, Nick, is one of these hooligans you want arrested. I've never heard him or any of his friends talk about breaking into The Castle. They know better." The red on Sadie's face rivaled Josh's. She stood and pointed her finger at Josh sitting across from her. "You like causing trouble."

After setting the full carafes on the table, I put my hand on Sadie's shoulder, easing her back into her chair. "This topic needs to be tabled until the next meeting. We'll invite Detective King to attend to address Mr. Thomas's concerns about property safety. Bill, do you want to get us back on track with the agenda?" I threw a lifeline to Bill Simmons, our council chair and owner of South Cove Bed-and-Breakfast on Main Street.

Bill shot me a grateful smile. "I'm sure Jill is anxious to get the meeting over and get back to business. As a side note, the mayor has reappointed Ms. Gardner as the chamber's liaison for next year. Mr. Thomas, if you have questions about our procedures, she will be happy to work with you."

Okay, now I officially hated Bill Simmons. Taking a deep

breath, I pasted on a flight attendant smile and nodded. "Of course, I'll stop by and visit with Josh this week."

Josh didn't seem pleased with the idea of spending quality time with me, either. Cool, I could plan on the visit being quick.

Bill's relief at regaining control swept across the room, calming everyone, except me and Josh. "Let's move on. The Annual Summer Festival starts up next month. Can we get a report from the committee on how the preparations are going? Darla?"

As the owner of the local winery explained the committee's goals, I took a seat next to Sadie. "Thanks," she whispered.

"Not a problem." I liked Sadie. She and I had become friends in the last year, mostly over coffee after the Business to Business meetings. In her forties, the woman was a single mom, led the women's group at her church, and ran a small business. She got more done in two hours than I accomplished in eight. She'd been a rock for me when I'd been put in charge of Miss Emily's funeral earlier this year. Without Sadie's help, my friend would have been sent to the afterlife without a proper good-bye.

My coffee shop/bookstore was the best customer for her business, Pies on the Fly. She was easygoing and would give you her left arm if you needed it. But no one messed with her kid.

Nick Michaels chaired the school debate team, served as youth leader for his church's Boy Scout troop, and led the high school football team as an all-star quarterback. Calling him a hooligan was like saying the pope ran around throwing rocks through windows. Trouble wasn't in the boy's DNA.

Somehow Bill pushed the last two items off until the next meeting, and before I knew it, the meeting adjourned. Sadie stayed around to help clean up after the others refilled their cups with a last free coffee and said their good-byes. I started wiping down the hodgepodge of tables we'd moved together for the meeting. Sadie shoved paper plates and used napkins into a sack with a gale wind force.

"I can't believe that man." Sadie crumpled a leftover paper cup and shoved it into a trash sack. "He doesn't like kids. That's all. He's so used to working with the past, he can't see the future right in front of him."

"He's a character, I'll agree with you on that point." I wiped a table clean and returned it to a spot near the window. Pulling chairs around the table, I watched my friend's face as I said the words she didn't want to hear. "Listen, Craig's been complaining to everyone the town kids are sneaking in after-hours. Greg's been out on calls there three times this month."

Detective Greg King had returned to town after his divorce to serve as the town's lead police officer. Greg was also my boyfriend. The word still rankled when I thought it, let alone said, *boyfriend*. Seriously, wasn't there a grown-up word a thirty-two-year-old could call the hunk of boy toy she dated?

"You don't think my Nick would be part of anything like that, do you? He knows better." Sadie's eyes filled with tears. She'd raised Nick alone after her husband was killed on an off-shore oil rig when their son was five. His mom's eagle eye kept the boy in line, but sometimes I wondered if he wasn't too controlled. Boys needed a wild side, and breaking in to swim in the most expensive pool in town could be Nick's way of getting his freak on. So to speak.

"Wouldn't be the worst thing for the boy," Aunt Jackie called from behind the counter where she stood making a pot of coffee and eavesdropping. "Maybe he's getting lucky with some girl."

"Aunt Jackie!" I glanced over at Sadie, whose face had turned whiter than the wash towel in her hand. I tried to console her. "I'm sure it's not Nick."

"Now, Jill Gardner, you know as well as I do boys will be boys." My aunt huffed and left for the back of the store.

After making sure Jackie had left, I glanced at my friend. Her face now appeared mottled gray. "Sorry, you know how she is. Talk first. Think later."

"That's the thing. I'm not sure Nick's innocent." Sadie slumped down into a chair.

"Problems?" I sat at the table with her.

"There's a new girl at church. Her folks moved the family here from LA. The girl got kicked out of the last prep school she attended." Sadie scanned the room to see if anyone had remained, and then she paused from wiping the same spot on the table for the tenth time. She whispered, "Drugs."

"I'm sure that's a rumor." I gently took the rag from her hand. There'd be no varnish left on the tabletop if I didn't intervene.

She shook her head. "It's not a rumor. Cindy told me and she heard it from Gladys, the church secretary. She'd overheard the girl's folks telling Pastor Bill." Sadie reached out for my hand. "She works at The Castle giving tours." She uttered the words that she must have thought hammered the nails into Nick's prison cell.

I watched Sadie leave the coffee shop a few minutes later, a pie order for next week in her hand and her heart on her sleeve. Sighing, I sat down with the book catalogue and made a list for Jackie to order later that night.

Nearly two hours later, glancing around the still-empty dining room, I picked up the phone and called Amy, South Cove's city planner, secretary to Mayor Baylor, and my best friend—roles that had gotten her kidnapped and stranded on a remote Mexican island a few months ago. But true to Amy's character, she'd been more excited by the mondo waves she'd ridden to worry about rescue.

"South Cove City Hall." Amy's perky voice came over the speakerphone.

"Lunch today?" I nodded at Toby Killian, who'd entered the shop for his afternoon shift. Toby worked for me during the day and for Greg most evenings as one of South Cove's finest. I pulled off my apron and glanced into the mirror behind the coffee bar. My makeup had disappeared, leaving my face pale and blotchy, and the curl in my black hair rivaled Little Orphan Annie's without the flame red. I finger-combed my curls into a controlled chaos, the phone still cradled between my shoulder and my ear.

"Eleven-thirty, I'm finishing last night's council notes." Amy disconnected the call. No good-bye, and since we only had one restaurant in town, no need to plan any further.

"Hey, boss." Toby came around the counter and put on an apron with *Wired Up?* printed on the front. Aunt Jackie's newest promotion for the coffee shop focused on the free Wi-Fi we offered our customers. From what I saw, after adding the service we'd gained a lot of the hooligan teenage crowd Josh had been complaining about. Our sales had increased in the late afternoon hours, so I wasn't complaining.

"Do we have problems with the after-school crowd? Anything I should know about?" I leaned against the counter, watching Toby start a fresh pot of decaf.

"Like what?" Toby pushed the button to brew and flipped a clean rag over his shoulder. He rocked the indie-barista look and knew it.

"With the teenagers. Josh Thomas said he'd had some run-ins." I was pretty sure Josh had overreacted.

"Kids are kids. They don't give me any guff. Probably afraid I'll arrest them if I see them later." Toby straightened the flyers for the next Mystery Book Club meeting on Friday. "I can talk to a few of them if you'd like. But as long as he keeps yelling because they walk by his shop, he's going to get crap back."

"Keep your ears open. Josh said some have been sneaking into The Castle grounds for after-closing swim parties." I glanced at the clock and took off my apron, my shift done. I'd been hesitant to hire anyone before Aunt Jackie had started working with me; now I had two employees and a lot of spare time.

South Cove sat inland on the central California coastline. Summer weather meant highs in the seventies, a lot like the weather forecast in spring, fall, and, thankfully, winter. Fog tended to disappear by noon, and the day turned to shirtsleeve weather. Today was glorious. The flower boxes lining the sidewalks bloomed with bright colors, the flowers' sweet smell filling the morning air.

Walking past Antiques by Thomas, I noticed Josh moving a walnut side table into his store display window. I waved, but he glared back. My lack of support during the meeting hadn't gone unnoticed. I'd stop by the shop later this week with a box of cookies in an attempt to mend fences.

Cookies could fix anything, and good fences make good neighbors. Or at least I hoped the old wisdom held true. Maybe I'd send Aunt Jackie over. She could charm a cobra, which she'd actually done on one of her senior hostel trips to India.

Having Aunt Jackie helping with the business had been hard to accept at times. But I had to admit, her ideas paid off. The local author readings she'd started tripled business in both the book side and the coffee shop on what used to be Dead Wednesday. Lille's diner traffic increased, as well, with customers migrating there for a meal after the readings ended.

Next month, a famous mystery author was scheduled to speak at the bookstore. Partnering with Bill at South Cove Bed-and-Breakfast, our only cost so far amounted to half the author's plane fare. Though I signed the checks, my aunt still kept the mystery author's identity a secret.

This marketing tactic might be her first big failure. Who would come to hear someone they didn't know? When I complained, she shooed me off.

"That's part of the fun. It's a mystery."

"We do have an author scheduled, right?" My stomach turned at the thought.

"Of course. He or she's already agreed to come and read. Their new book is arriving that week, and we are hosting the book's homecoming."

"You mean launch." Sometimes she scared me how much she didn't know about the bookselling business.

"Yeah, that's the word. I knew he said it had something to do with a cruise."

"But what if no one comes?" I tried one more time. The author was a man. She'd let that slip. My mind raced through the upcoming new releases I'd ordered last week. Had I overstocked one book?

"Pish. You worry too much." She'd walked away, the conversation over. The shadowed flyers told people the date, the time, and that they would love this author, but the rest remained as the sign said, "Cloaked in Mystery."

Diamond Lille's was a block down on Main Street, and I was in front of it before I realized I'd arrived. I shook my head clear of the book launch worries and put on a receptionist smile before I entered the diner. Believe me, gossip travels fast in South Cove. If I'd walked in with a frown, people would be betting on hearing some bit of bad news within a day. I'd either be dying of cancer, had found Greg cheating with a stripper from Bakerstown, or my business was on the ropes. And even though none of those things was going to happen anytime soon, truth didn't stop tongues from wagging.

Amy sat in our favorite booth. She'd already ordered our drinks, and a large glass of iced tea waited for me while she sipped on a soda.

"What, no ice cream shake?" I slipped into the bench seat across from her. Today, the lunch special featured potato soup. Adding a dinner salad to go with the bowl of creamy goodness topped with shredded cheddar cheese and a generous dollop of sour cream, made the meal appear somewhat healthy and part of my ongoing diet.

Amy's face turned red. "Am I that predictable?"

"If it's Tuesday, it's strawberry shake day. If we meet on Friday, you order a fish sandwich and chocolate shake."

Grinning, Amy nodded. "Why mess with routine? Actually, they were backed up in the kitchen. Somebody bailed on their shift. Carrie got me this while I waited."

"Who didn't show?"

"Sadie's kid, Nick." Amy's voice came from behind the menu she studied. Not like she hadn't read the same list of items three times a week for the last year. "I think I'll get the grilled pastrami on rye today."

"No club on wheat with a side of chicken noodle soup?" I recited Amy's usual Tuesday lunch order.

She swatted at me with the menu. "Hank and I found the best New York–style deli when we were in the city last weekend. I've been craving pastrami since Sunday."

Carrie showed up to take our orders. "I'm sure I could let the kitchen know you're both here. But let's go through the motions. What can I get for you?" She regarded me first.

"I'm having a house salad, blue cheese dressing on the side, and a bowl of loaded potato soup. But Amy's going to surprise you."

"God, you'd think I shaved my head and become a Buddhist." Amy kicked me under the table. "I'll have the grilled pastrami on rye with a side salad. And a strawberry milk shake."

"Crap, I forgot about the shake. No problem. But no club?" Carrie reached out to touch Amy's forehead to see if she felt hot.

"Did I say I wanted a club? Jeez, people change their minds." Amy pulled her head back out of Carrie's reach.

Carrie yanked the menus off the table. "Don't get huffy. I have enough to do with Nick out."

"Did Nick call in sick?" After the talk I'd had with Sadie, I didn't want to hear the answer, but like looking at a car wreck on the side of the road, I couldn't stop from asking.

"Nope. The kid didn't show. Lille's hopping mad. She got called in on her day off to wash dishes. He's going to get an earful tomorrow." Carrie turned and headed back to the kitchen, picking up plates and taking refill drink orders on the way.

"Looks like it's going to be a leisurely lunch hour." Amy leaned back. "So, you probably want to know about Hank and the weekend."

"Actually, I wanted to know if anyone at The Castle complained to the council about teenagers."

I knew Amy wanted to talk about Hank. The four of us drove to the city for dinner as a double date two weeks ago. Hank dominated the conversation from the time we got in the car to the time Greg dropped the couple off at Amy's apartment. Hank was a disaster. I avoided the subject at all costs, but one day, the Hank discussion would happen. Then Amy would be crushed I didn't see his warm and loving side. But that conversation wasn't happening today.

"The Castle?" Amy tapped her fingers on the table, thinking. "Actually, Craig had an appointment with the mayor last week. I figured he was arguing for more advertising funding from the city. You know he thinks the only reason anyone comes to South Cove is to visit The Castle."

I knew. All the business owners knew Craig Morgan's opinion of them. In fact, Craig wasn't shy about calling us bloodsucking parasites to our faces. Sure, visitors to The Castle brought in shoppers. But sometimes, the traffic happened to flow from the town to The Castle. God knows I'd sent my share of tourists to his door. And still he wanted the entire allotment of the chamber's marketing money? He even refused to come to the Business Basics meetings because he was busy, running a real company. Like I wasn't?

Well, I guess with Aunt Jackie and Toby working the floor, I wasn't quite as busy as I'd been. But the shop was hopping. I'd filled my empty time finishing renovating the house I'd inherited from Miss Emily. Not to mention hours working with the historical commission on certifying the stone wall in the back of the property as the "real" South Cove mission site. If the certification ever came through, South Cove would have a second historic site to promote. Craig wasn't happy about sharing the marketing money now. His reaction to sharing the budget with the mission site wouldn't be pretty.

"You don't think he's working the historical commission against certifying the site, do you?" Fear gripped my stomach. If the commission even smelled a whiff of community discordance around the project, they'd back off the process.

"I wouldn't put it past him. Ever since you shut down Eric's development plans, the mayor hasn't been too happy with you." Amy scanned the packed diner. Most tables were still without food.

"I didn't shut down Eric Ammond's development. His lying, stealing, murdering girlfriend handled that on her own!" I couldn't believe Amy was blaming me for the development shutting down. If I hadn't found her, she'd still be surfing on a reclusive island off the coast of Mexico. Okay, well, she could blame me a little. Surfing would be more calming than trying to manage all the jobs she had going here in town. But still, you'd think she'd be a little grateful.

"Everyone knows the crazy ex-schoolteacher bombed the project. Except, His Honor The Mayor. Marvin still can't say your name without spitting." Amy nodded to Carrie on her way over with a tray. "Maybe we're getting lucky."

We were. Carrie dropped off food for us and the next table over. She stopped at the booth for a quick second. "Nick finally showed. He claimed his girlfriend needed a ride into the city, and he thought they'd be back long before his shift started." Carrie leaned down and whispered, "You can bet what she wanted. She's going to ruin his reputation. Mark my words."

Amy watched Carrie walk away, then brightened as if she remembered something. "Oh, Esmeralda says to tell you hello. She wants you to come in for a reading." Amy laughed. "She said she threw your cards or whatever mumbo jumbo."

Esmeralda was South Cove's fortune-teller and police dispatcher. If my house won the prize for being the oldest building in town, Esmeralda's came in a quick second. The mayor loved her. As long as she kept foreseeing a great future for the man, he left her housing code issues alone. She'd done a quick read on me once in the mayor's lobby. Now, the fortune-teller and I were best friends, not. "What did the cards say this time?"

Amy grinned. She pointed her French fry at me and said in a lowered imitation of Esmeralda's voice so good, the words gave me goose bumps: "Death surrounds you again."

Printed in the United States
by Baker & Taylor Publisher Services